Fiona McA... ... ...es
in the country and loves to dream. W... ... ...cal
Romance gives Fiona the scope to write about all the
wonderful aspects of romance, adventure, medicine
and the midwifery she feels so passionate about.
When she's not catching babies, Fiona is with her
husband Ian, off to meet new people, see new places
and have wonderful adventures. Drop in and say hi at
Fiona's website: Fionamcarthurauthor.com.

Jennifer Taylor has written for several different
Mills & Boon series, but it wasn't until she
'discovered' Medical Romances that she found
her true niche. Jennifer loves the blend of modern
romance and exciting medical drama. Widowed, she
divides her time between homes in Lancashire and the
Lake District. Her hobbies include reading, walking,
travelling and spending time with her two gorgeous
grandchildren.

HEALED BY THE MIDWIFE'S KISS

FIONA McARTHUR

REUNITED BY THEIR BABY

JENNIFER TAYLOR

MILLS & BOON

First Published in Great Britain 2018
by Mills & Boon, an imprint of HarperCollins*Publishers*
1 London Bridge Street, London, SE1 9GF

Healed by the Midwife's Kiss © 2018 by Fiona McArthur

Reunited by Their Baby © 2018 by Jennifer Taylor

ISBN: 978-0-263-93345-1

MIX
Paper from
responsible sources
FSC® C007454

FSC
www.fsc.org

This book is produced from independently certified FSC™ paper
to ensure responsible forest management.
For more information visit www.harpercollins.co.uk/green.

Printed and bound in Spain
by CPI, Barcelona

HEALED BY THE MIDWIFE'S KISS

FIONA McARTHUR

MILLS & BOON

Dedicated to Finn, author Kelly Hunter's legend
of a four-legged friend, who went to doggy heaven
while I was writing this book.

It just seemed right to say
there are Finn heroes everywhere.

Vale Finn.

PROLOGUE

AT SIX A.M. on a Thursday, Lighthouse Bay's maternity ward held its breath. Midwife Catrina Thomas leaned forward and rubbed the newborn firmly with a warmed towel. The limp infant flexed and wriggled his purple limbs and finally took a gasping indignant lungful.

The baby curled his hands into fists as his now tense body suffused with pink. 'Yours now, Craig. Take him.' She gestured to the nervous dad beside her and mimed what to do as she encouraged Craig's big callused hands to gently lift the precious bundle. One huge splashing silver tear dropped to the sheet from his stubbled cheek as he placed his new son on his wife's warm bare stomach.

Craig released a strangled sob and his wife, leaning back on the bed in relief, half laughed in triumph, then closed her hands over her child and her husband's hands and pulled both upwards to lie between her breasts.

For Catrina, it was this moment. This snapshot in time she identified as her driver, the reason she felt she could be a midwife for ever—this and every other birth moment that had come before. It gave her piercing joy when she'd thought she'd lost all gladness, and it gave her bittersweet regret for the dreams she'd lost. But mostly, definitely, it gave her joy.

An hour later Catrina hugged her boss awkwardly, because Ellie's big pregnant belly bulged in the way as they came together, but no less enthusiastically because she would miss seeing her friend in the morning before she finished her shift. 'I can't believe it's your last day.' She rolled her eyes. 'Or my last night shift tomorrow.'

'Neither can I.' Ellie's brilliant smile lit the room even more than the sunlight streaming in through the maternity ward windows.

Trina marvelled at the pure happiness that radiated from a woman who had blossomed, and not just in belly size but in every way in just one year of marriage. Another reason Trina needed to change her life and move on. She wanted what Ellie had.

A family and a life outside work. She would have the latter next week when she took on Ellie's job as Midwifery Unit Manager for Ellie's year of maternity leave.

She'd have daylight hours to see the world and evenings to think about going out for dinner with the not infrequent men who had asked her. The excuse of night shift would be taken out of her grasp. Which was a good thing. She'd hidden for two years and the time to be brave had arrived.

She stepped back from Ellie, picked up her bag and blew her a kiss. 'Happy last day. I'll see you at your lunch tomorrow.' Then she lifted her chin and stepped out of the door into the cool morning.

The tangy morning breeze promised a shower later, and pattering rain on the roof on a cool day made diving into bed in the daylight hours oh, so much more attractive than the usual sunny weather of Lighthouse Bay. Summer turning to autumn was her favourite time of year. Trina turned her face into the salty spray from the sea as she walked down towards the beach.

She slept better if she walked before going up the hill to her croft cottage, even if just a quick dash along the breakwall path that ran at right angles to the beach.

Especially after a birth. Her teeth clenched as she sucked in the salty air and tried not to dwell on the resting mother lying snug and content in the ward with her brand-new pink-faced baby.

Trina looked ahead to the curved crescent of the beach as she swung down the path from the hospital. The sapphire blue of the ocean stretching out to the horizon where the water met the sky, her favourite contemplation, and, closer, the rolling waves crashing and turning into fur-like foam edges that raced across the footprint-free sand to sink in and disappear.

Every day the small creek flowing into the ocean changed, the sandbars shifting and melding with the tides. The granite boulders like big seals set into the creek bed, lying lazily and oblivious to the shifting sand around them. Like life, Trina thought whimsically. You could fight against life until you realised that the past was gone and you needed to wait to see what the next tide brought. If only you could let go.

Ahead she saw that solitary dad. The one with his little girl in the backpack, striding along the beach with those long powerful strides as he covered the distance from headland to headland. Just like he had every morning she'd walked for the last four weeks. A tall, broad-shouldered, dark-haired man with a swift stride.

Sometimes the two were draped in raincoats, sometimes his daughter wore a cheery little hat with pom-poms. Sometimes, like today, they both wore beanies and a scarf.

Trina shivered. She could have done with a scarf. When she was tired it was easy to feel the cold. It would be good to move to day shifts after almost two bleak years on nights, but falling into bed exhausted in the daytime had been preferable to the dread of lying lonely and alone in the small dark hours.

She focused on the couple coming towards her. The little girl must have been around twelve months old, and seemed to be always gurgling with laughter, her crinkled eyes, waving fists and gap-toothed smile a delight to start the day with. The father, on the other hand, smiled with his mouth only when he barely lifted his hand but his storm-blue eyes glittered distant and broken beneath the dark brows. Trina didn't need to soak in anyone else's grief.

They all guessed about his story because, for once, nobody had gleaned any information and shared it with the inhabitants of Lighthouse Bay.

They drew closer and passed. 'Morning.' Trina in-

clined her head and waved at the little girl who, de-
lightfully, waved back with a toothy chuckle.

'Morning,' the father said and lifted the corner of
his lips before he passed.

And that was that for another day. Trina guessed
she knew exactly how he felt. But she was changing.

CHAPTER ONE

Finn

AT SEVEN-THIRTY A.M. on the golden sands of Lighthouse Bay Beach Finlay Foley grimaced at the girl as she went past. Always in the purple scrubs so he knew she was one of the midwives from the hospital. A midwife. Last person he wanted to talk to.

It had been a midwife, one who put her face close to his and stared at him suspiciously, who told him his wife had left their baby and him behind, and ran away.

But the dark-haired girl with golden glints in her hair never invaded his space. She exuded a gentle warmth and empathy that had begun to brush over him lightly like a consistent warm beam of sunlight through leaves. Or like that soft shaft of light that reached into a corner of his cottage from the lighthouse on the cliff by some bizarre refraction. And always that feather-stroke of compassion without pity in her brown-eyed glance that thawed his frozen soul a little more each day when they passed.

She always smiled and so did he. But neither of them stopped. Thank goodness.

Piper gurgled behind his ear and he tilted his head to catch her words. 'Did you say something, Piper?'

'Mum, Mum, Mum, Mum.'

Finn felt the tightness crunch his sternum as if someone had grabbed his shirt and dug their nails into his chest. Guilt. Because he hadn't found her. He closed his eyes for a second. Nothing should be this hard. 'Try Dad, Dad, Dad, Dad,' he said past the tightness in his throat.

Obediently Piper chanted in her musical little voice, 'Dad, Dad, Dad, Dad.'

'Clever girl.' His mouth lifted this time and he felt a brief piercing of warmth from another beam of light in his cave-like existence.

Which was why he'd moved here. To make himself shift into the light. For Piper. And it did seem to be working. Something about this place, this haven of ocean and sand and cliffs and smiling people like the morning midwife soothed his ragged nerves and restored his faith in finding a way into the future.

A future he needed to create for Piper. Always the jolliest baby, now giggling toddler and all-round ray of puppy-like delight, Piper had kept him sane mainly because he had to greet each day to meet her needs.

His sister had said Piper had begun to look sad. Suspected she wasn't happy in the busy day care. Didn't see enough of her dad when he worked long hours. And he'd lifted his head and seen what his sister had seen.

Piper had been clingy. Harder to leave when he

dropped her off at the busy centre. Drooping as he dressed her for 'school' in the morning. Quiet when he picked her up ten hours later.

Of course he needed to get a life and smile for his daughter. So he'd listened when his sister suggested he take a break from the paediatric practice where he'd continued as if on autopilot. Maybe escape to a place one of her friends had visited recently, where he knew no one, and heal for a week or two, or even a month for his daughter's sake. Maybe go back part-time for a while and spend more time with Piper. So he'd come. Here. To Lighthouse Bay.

Even on the first day it had felt right, just a glimmer of a breakthrough in the darkness, and he'd known it had been a good move.

The first morning in the guesthouse, when he'd walked the beach with Piper on his back, he'd felt a stirring of the peace he had found so elusive in his empty, echoing, accusing house. Saw the girl with the smile. Said, 'Good morning.'

After a few days he'd rented a cottage just above the beach for a week to avoid the other boisterous guests—happy families and young lovers he didn't need to talk to at breakfast—and moved to a place more private and offering solitude, but the inactivity of a rented house had been the exact opposite to what he needed.

Serendipitously, the cottage next door to that had come up for sale—*Would suit handyman*—which he'd never been. He was not even close to handy. Impulsively, after he'd discussed it with Piper, who had smiled and nodded and gurgled away his lack of handyman skills with great enthusiasm, he'd bought it. Then and there. The bonus of vacant possession meant an immediate move in even before the papers were signed.

He had a holiday house at the very least and a home if he never moved back to his old life. Radical stuff for a single parent, escaped paediatrician, failed husband, and one who had been used to the conveniences of a large town.

The first part of the one big room he'd clumsily beautified was Piper's corner and she didn't mind the smudges here and there and the chaos of spackle and paint tins and drip sheets and brushes.

Finally, he'd stood back with his daughter in his arms and considered he might survive the next week and maybe even the one after that. The first truly positive achievement he'd accomplished since Clancy left.

Clancy left.

How many times had he tried to grasp that fact? His wife of less than a year had walked away. Run, really. Left him, left her day-old daughter, and disappeared. With another man, if the private investigator had been correct. But still a missing person. Someone who in almost twelve months had never turned up in a hospital, or a morgue, or on her credit card. He had even had the PI check if she was working somewhere but that answer had come back as a no. And his sister, who had introduced them, couldn't find her either.

Because of the note she'd given the midwives, the police had only been mildly interested. Hence the PI.

Look after Piper. She's yours. Don't try to find me. I'm never coming back.

That was what the note had said. The gossip had been less direct. He suspected what the questions had been. Imagined what the midwives had thought. *Why did his wife leave him? What did he do to her? It must have been bad if she left her baby behind...*

The ones who knew him well shook their heads and said, *She'd liked her freedom too much, that one.*

At first he'd been in deep shock. Then denial. She'd come back. A moment's madness. She'd done it before. Left for days. With the reality of a demanding newborn and his worry making it hard for him to sleep at all, his work had suffered. But his largest concern had been the spectre of Clancy with an undiagnosed postnatal depression. Or, worse, the peril of a postnatal psychosis. What other reason could she have for leaving so suddenly so soon after the birth?

Hence he'd paid the private investigator, because there were no forensic leads—the police were inundated with more important affairs than flighty wives. But still no word. All he could do was pray she was safe, at least.

So life had gone on. One painful questioning new morning after another. Day after day with no relief. He hadn't been able to do his job as well as he should have and he'd needed a break from it all.

Buying the cottage had been a good move. Piper stood and cheered him on in her cot when he was doing something tricky, something that didn't need to have a lively little octopus climb all over him while he did it, and she waved her fists and gurgled and encouraged him as he learnt to be a painter. Or a carpenter. Or a tiler.

Or a cook. Or a cleaner. Or a dad.

He was doing okay.

He threw a last look out over the beach towards the grey sea and turned for home. 'That's our walk done for this morning, chicken. Let's go in and have breakfast. Then you can have a sleep and Daddy will grout those tiles in the shower so we can stop having bird baths in the sink.'

Piper loved the shower. Finn did too. When he held her soft, squirming satin baby skin against his chest, the water making her belly laugh as she ducked her head in and out of the stream always made him smile. Sometimes even made him laugh.

So he'd spent extra time on the shower. Adding tiles with animals, starfish, moon shapes and flowers, things they could talk about and keep it a happy place for Piper. And he'd made a square-tiled base with a plug. Soon she could have a little bath. One she could splash in even though it was only the size of the shower.

Doing things for Piper kept him sane. He didn't need the psychologist his sister said he did, or the medication his brother-in-law recommended. Just until he'd climbed out of the hole he'd dug himself to hide in, he would stay here. In Lighthouse Bay. Where nobody pointed or pitied him and every corner didn't hold a memory that scraped like fingernails on the chalkboard of his heavy heart.

Except that around the next corner his heart

froze for a millisecond to see the morning midwife crouched on the path in front of him.

He quickened his pace. 'Are you okay?'

She turned to look up at him, cradling something brightly coloured against her chest, and with the shift of her shoulders he saw the bird cupped in her hands. 'She flew into that window and knocked herself out.'

The lorikeet, blue-headed with a red and yellow chest, lay limp with lime-green wings folded back in her hands. A most flaccid bird.

Still, the red beak and chest shuddered gently so it wasn't dead. 'How do you know it's a girl?' He couldn't believe he'd just said that. But he'd actually thought it was her that had been hurt and relief had made him stupid.

She must have thought he was stupid too. 'I didn't actually lift her legs and look. Not really of major importance, is it?'

Just a little bit of impatience and, surprisingly, it was good to be at the receiving end of a bit of healthy sarcasm. So much better than unending sympathy.

He held up his hands in surrender and Piper's voice floated over both of them from his back. 'Dad, Dad, Dad!'

The girl sucked in her breath and he could see her swan-like neck was tinged with pink. 'Sorry. Night duty ill temper.'

'My bad. All mine. Stupid thing to say. Can you stand up? It's tricky to crouch down with Piper on my back. Let's have a look at her.'

The morning midwife rose fluidly, calves of steel obviously; even he was impressed with her grace—

must be all those uphill walks she did. 'She's not flut-
tering her wings,' she said, empathy lacing a voice
that, had it not been agitated, would have soothed the
bird. He shook himself. She was just being a typical
midwife. That was how most of them had spoken to
him when Clancy had disappeared.

'Still breathing.' He stroked the soft feathers as
the bird lay in her small hands. 'She's limp, but I
think if you put her in a box for a couple of hours in
the dark, she'll rouse when she's had a sleep to get
over the shock.'

'Do you think so?'

'I do. She's not bleeding. Just cover the box with a
light cloth so she can let you know she can fly away
when she's ready.'

'Do I have to put food or water in there?'

'Not food. A little water as long as she doesn't
fall into it and drown.' He grimaced at another stupid comment.

She grinned at him and suddenly the day was
much brighter than it had been. 'Are you a vet?'

'No.'

'Just a bird wrangler?'

She was a stunner. He stepped back. 'One of my
many talents. I'll leave you to it.'

'Thank you.'

'Bye.'

She looked at him oddly. Not surprising. He was
odd. He walked on up the hill.

Her voice followed him. 'Bye, Piper.' He heard
Piper chuckle.

CHAPTER TWO

Trina

TRINA FINISHED HER night shift at seven a.m. on Friday and picked up her mini-tote to sling it on her shoulder. Her last night done, except for emergencies, and she did a little skip as she came out of the door. At first, she'd been reluctant to take the night shift to day shift change that Ellie had offered her because change could be scary, but it had started the whole paradigm inversion that her life had needed. Look out daylight. Here she comes.

Yes. She'd come a long way in almost two years since Ed had died.

Not just because on Monday morning she'd return as acting Midwifery Unit Manager, an unexpected positive career move for Trina at Lighthouse Bay Maternity.

But things had changed.

Her grief stayed internal, or only rarely escaped under her pillow when she was alone in her croft on the cliff.

And since Ellie's wedding last year she'd begun

to think that maybe, some time in the future, she too could look at being friends with a man. If the right one came along.

Not a relationship yet. That idea had been so terrifying, almost like PTSD—the fear of imagining what if history repeated itself; what if that immense pain of loss and grief hit her again? What then?

She'd been catatonic with that thought and to divert herself she'd begun to think of all the other things that terrified her. She'd decided to strengthen her Be Brave muscle.

Last week she'd had her first scuba lesson. Something that had fascinated but petrified her since she'd watched the movie *Finding Nemo* with the daughter of a friend. And in the sparkling cove around the corner from Lighthouse Bay the kindly instructor had been so reassuring, so patient, well… Maybe she'd go back on Saturday for another lesson.

And when she'd mastered that she was going out on a day of deep-sea fishing. The captain's wife had not long delivered a late-in-life baby and Trina had been the midwife. Even though he'd fainted again, he'd promised her a day of deep-sea fishing when he felt better. She'd bought seasickness bands and stored them in her drawer just in case.

She wasn't sure about the parachuting. The girls at work had all joined the idea factory and brochures and social media tags of extreme sports and adventure holidays appeared like magic in her pigeonhole and on her private page. Parachuting? She didn't think so but she'd worry about that later.

Her aim to do one challenge a month seemed possible to allay the fear that she was relying on work to be her whole world. Though not too adventurous—she didn't want to kill herself. Not now.

Her friends were cheering. Thinking of the midwives of Lighthouse Bay…well, that made her whole world warm into a rosy glow. A fiercely loyal flotsam of women tossed here by the fickle cruelty of life, forging into a circle of hands supporting birthing women and each other. All acutely aware of how fortunate they were to have found the magic of the bay.

There was something healing about that crescent of sand that led to the cliffs.

A mystical benevolence about the soaring white lighthouse on the tallest point that looked benignly over the tiny hamlet of coloured houses and shone reassuring light.

And the pretty pastel abodes like a quaint European seaside town were a delight, a new trend that had taken off with the gentle crayon façades dipping in colour like playful toes into the sea.

Crazy coloured houses, and if she could do all those crazy-coloured feats of bravery then just maybe she could be brave enough to begin a real conversation with a man. Like yesterday. She'd almost forgotten the handsome dad was a man when she'd snapped at him. They'd almost had a whole conversation. She wouldn't mind another one so he didn't think she was a short-tempered shrew but she had been concerned about the bird. The one that had flown away two hours later, just like he said it would.

If she could talk to a man she could try again to go

out with one. At least once. She'd been turning them down for six months now. None of them had been Ed.

Now there were more midwives around to lessen the on-call restrictions. Four new midwives had come on board to swell their ranks with the shift to a midwife-led unit. They still had old Dr Southwell in the hospital for non-maternity patients and maternity emergencies, but all the midwives had moved to four days of ten-hour shifts and caring for a caseload of women, so suddenly there was more time for life with an extra day free and people to cover you if needed. And she'd scored the admin side Monday to Thursday, daylight hours, for a year. Starting Monday. Imagine.

So she'd better get out there and grab that exciting life before it drifted past in a haze of regrets. She lifted her head and sucked in a pure lungful of gorgeous sea air.

Without realising it her feet had followed the well-beaten path down to the beach and just as she turned to start her morning breakwall walk she saw the dad and his little girl come up off the beach.

He looked happier today. Nice. It made her smile warmer. 'Beautiful morning.'

He looked startled for a minute. 'Yes, it is.' Almost as if he was surprised. 'Good morning—how is your bird?'

'Flew away two hours later. Didn't look any worse for wear.'

He gave her the first real smile she'd seen. 'That's good.'

Then he was past. Trina turned her head to glance back and the little fair-haired girl waved.

Trina smiled and yawned. She should go to bed and get a couple of hours' sleep before Ellie's farewell lunch. Just a quick walk.

CHAPTER THREE

Finn

THE EARLY-MORNING BREEZE off the ocean seemed cooler. The water had taken till now to shine like a jewel. She'd been late this morning. Finn had waited a minute, hoping she wouldn't see him do it, and strangely the minute seemed to take for ever, then he'd looked back. He'd been thinking of her last night. Wondering if she were sad about a dead bird or happy when it flew away.

He thought back to her response. Now that was a smile. He could see it in his retina like a glance at the sun. Warm and glowing. Saw her walking quite a way in the distance—she'd moved fast. He'd noticed that before, that her pace ran to brisk rather than dawdling. Nurses often did walk briskly. Couldn't seem to slow themselves enough to meander even on a seaside walk. He tore his eyes away.

He'd done the breakwall walk she did a couple of times when he'd first come here but he liked the effort of walking through the sand with Piper on his back. If nothing else he'd become fit and tanned and physically healthier here in a month. And Piper too had sun-kissed limbs and sparkling eyes that exuded health.

His sister would be pleased when she came today. His first visitor. He shied away from that intrusion into his safe world and thought again of the young midwife. Maybe not so young because he'd seen the signs of loss and life in her big coffee eyes—even in those brief glances they'd shot at each other. For the first time he wondered if other people had suffered as much as he had? Well, that at least seemed a positive sign that he could reconnect with his inherent compassion that he'd seemed to have lost.

The thought made him wonder what it would be like to talk to someone who could actually begin to understand his hell, and then called himself crazy for making up a past about someone he didn't know. Poor woman probably had never had a sad day in her life. But something told him otherwise.

Just before one p.m. his sister stepped out of her red convertible and through his front gate. 'It's beautiful, Finn. I can't believe you've done all this yourself!' Her perfectly pencilled brows were raised as she gazed at the pale pink external walls of the house and the rose-red door.

He'd been a little surprised himself. And the front path bordered by pansies and baby's breath looked as if it belonged to some older lady with a green thumb—not a guilt-deranged paediatrician running from life.

She rocked her head slowly. He'd expected disbelief but not this patent incredulity. He felt strangely offended. 'I didn't even know you like to garden!'

He shrugged, urging her towards the door. 'Neither did I. But Piper loves being outside and we needed to do something while we're out here.'

Frances rubbernecked her way up the path, nice and slow for the neighbours, he thought dryly, and sighed while she gushed. She gushed when she didn't know what to say, though what the problem was he had no idea.

'And the house. Freshly painted? You actually painted?' She glanced around. 'Pastel like the others in the street. It's gorgeous.'

Finn looked at the stucco walls. They'd been a pain to paint. 'Piper chose the colour. I would have preferred a blue but, given the choice, she went for pink every time. Never thought I'd have a stereotypical daughter.'

Frances laughed and waved her hand dismissively. 'Piper's too young to choose.'

'No, she's not,' he said mildly. 'How can you say it's not her choice if I give her four colours and she keeps choosing pink?'

Frances looked at him as if he needed a big dose of sympathy for his feeble brain. 'You didn't pretend she was choosing?'

'Who else was I going to ask?' He heard the edge in his voice. And his sister shut up. So then he felt mean.

It was always like this. On and on until he shut her down. She meant well, but for heaven's sake. He wanted her gone already.

They finally made it to the front door.

In an attempt to lighten the mood he stopped to show her something else. 'Piper helped everywhere.' He kissed the top of his daughter's head as she perched on his hip. Quiet for a change because she hadn't quite found her ease with her aunt. Or maybe she was picking up Finn's nervous vibes. Either way she leaned into him, unusually subdued.

He pointed to a handprint on the front step that he'd finished with instant cement. Using a layer of cling wrap over the wet surface, he'd pressed her starfish hand into the step on each side while holding her clamped to his side. The little palm prints made him smile every time he opened the door.

'Come in.' He heard the pride in his voice and mocked himself. Finn the decorator. 'There's still the kitchen and laundry, but I've finished Piper's corner, the bathroom and the floating boards on the floor because she'll need a solid surface to learn to walk on.'

Frances rotated her neck, as if stuck to the step and that was the only part of her body she could move. 'It's tiny.'

He frowned. 'Yes. It's a beach cottage. Not a mansion.'

She blinked. Shifted uneasily. 'Oh, yes. Of course. But your other beautiful house…'

'Is on the market.'

Now the shock was real. Frances had approved mightily of his imposing residence on top of the hill. Two hills over from her imposing residence. He'd only liked it because Clancy, his missing wife, had loved it.

Frances spluttered, 'You're buying a new house?'

'I've bought a new house.' He put out one hand and gestured. 'This house. I'm staying here.'

'I… I thought you'd done this for the owners. That you rented?'

'I am the owner.' *A little too fierce, Finn,* he chided himself.

Frances leaned towards him pleadingly. 'But your work?'

'Will be here too when I'm ready. One of the GPs here has offered me a place in his practice when I'm ready. I'll specialise in children but do all the GP stuff I've almost forgotten. It'll be good.' He wasn't sure who he was convincing, Frances or himself. 'It won't be yet because I'm in no hurry.'

'But…'

'But what?'

His sister turned worried eyes on his. 'You were only supposed to come here for a few weeks and then come back. Come home.'

'Home to where, Frances? To what? To an empty castle on a hill full of ghosts and pain. To a clinic with not enough hours in the day so I had to keep my daughter in long day care?'

Frances looked stricken and he leaned in and shared a hug with her, Piper still a limpet on his other hip. Frances meant well and she truly loved him. And now that Mum was gone she was all the family he had. Of course she'd never understood him with the ten-year age difference. Frances hadn't understood Mum either, if they were being honest. 'It's okay. This is a magic place to live and for Piper and me this is the right place at the right time. We're staying.'

Frances almost wrung her hands. 'You won't meet any eligible women here.'

He could feel his mood slip further. His irritation rise. His disappointment deepen. His sister didn't understand his guilt couldn't be fixed by an eligible woman. 'Eligible for what, Frances? I'm no good for any woman at the moment and won't be...' he didn't say *ever* '...for a very long time.'

He decided not to demonstrate the shower. Or point anything else out. Ditched the plans to take a picnic to the beach.

Instead he took Frances to the most expensive restaurant in town, where Piper slept in her stroller beside the table despite the noise of conversations and laughter all around, and listened to her stories of droll people and dire events in her husband's practice.

In the corner of the restaurant he noticed a very attractive brunette. She nodded at him and he realised it was his morning midwife, elegantly dressed—*sans* scrubs—and made-up like a model, her brown hair blow-dried and shining, the glints catching the sun. Looking like a million bucks. Other men were looking at her. He preferred the windblown version.

She sat, a little isolated, in a lively group of people, all chinking champagne flutes to celebrate. Frances would approve of the clientele, he thought dryly, but recognised the older doctor he'd mentioned to his sister, and noted the stylish older woman next to him who leant into his shoulder, probably his wife. Another young woman he hadn't seen around was chatting to the vibrantly glowing woman in the latter stages of pregnancy who drank water, and next

to her a man hovered protectively, obviously the doting father-to-be.

He wished him better luck than he'd had. Finn felt
his heart twist in self-disgust. He'd tried that. A lot
of good that had done him.

'Finn?'

His sister's voice called him back to the present
and he jerked his face away from them. 'Sorry. You
were telling me about Gerry's partner?'

Frances hovered over being cross for a moment and
thankfully decided to forgive graciously. 'I was saying she has no idea how a doctor's wife should dress.'

The lunch dragged on until finally Piper woke up
and gave him an excuse to pay the bill.

They waved Frances goodbye after lunch with
much relief. 'Seriously, Piper. Your aunt is getting
worse. We're lucky to be so far away.'

They took the sand buckets and spade back down
to the beach in the afternoon because Piper's routine
had been disrupted and she needed to get some play
time in and wear herself out before bedtime.

To his surprise, and with a seagull-like swoop of
uplifting spirits, the morning midwife sat there on the
breakwall, back in beach clothes and mussed by the
wind. He smiled at her like a long-lost friend. After
the visit from his sister he felt as if he needed a pal.

CHAPTER FOUR

Trina

TRINA SAT SWINGING her legs on the breakwall down on the beach and breathed in the salt. The sea air blew strands into her eyes but it felt too good to worry about that. She saw him before he saw her and a deep, slashing frown marred his forehead. Different to this morning. Then his expression changed as he saw her, the etched lines disappeared and an unexpected, ridiculously sexy, warmly welcoming smile curved in a big sweep. *Goodness.* What had she done to deserve that?

'Lovely afternoon,' he said and the little girl waved.

Trina's mouth twitched as she waved back. 'Beautiful. I saw you at lunch. That's three times in a day.'

'A new world record,' he agreed and she blushed. No idea why.

He paused beside her, another world record, and looked down from far too high. Up close and stationary, told herself again, he would be a very good-looking man—to other women. She studied him almost dispassionately. Long lashes framed those bril-

liant blue eyes and his dark brown wavy hair curled
a tad too long over his ears. His chin was set firm
and his cheekbones bordered on harsh in the bright
light. She could see his effort to be social cost him.
She knew the feeling.

'I'm Catrina Thomas.' She didn't enlarge. He could
ask if he was interested, but something told her he
wasn't so much interested as in need of a friend.
Which suited her perfectly.

'Finlay Foley. And you've met Piper. My daughter.'
The little girl bounced in the backpack.

You could do nothing but smile at Piper. 'Piper
looks like she wants to get down amongst the sand.'

'Piper is happiest when she's caked in sand.' His
hand lifted to stroke the wiggling little leg at his
chest. Strong brown fingers tickling a plump golden
baby ankle. 'We're going to build sandcastles. Piper
is going to play hard and long and get extremely tired
so she will sleep all night.' Trina wasn't sure if he was
telling her or telling Piper. She suspected the latter.

'Nice theory,' Trina agreed judiciously. 'I see you
have it all worked out.'

He began to fiddle with the straps as he extricated
his daughter from the backpack and clinically she
watched the muscle play as man power pulled his
loose white shirt tight. His thick dark hair tousled in
the wind and drew her eyes until she was distracted
again by the wriggling child. Finlay popped her down
in the sand on her bottom and put a spade and bucket
beside her.

'There, miss.' He glanced up at Trina. 'Her aunt
came today and she's ruined our sleep routine.' He

paused at that. 'Speaking of routines, this is late in the day for you to be on the beach.'

'Nice of you to notice.' She wasn't sure if it was. There had been a suspicious lift of her spirits when she'd realised the woman he'd shared lunch with was his sister. What was that? She didn't have expectations and he wouldn't either—not that she supposed he would have. She wasn't ready for that. 'Don't get ideas or I'll have to leave.' Almost a joke. But she explained.

'Today is my first official Friday off for a long time. I'm off nights and on day shifts for the next year. Monday to Thursday.' She looked around at the little groups and families on the beach and under the trees at the park. Pulled a mock frowning face. 'I'll have to talk to people and socialise, I guess.'

'I know. Sucks, doesn't it.' The underlying truth made them both stop and consider. And smile a little sheepishly at each other.

Another urge to be truthful came out of nowhere. 'I'm a widow and not that keen on pretending to be a social butterfly. Hence the last two years on night duty.'

He said more slowly, as if he wasn't sure why he was following suit either, 'My wife left us when Piper was born. A day later. I've morphed into antisocial and now I'm hiding here.'

Died? Or left? How could his wife leave when their daughter was born? She closed her mouth with a snap. Not normal. Something told her Piper's mum hadn't died, though she didn't know why. Postnatal depression then? A chilling thought. Not domestic violence?

As if he read her thoughts, he added, 'I think she

left with another man.' He seemed to take a perverse pleasure in her disbelief. 'I need to start thinking about going back to work soon. Learn to stop trying to guess what happened. To have adult conversations.'

He shrugged those impressive shoulders. Glanced around at the white sand and waves. 'I'm talking to Piper's dolls now.'

Still bemused by the first statement, the second took a second to sink in. Surprisingly, Trina giggled. She couldn't remember the last time she'd giggled like a schoolgirl.

He smiled and then sobered. 'Which means Piper and her dolls must go into day care if I go back to work.'

'That's hard,' Trina agreed but wondered what sort of work he could 'start thinking about going back to'. Not that there were screeds of choices around here. 'Maybe part-time?'

'I think so.'

'Are you a builder? The house looks good.'

He laughed at that. 'No. Far from it. Piper's taught me everything I know.'

Trina giggled again. *Stop it.* She sounded like a twit. But he was funny. 'I didn't have you pegged as a comedian.'

His half-laugh held a hint of derision at himself. 'Not usually. Remember? Antisocial.'

She nodded with solemn agreement. 'You're safe with me. If you need a protected space to tell your latest doll story you can find me.' She waited until his eyes met hers. 'But that's all.'

'Handy to know. Where do I find you? You know

where I live.' Then he turned away as if he regretted asking.

'Of course I know where you live. It's a small town and single men with babies are rare.' Trina looked at him. 'I meant…find me here. But I'll think about it. I'm happy to have a male friend but not a stalker.'

She felt like an idiot saying that but thankfully he just looked relieved. 'Hallelujah. And I promise I will never, ever turn up uninvited.'

'We have that sorted.' She glanced at Piper, who sat on the sand licking white granules off her fingers, and bit back a grin. 'It's good when children will eat anything.'

Finn focused instantly on his daughter and scooped her up. Trina could see him mentally chastising himself. She imagined something like, *See what happens when you don't concentrate on your daughter*, and she knew he'd forgotten her. Was happy for the breathing space because, speaking of breathing, she was having a little trouble.

She heard his voice from a long way away. 'Sand is for playing—not eating, missy.' He scooped the grains from her mouth and brushed her lips. His quick glance brushed over Trina as well as he began to move away. 'Better go wash her mouth out and concentrate. Nice to meet you, Catrina.'

'You too,' she said, suddenly needing to bolt home and shut her door.

Ten minutes later the lock clunked home solidly and she leant back against the wood. Another scary challenge achieved.

Not that she'd been in danger—just a little more challenged than she'd been ready for. And she had been remarkably loose with her tongue. Told him she was a widow. About her job. The hours she worked. What had got into her? That was a worry. So much so that it did feel incredibly comforting to be home. Though, now that she looked around, it seemed dark inside. She frowned. Didn't just *seem* dark.

Her home was dark.

And just a little dismal. She frowned and then hurried to reassure herself. Not tragically so, more efficiently gloomy for a person who slept through a lot of the daylight hours. She pulled the cord on the kitchen blind and it rolled up obediently and light flooded in from the front, where the little dead-end road finished next door.

She moved to the side windows and thinned the bunching of the white curtains so she could see through them. Maybe she could open those curtains too. Now that she'd be awake in the daytime. Moving out of the dark, physically and figuratively.

So, she'd better see to lightening it up. Maybe a few bright cushions on her grey lounge suite; even a bright rug on the floor would be nice. She stared down at the grey and black swirled rug she'd bought in a monotone furnishing package when she moved in. Decided she didn't like the lack of colour.

She crossed the room and threw open the heavy curtains that blocked the view. Unlocking the double glass doors and pushing them slowly open, she stepped out onto her patio to look out over the glittering expanse of ocean that lay before her like a big blue shot-thread quilt as far as the eye could see. She didn't look down to the beach, though she wanted too. Better not see if there was the figure of a man and a little girl playing in the waves.

Instead she glanced at the little croft to her right where Ellie and Sam lived while Sam built the big house on the headland for their growing family. She wondered if they would keep the croft, as they said they would. It would be strange to have new neighbours on top of everything else.

The three crofts sat like seabirds perched on a branch of the headland, the thick walls painted white like the lighthouse across the bay and from the same solid stone blocks. Trina's veranda had a little awning over the deck the others lacked. A thick green evergreen hedge separated the buildings to shoulder height.

On the other side of her house lay Myra's croft. Originally from Paddington in Sydney, stylish Myra ran the coffee shop at the hospital and had recently married the older Dr Southwell—her boss Ellie's father-in-law.

Two brides in two months, living each side of her, and maybe that had jolted her out of her apathy as much as anything else. Surrounded by people jumping bravely into new relationships and new lives had to make a woman think.

She stepped out and crossed to the two-person swing seat she'd tussled with for hours to assemble. Her last purchase as a flat-pack. Last *ever*, she promised herself.

She'd never seen so many screws and bolts and instructions in one flat-pack. Then she'd been left with a contraption that had to be dragged inside when it got too windy here on top of the cliffs because it banged and rattled and made her nervous that it would fly into the ocean on a gust. It wasn't really that she thought about the fact it needed a second person. Not at all.

She stepped back inside, glanced around then picked up the sewing basket and dug in it for the ribbons she'd put away. Went back to the double doors and tied back the curtains so they were right off the windows. Not that she was getting visitors—her mind shied away from the mental picture of a man and his baby daughter.

No. She'd lighten it because now she didn't need to exclude the light to help her sleep. She was a day-shift person. She was brave. And tomorrow she'd scuba again, and maybe talk to Finlay and Piper if she saw them because she was resurrecting her social skills and stepping forward. Carefully.

CHAPTER FIVE

Finn

FINN GLANCED BACK to the rocky breakwall once, to the
spot where Catrina—nice name—had disappeared,
as he crouched with Piper at the edge of the water to
rinse her mouth of sand. It seemed other people did
hurt like he did. And were left with scars that im-
pacted hugely on how they lived their lives.

Two years working on night duty. He shuddered
but could see the logic. Side-stepping the cold space
beside you in the bed at night and avoiding that feeling of loss being the first thing you noticed in the day.
Maybe he should have given that a go.

But the way she'd said she hadn't pegged him as
a comedian surprised him out of his usual lethargy.
He'd made her laugh twice—that was pretty stellar.
Apart from his daughter, whose sense of humour ran
to very simple slapstick, he hadn't made anyone giggle for a long time. He could almost hear her again.
Such a delicious giggle. More of a gurgle really.

So—a widow? Lost like him, for a different reason. He wondered how her husband had died but in

the end it didn't really change her pain. He was gone. For ever. Unlike the uncertainty he lived with.

Would Clancy ever come back? In a year. In ten years? Was she even alive? But, most of all, what would he tell Piper when she grew up? How could he say her mother loved her when she'd walked away and never asked about her again? The pain for Piper's future angst had grown larger than his own loss and he had no desire to rush the explanations.

Milestones with Piper never passed without him singeing himself with bitterness that Clancy wasn't there to see them. First tooth. First word. First step last week—though she still spent most of her time on her bottom. And on Sunday—first birthday. He felt his jaw stiffen. That would be the day he said *enough*. Enough holding his breath, expecting Clancy to walk through the door.

A milestone he'd never thought he'd get to. He hadn't decided whether to stay in Lighthouse Bay for the day with their usual routine; he was leaning towards taking Piper shopping, something he loathed, so that the logistics of strollers and car parking and crowd managing with a toddler drowned out the reminders of the best day of his life twelve months ago that had changed so soon after.

He wondered suddenly if he could ask Catrina to come. As a diversion, a pseudo-mother for the day, and then found himself swamped by such intense anger at Clancy for leaving their daughter he almost moaned. Piper clutched his hand and he looked down to see his daughter's eyes staring up at him as if she could sense his pain.

He scooped her up and hugged her, felt the lump in his chest and willed it away. Whatever they did, he needed to remember it was a celebration of this angel in his arms, not of the woman who'd left them.

'I'll always love you, darling.' The words came out thickly. 'What would you like to do on Sunday, Piper?'

'Mum, Mum, Mum, Mum.'

He groaned and buried his face in her shimmering golden cloud of hair. Fine mist-like hair that floated in the breeze and tangled if he didn't tie it back but he couldn't bring himself to get it cut. His gorgeous little buttercup with her fine-spun headache of hair.

'Mum, Mum, Mum,' Piper chirped.

The last thing he needed to hear at this moment. 'Oh, baby, don't. Please.'

She squirmed and the baby voice drifted up to him. Uncertain. 'Dad, Dad, Dad, Dad?'

Pull yourself together. He lifted his head and looked into the soft dimpled face so close to his. 'Yes. Dad, Dad, Dad, Dad.' He carried her into the waves to dangle her feet and she wriggled happily. He concentrated on his fingers holding her as he swept her ankles through the waves and the foam ran up her knees as she squealed in delight. Guilt swamped him all over again. 'You can say *Mum, Mum, Mum* any time, my darling. Of course you can. Daddy's being silly.' *Stupid!*

Piper gurgled with laughter. 'Dad, Dad, Dad, Dad.' Finn could feel his heart shattering into a million pieces again and any lingering thoughts of Catrina the midwife washed into the sea with the grains of sand stuck to Piper's feet.

CHAPTER SIX

Trina

THE EARLY-MORNING SUNBEAM poked Trina in the eye with an unfamiliar exuberance and she groaned and threw her hand up to cover her face. *Who left the curtains open?* Only one answer to that. The twinge of morning memory and loss made her breath hitch and she forced herself to breathe calmly.

Saturday morning. Scuba lesson. She groaned again and all the doubts and fears from last week came rushing back to twist her stomach. Why had she said she wanted to do this again? Why the need to push herself to extremes she didn't feel comfortable with?

She flung the bedclothes back and swung her legs. The floor was warmed a little under her feet from the sun. That too seemed different.

Okay. Why was she fighting this? This was a new chapter in her life. Same book. She wasn't removing any of the pages—just going forward.

She squinted at the morning beams painting the inside of her one-room croft in golden stripes and decided they were quite lovely. Not worth groaning about at all.

She padded across to the uncurtained double doors looking out over the ocean and decided the light streaming in shone still a little too bright until she'd made an Earl Grey to start the day and turned her back.

As she busied herself in the tiny kitchen nook, she pondered on yesterday and the advances she'd made towards holding a sensible conversation with an eligible male. Though technically she guessed he wasn't eligible. But probably safe to practise on, as long as he was okay with it.

Not that she had any long-term intentions but she'd done all right. Beaten the bogeyman, and so had he. That made it a little easier. And no doubt different for him, as his wife had chosen to go. How on earth could a woman leave her baby? And why would she leave Finlay? That too was a teensy worry.

Trina thought back to where she'd been a year ago. Still in a black fog with a bright shiny mask on her face for work.

She didn't believe that time healed all wounds, but maybe it scabbed over some of the deeper lacerations. The problem with losing your true love was they were never really gone, always hovering, a comfort, and an ache that flared into pain that burned right through you.

Boy, did she recognise the symptoms of reluctantly dipping a toe into the real world after the misty haze of deep grief. There were some aspects of her loss of Ed that would never disappear but in other ways she could, and would, live a happy life. She didn't think that Finlay Foley had reached that stage yet. Which was a tiny shame.

But she'd better get on and prepare for her scuba lesson. She'd eat when she came back.

By the time Trina left her croft on the cliff she knew she'd be late if she didn't hurry and her steps skipped as she descended to the beach with her towel and specially fitted snorkelling mask. That was one good thing about living right on the beach—she didn't need to carry much because home was always a few steps away.

The path stopped at the sand and Trina began walking quickly around the headland. She'd glanced once towards the curve of the bay but no Finlay and Piper there, no sign of him, so tall and broad and unmistakable, so no golden-haired Piper on his back either, and fancifully it felt strange to be hurrying away without seeing them.

She forced herself to look forward again and concentrated on the scuba lessons she'd learnt last week from old Tom, running through the procedures.

'Nice even breathing through the mouthpiece; no holding your breath. This is how to replace a regulator in your mouth if it gets knocked out. This is how to control the speed of your ascent and descent by letting air in and out via the buoyancy control, so your ears don't hurt. Nothing to be nervous about. We'll go as slow as you need.'

Two hours later as she walked home in a much more desultory fashion a glow of pride warmed her as she remembered old Tom's quiet pleasure in her. 'You're a natural,' he'd told her.

A natural scuba diver? Who would have known? But today he'd taken her to the little island just off the beach and they'd dived slowly around the tiny inlets and rocks and seen colourful fish, delicate submarine plant life that swayed with the rhythm of the ocean, once a small stingray and one slightly larger shark, and it had all been Technicolor brilliant. Exciting. And, to her absolute delight, she'd loved it.

Her mind danced with snapshots of the morning and she didn't see the man and little girl sitting in a shallow rock pool under the cliff until she was almost upon them.

'Oh. You. Hello,' she stammered as she was jerked out of her happy reveries.

'Good morning, Catrina,' Finlay said. Though how on earth he could remain nonchalant while sitting in a sandy-bottom indent in the rock where the water barely covered his outstretched legs, she had no idea. 'You look very pleased with yourself.'

She regarded them. She liked the way they looked—so calm and happy, Piper dressed in her frilly pink swimsuit that covered her arms and legs. And she liked the way he called her Catrina. Ed had always called her Trina and she wasn't ready for another man to shorten her name. 'Good morning to you, Finlay.'

'Finn. Please. I'm usually Finn. Don't know why I was so formal yesterday.'

'Finn.' She nodded and smiled down at Piper. 'Hello, Piper. What can you see in the rock pool?'

The little girl turned her big green eyes back to the water. Pointed one plump finger. 'Fiss,' Piper said and Finn's eyes widened.

His mouth opened and closed just like the word his daughter had almost mouthed.

'She said fish!' His eyes were alight with wonder and the huge smile on his face made Trina want to hug him to celebrate the moment of pure joy untinged by bitterness. 'I can't believe she said fish.'

'Clever girl,' Trina said and battled not to laugh out loud. She'd thought it had been more like a mumbled *fiss*. But she was sure her father knew better. Her mouth struggled to remain serious. In the end she giggled. Giggled? Again? *What the heck?*

She'd never been a giggler but this guy made her smiles turn into noises she cringed at.

To hide her idiotic response she said, 'I've seen fish too, Piper.'

Finn glanced at her mask. 'You've been snorkelling?'

Trina spread her arms and said with solemn pride, almost dramatically, 'I have been scuba diving.'

'Have you? Go you. I used to love to scuba.' He glanced around. 'Would you like to join us in our pool? There's no lifeguard except me but if you promise not to run or dive we'll let you share.'

Trina scanned the area too. Nobody she knew. She'd look ridiculous, though a voice inside her head said he looked anything but ridiculous in his skin-tight blue rash shirt and board shorts that left not one gorgeous muscle top or bottom unaccounted for.

She put down her mask and the sandals she carried, folded her towel to sit on, hiked up her sundress so it didn't drag in the water and eased herself down at the edge of the pool and put her feet in. The water felt deliciously cool against her suddenly warmer skin.

Finn watched her and she tried not to be aware of that. Then Piper splashed him and the mood broke into something more relaxed. 'So where did you go to scuba?'

She glanced the way she'd come. 'Have you been around the headland?'

He nodded. 'Around the next two until Piper started to feel like a bag of cement on my back.'

Trina laughed. She could so imagine that. She smiled at him. 'The next bay is called Island Bay and the little rocky island that's about four hundred metres out is called Bay Island.'

He laughed. 'Creative people around here.'

She pretended to frown at him. 'I like to think of it as being whimsical.'

'Whimsical. Right.'

She nodded at him. 'Thank you. So, Bay Island is where I did this morning's lesson. Old Tom takes beginners out.'

Piper sat between Finn's legs and he had his big brown long-fingered hands around her tiny waist so she couldn't slip. She was splashing with her starfish hands and silver droplets of water dripped in chasing drops down her father's chest. An unexpected melancholy overwhelmed Trina because the picture made her ache for lost opportunities she should have had with Ed. Opportunities Finn should have had with his wife. She wondered when these thoughts would stop colouring her every experience.

Finn smiled. 'Let me guess. His business is called Old Tom's Dive Shop.'

She jerked back to the present. Her brows crinkled in mock disbelief and she drew the sentence out slowly. 'How did you know that?'

'I'm psychic.' His expression remained serious.

'Really?' She tried for serious too but he was doing it again and her mouth twitched.

'Mmm-hmm. True story.'

'Wow.' She noted the little girl had found a treasure. 'So you can see your daughter is about to put a shell in her mouth?'

Without taking his eyes off Trina's face, his hand came up gently and directed Piper's hand away from her lips. Brushed her fingers open until she dropped the shell and bent down and kissed the little fingers. 'Absolutely.'

'That's fascinating.' And it was. Watching this big bronzed man being so gentle and connected to this tiny girl-child. The bond between them made tears sting Trina's eyes and she pretended she'd splashed water in them. Until she felt, and heard, her tummy rumble with sullen emptiness and seized on the excuse.

'Well, as lovely as your private ocean pool is, I need to have food. I missed breakfast and I'm starving.'

'Ah. So that's what the noise was,' he teased. 'I thought it was an outboard motor.'

She flicked tiny droplets from her damp fingers at him. 'Too rude.'

He rolled his eyes at her, then shifted Piper from between his legs to sit in the shallow pool and stood up easily. He leant down to offer her his hand. 'Piper's hungry. I should feed her too.'

She barely heard him. His so casually offered fingers were a stumbling block and she hesitated. Piper splashed and she knew she was holding them up. Reluctantly she put out her hand to his and his strong brown fingers closed over hers to lift her smoothly. Way too easily. But the touch of his fingers on hers created such a vibration between them that their eyes met. One pair as startled as the other.

When she was standing he let go quickly and bent down to hoist his daughter into his arms. His face stayed hidden as he tickled her and Trina straightened her own shocked features into a mask of politeness as Piper giggled.

'Well,' she said awkwardly, still rocked by the frisson of awareness that had warmed her whole hand. Her whole arm really. 'Thanks for the swim.'

'Can we walk back with you?'

No, she thought. 'Of course,' she said. And resisted the urge to hold her tingling hand in the other. She bent down and picked up her sandals and mask, slung her towel over her shoulder and resolutely faced the bay until they began walking beside her.

'Would you like to have lunch with us?'

No, she thought. *I can't. I don't know what I'm feeling and it's making me more nervous than scuba diving ever did.* But that was the idea of these new

challenges. To challenge things that seemed daunting.
And Finn was safe. It took her a long time to answer
but strangely she didn't feel pressured to make that
snap decision. So she thought about it some more.
It was just an impromptu lunch. And Piper made it
much easier than if there were just the two of them.
'Okay. Where?'

'How about the beach shop? They have a closed-in
play area that Piper loves to crawl around. It's shady
and the breeze is always good there.'

'Sounds easy. But how about I meet you there? I
didn't bring my purse. I can just run up to the croft
and get it.'

He looked a little crestfallen. 'Piper may not last
that long. She's nearly ready for her sleep. I could
shout you. You could pay for ice creams or something next time?'

Next time? They hadn't tried this time yet. This
was all happening way too fast. And wasn't he having as much trouble as she was, putting a toe in the
water of opposite sex conversation? Panic built like
a wave rising from the ocean to her left. She tried to
ride it and not be dumped.

He must have seen the indecision on her face because his features softened in understanding. 'It's
okay. We can do a rain-check for another day.'

Disappointment dipped in her stomach. Did she
want that? Why was everything so hard? 'No. Let's
not. Thank you. I'll just buy the next one, if that's
okay. A quick bite would be nice with company.'

They sat under the umbrellas and watched Piper
play with a stand of coloured balls, then crawl im-

portantly to steer a pretend ship with a bright blue Captain's wheel. Every time the conversation flagged, Piper sparked a new discussion with some cute little parody of life in her determination to experience all that the colourful play area offered.

Trina could do with her enthusiasm. Considered that fact. 'Babies should be compulsory on all outings. You could watch her all day.'

Finn laughed. Then, more seriously, said, 'I do. She keeps me sane. Makes me get out of bed in the morning.'

Trina knew that feeling. 'Well, you've certainly been busy since you got here. Your cottage is pretty in pink.'

'Piper chose the colour,' he said and then looked at her as if expecting her to laugh.

'So she's a pink girl. I can believe that. It looks good on her.' Trina rested her cheek on her hand to watch his face, trying to understand why he should be so wary. 'How did you get her to choose?'

'I gave her swatches. I was hoping for blue but she took the pink every time.'

Too funny. Trina laughed. 'Great idea. I can see that too.' She looked at his face and his beautiful smile. She shook her head. 'Her decision. You were stuck with it. Nothing you can do about that, then.'

He shrugged, his expression light and relaxed. It made her warm that he could be that way around her. 'I'm used to it now. I've been learning to be a handyman. And quite enjoying the challenge.'

Handyman. Or woman. The bane of her life. She rolled her eyes. 'Boy, have I had some repair challenges in the last two years? I've had to learn that too. Maybe I should paint my croft. Just yesterday I was thinking it looks very dark inside.' She shut her mouth. Now, why did she say that? Almost an invitation for help.

Finn's voice was light—lighter than her thoughts. 'I can send Piper up if you like. To talk colours with you.'

Trina felt herself relax. He got it. Her expression had probably telegraphed the message that she'd regretted being so open. 'I might take you up on that one day.' She could hear the relief in her voice. Hoped he couldn't.

They'd finished their roast beef sandwiches and iced coffee and Trina desperately needed some distance to think about the morning with Finn but the moment passed.

A commotion at the next table made them both turn. A woman had overturned her chair and the crash turned every head her way. She shook a small child hysterically. 'Spit it out. Come on.' She glanced around wildly. 'He swallowed a button.'

The child gasped weakly, tried to cry and couldn't find enough air to do so as he gulped and coughed. His face was tinged an alarming shade of blue as his mouth quivered.

Finn rose from their table and crossed the space in two strides. 'May I? I'm a doctor.' He didn't wait long.

The woman sagged, nodded and, sobbing in panic, watched as Finn took the child from her. Trina had followed him and righted the woman's chair and urged her back into it. Finn was a doctor. *Wow.* He'd said he wasn't a vet.

Finn sank into the nearest seat and lay the little boy, head down, across his knees and patted his mid back firmly in slow pats.

Trina leaned towards him. 'Can I help?'

Finn shook his head and concentrated on the boy. He patted again, then tipped him further. 'Come on now, mate. Everything is fine. Cough it up.'

To Trina's relief a sudden plop heralded the arrival of the button as it flew out onto the floor, initiating a collective sigh of relief from the entire café. And her. *Wow. Calmness is us.*

Finn righted the little boy and gave him a reassuring squeeze. Then he stood up with the exhausted child in his arms and passed him to his mother as if nothing had happened.

'He'll be fine. Just needs a minute to get his breath back.' He rested his hand on her shoulder and spoke quietly into her ear. Trina couldn't hear what he said but the woman nodded. Once. Twice. Glanced at the boy in her arms and squeezed him tighter. Then looked back at Finn with a vehement nod. 'Thank you.' The words were heartfelt.

Trina felt her eyes sting. Her heart still thudded from the spectre of a child choking to death in front of them all. She had no doubt everyone there had felt for the fear of the mother, though Trina would have liked to have given her a few pointers about first aid manoeuvres.

She glanced to where Piper played contentedly, oblivious to the drama she'd missed, and oblivious to the fact her daddy had quite possibly just saved a little boy's life. Trina wanted to go home. She felt too emotional to be out in public. Though she suspected she would still be thinking about Finn even if she was away from him.

When Finn sat back down and the conversations around them had begun again she nodded towards the woman, who was paying her bill and leaving with her little boy hugging her leg as he waited.

'Good job. What did you say to her?' She didn't mention he'd said he was a doctor. It didn't matter what he was.

'I asked if she'd seen what I did and, if there was a next time, to try that instead. That shaking didn't help and was actually dangerous. That calm speaking would relax the oesophagus as well.'

'I'm impressed. Discreet and direct.' The guy did everything right. But she still needed to get away from the emotionally charged atmosphere. She collected her mask and towel from the ground beside her and pushed her chair back. 'Before all the excitement I was about to leave. So thank you for lunch.' She glanced at his daughter, who had apparently wrung every conceivable amusement out of the play area and looked to be ready to depart as well.

'Maybe next weekend I could repay the favour.' Piper wailed. 'As long as Piper is free?'

Finn stood up to rescue his daughter. 'I'll look in her calendar and let you know.'

Their eyes connected for a moment, both a little bemused by the ease of their conversation. 'That would be lovely. Thank you, Finn.'

'Thank you, Catrina.' He watched her again and she knew he didn't want her to go. His approval circled her like a whisper of flame crackling and warming her around the base of her lost confidence. But the lure of time away from this new and challenging situation beckoned enticingly.

She stood and waved to the tiny girl. 'Bye, Piper.'

CHAPTER SEVEN

Finn

FINN WATCHED HER walk swiftly across the car park to the path. Almost hurrying away from him. Was it the incident with the little boy? That had turned out okay. Poor terrified little kid and mum—but all right now.

His eyes followed Catrina as Piper leaned into his neck. Maybe she'd left because she felt he was pushing for her company? He was. Why was he pressuring her? If someone had pushed him like he was pushing her he'd have run for the hills. Or a croft. Which she did.

Maybe he was sabotaging himself and hoping she'd stop it before he did? But there was no getting over the fact he'd been a little desperate for Catrina to stay.

And then there had been that jolt when he'd helped her stand at the rock pool. Unconsciously his hands came together to replicate the action, as if to see if he could still feel that vibration that had taken them both by surprise. It had been bizarre, and he'd seen the shock in her face—apparently he hadn't been the only one to feel it—before he'd picked up Piper to give himself a moment to recover.

He wished he'd told her it was Piper's birthday tomorrow. Because at lunch, after an initial stiffness, conversation had felt so easy. It had been strangely healing to have her sitting opposite him as they both watched his baby playing. When Catrina was there it was easier not to think about where Piper's mother would be tomorrow.

The guilt hit him like a fist in the chest and he sucked in his breath. What was he doing? How could he think that? He was a coward and tomorrow he'd celebrate Piper—he needed to be man enough not to cower in a corner feeling sorry for himself. He paid the bill and gathered Piper up in his arms.

Tomorrow he'd survive and Monday he'd see about getting a job.

Sunday morning Finn woke with a headache. Unusually, Piper had been unsettled most of the night and he wondered if they were both coming down with a cold. Or if the emotion of the coming anniversary of Clancy's desertion was rubbing off him and onto Piper.

He took two paracetamol and a vitamin tablet, and hand-squeezed an orange to give Piper with her breakfast. Because she was still asleep, he decided they wouldn't go out for the day if they were both unwell. He looked at the two wrapped presents he had for Piper. One was a tiny gardening set in a flower-decorated garden basket and the other a push-along block set for inside or out.

The cupboard above the sink drew his eyes and

he crossed the room and searched for the packet cake mix he'd thrown in there a month ago in case he needed to make Piper's birthday cake. The packet mix came with little blue cupcake wrappers, pink frosting and fairy princess stickers to press into the icing after they'd been cooked.

The instructions seemed basic and he set it all out, with the candle, for later when he could make some noise. He glanced across at Piper but she snored gently and he wandered to the front of the beach house and stared out at the waves across the bay.

He could see Catrina walking along the break-wall and watched her brisk walk as she strode further away, the wind whipping her hair across her face. He wanted to wave and call her and share the burden and the blessing of this day with her, but knew he wouldn't.

'Last thing she needs,' he told himself out loud, keeping his voice quiet.

'Boo,' said a little voice from behind him and he turned to see Piper standing in her cot with her bunny cuddle blanket over her face.

Despite his aching heart, he smiled. 'Where's Piper?'

Piper pulled the blanket off her head and appeared like magic. Her eyes crinkled with delight at her own cleverness. 'Boo.'

'There she is.' He crossed the room to her but before he arrived he put his hands over his face and then pulled them away. 'Boo to you too, missy. Happy birthday, Piper!' He lifted her up out of her cot and hugged her. She gurgled with squirming delight and he had to force himself not to squeeze her too tight.

He began to sing 'Happy birthday' but faltered halfway through when he thought of Clancy and all she was missing. Forcing himself to finish the song, he carried Piper over to the window. 'It's a breezy sunny day for your birthday. What would you like to do?'

Piper put her head on his shoulder and snuggled in.

Suddenly it was okay again. They could do this. 'You feeling a little fragile today, poppet? Me too. But I'm making you a cake this morning. You can help by pushing on the stickers. It will be our first cake but your daddy is a doctor and supposed to be very smart. I'm sure we can manage little pink cakes for our birthday girl.' She bounced with a little more enthusiasm in his arms.

'Then we can sit outside and let the sunshine and fresh air kill all the germs, if there are any. No work today. Lazy day.'

He put Piper down on the floor and she crawled away from him to her box of toys in the corner with just a little less than her usual surprising speed.

He watched her go and thought about looking for childcare tomorrow. If he couldn't find anything then they'd leave it all for a while longer. That thought brought comfort. Surely it would be hard to find someone in a small town like this at such short notice.

He glanced out of the window again down to the beach and saw Catrina was on her way back. She didn't pass his house, or hadn't in the past or he would have noticed, and he leaned towards the window and saw her moving up the hill towards the cliff opposite the lighthouse. She'd said 'croft' yesterday. Maybe she was in one of those three little cottages on the cliffs that matched the lighthouse. All white stone.

He'd liked the look of them but the real estate agent had said they weren't for sale. He'd never actually gone up that way towards the hospital along the cliff path. Maybe it would be a nice place to go for a change when he went walking with Piper. Just in case he was missing out on a good walk, he reassured himself. But not today. He had promised he'd never drop in uninvited and had no intention of doing so.

Except the morning dragged. They went to the beach but the wind was a little cool to get wet and if Piper was coming down with a cold he didn't want to make it worse. Before long they went home and played inside. But he felt closed in staying indoors. Piper seemed to have recovered and before lunch she'd become unusually bored.

So after lunch, full from eating little pink cakes and with a sealed bag holding an extra one, he hefted Piper onto his back and went for a walk up the hill.

Yes, he nodded to himself dryly, towards the cliff path, not totally directed to one of the crofts that he wondered might belong to Catrina, but certainly it felt good to be outside, with a fresh breeze blowing the cobwebs and fingers of darkness from his lowered mood.

'Dad, Dad, Dad,' Piper burbled from behind his ear—so Piper liked being outside too, and it was her birthday. He was supposed to be doing what she wanted. Each of his steps up the hill lightened his mood and the hill path was well maintained and solid under his feet. He could feel the exertion and decided Catrina could probably run up this hill if she did it a couple of times a day. He wasn't quite up to that yet.

The path forked towards the cottages one way and down onto a cliff edge path on the other and he realised the crofts had hedges around them for privacy from below.

That was good. He wouldn't want anybody to be able to peek into Catrina's house just by walking along the path, but it was a tiny bit disappointing that he couldn't see any of the buildings up close. Then he rounded a bend and the path snaked up again and as he trekked up the hill he realised they'd come out past the cottages.

Quite ingenious really. At the top they came out onto a little open area with a bench and an ancient telescope that had been cemented into the footpath to look out to sea.

He paused and bent down to peer through it, which was hard with Piper suddenly excited and bouncing on his back, when a voice spoke behind him.

'I bet Piper is heavier going uphill.'

He could feel the smile on his face as he turned— he hadn't imagined her.

'Hello there, Catrina.'

'Hello, you two, and what are you doing up here in the clouds?'

'We've never been here before. And it's Piper's birthday.'

Her face broke into a shining sunbeam of a smile and she stepped closer to drop a kiss on Piper's cheek.

'Happy birthday, sweetheart. I hope Daddy made you a cake.'

Piper bounced and crowed.

'Of course. Though really we made cupcakes with pink princess stickers.'

This time the smile was for him. 'I wish I could have seen them.'

It felt good to know he'd thought ahead. 'By a stroke of luck, we do have a spare one in our bag which I'm sure Piper would love to share with you?' He looked around and considered the logistics of Piper and a cliff edge. Maybe not.

It seemed that Catrina got it in one. 'It's too tricky here for a birthday girl. Come back and I'll show you the croft. We can sit on the balcony; it's well fenced and safe.'

CHAPTER EIGHT

Trina

TRINA TURNED ON the path and directed them along
the other fork back towards her house, beckoning
them to follow. Thankfully, facing the other way,
Finn couldn't see the expression on her face. She still
couldn't believe she'd invited them into her home.
So blithely. Since when had her bravery suddenly
known no bounds?

Well, she could hear Finn's springing footsteps
behind her as she led the way around the loop that
led to the cottages again and within seconds they'd
popped out onto the road outside the last croft, where
Myra and Dr Southwell lived. As they passed the door
opened and the older gentleman stepped out.

He smiled when he saw her, and then his face lit up
further when he saw who followed her. 'Trina. And
Finn. And Piper. Hello. Delightful. So, you've met.'

Trina could feel herself blush. 'Hello. Yes. At the
beach.' Glancing around for inspiration to change
the subject, she added, 'Lovely day.' Not only had
she invited a man back to her house but she'd been

caught in the act. Everyone would know. Dr Southwell wasn't a gossip but, seriously, Ellie's father-in-law? *Small blinkin' towns.*

Trina blushed again under Dr Southwell's pleased smile.

'The weather is super. Love to stay and chat but I'm off to the hospital.' He waved and strode off.

Trina shrugged off the awkwardness with determination. 'So that's who lives next door on this side and my boss, Ellie, and her husband, who happens to be an obstetrician, Dr Southwell's son, live on the other side.'

He looked around at the three crofts as they came to hers, and paused. 'You're well covered for medical help then.' He smiled a little awkwardly.

'Never too many in an emergency.' She smiled back, too concerned with whether she'd left the house tidy before he arrived to worry about trying to read his reaction to her neighbours. She indicated her own front path. 'Come in. It's small but compact, much like yours is, I imagine.'

'Yes. Tiny, but I like it. You'll have to come and see my renovations.'

Not your etchings? She thought it and smiled to herself. Didn't risk saying anything in case he heard the amusement in her voice. At least she could be amused by something that she would have run a mile from a month ago. In fact, she could have rubbed her knuckles on her chest. Darn proud of herself, really.

She pushed open the door and was glad she'd opened all the blinds this morning. With everything open the sea seemed to be a part of the room, with all eyes being drawn to the open French windows out onto the little terrace. She gestured him to walk that way.

'Great view,' Finn said after a low whistle. 'That's really magic.' He walked slowly to the French windows and absently began to undo Piper's straps.

Trina came up behind him and undid the other one. 'Here, let me help.' She lifted Piper out of the straps and set her down. 'There's nothing to climb on. I only keep the swing chair out there and it's against the house wall. It has to come in when it's windy.'

Piper crawled straight for the rails and her little hands grabbed on as she pulled herself up. She bounced on the balls of her feet. Finn followed her out and Trina stood back a little and admired them both.

A bouncy, healthy little girl and her gorgeous dad. She wasn't sure when he'd graduated from attractive to other women to gorgeous for her, but she had to admit he made an admirable picture with his big shoulders and strong back silhouetted against the ocean. His long fingers rested lightly and then the curved muscles in his arms bunched as he gripped the rail for a minute. She wondered what he was thinking about as he stood guard over his daughter, his powerful thighs either side of her as one hand left the rail and brushed her small head.

Then the penny dropped. Piper's birthday. And his wife had left soon after Piper's birth. That made this time of year a distressing anniversary as well as a day for celebration for Piper. Tough call. She hadn't even crawled out of bed on the anniversary of losing Ed.

Why hadn't he said something yesterday? Then

she chastised herself. Why would he share that with a stranger?

She swallowed past the lump that had suddenly formed in her throat. 'Would you two like a cold drink?' She managed to even her voice. 'I have a spill-proof cup I use for one of my friend's daughters.'

'Piper has her water here, thanks.' He came back in and bent down to Piper's pack. Pulled out a little pink pop-top bottle. 'She'll use hers.' Then he pulled out a Ziploc bag. 'Aha! Here's your part of Piper's birthday cake.'

He glanced back at his daughter. 'Probably best she doesn't see it as I had no idea she could gobble as many as she did and she'll be sick if she eats any more.'

Trina nodded and swiped the bag, turning her back to the veranda and opening the seal. She lifted out the little blue-papered cake and admired the rough pink icing and slightly off-centre sticker. 'It's magnificent.'

'Piper put the stickers on herself.'

'Clever girl.' She looked at him. 'Clever Daddy for the rest.'

He looked at her. Maybe saw the lingering distress in her eyes and he closed his own for a minute and then looked at her again. Nodded. 'So you've guessed it's a tough day?'

'You have a different set of triggers but I was just thinking I didn't even get out of bed when mine went past.' They needed to get out and fill the day with something. 'How about we go for a walk along the cliffs further? There's a really cool cave overlooking the ocean about a kilometre north I could show you.

And there's a sweet little dip of green grass Piper would love.' She smiled at the thought. 'She could probably log roll down the tiny hill. I watched some kids do that one day and it looked fun.'

She saw relief lift the creases from his brow. 'That does sound good. Is there somewhere you'd prefer me to change Piper before we go? I have a change mat.'

'You have everything!' And wasn't that true. 'Change mats are great. You can use my bed and save you bending down. I'll make a little snack for the meadow.' She turned away. Excited for the first time in a long while with a task she couldn't wait to play with.

She slipped in two small cans of mixer cordial that she'd bought on a whim. A packet of dates and apricots for Piper. She even had arrowroot biscuits, perfect for a little girl to make a mess with. Threw in some crisps, two apples and a banana. It all fitted in her little cool bag she carried to work each day, along with the tiny checked throw she had never had the opportunity to use for a picnic.

They set off ten minutes later, Piper bouncing on her daddy's back and Trina swinging along beside them as if she was a part of the little family. She winced at her instinctive comparison. No. Like a party of friends. Looking out for each other.

The sun shone clear and warm on their backs as they strode along the path. The sea breeze blew Piper's bright golden mist of hair around her chubby face as she chattered away. Trina decided Finn looked so much more relaxed out in the open. It made her feel good that she'd helped.

A cruise ship hugged the horizon and she pointed it out to Finn. Piper saw a seabird dive into the water far below and they had to stop and watch for a minute until it came out again with a fish in its beak.

Trina admired the skill of the surfers, bobbing and swooping like brilliant supple-bodied flying fish on the curling waves.

When she commented, Finn shared, 'I love surfing.'

'I've never tried.' Maybe she could add that to her adventure list.

Finn said, 'When Piper is old enough I'll teach her to surf. This looks a great place to do that.'

'Dr Southwell used to surf every morning before he was married. Though I have to admit he did come a cropper when he was washed off the shelf last year.'

He looked back the way they'd come. 'Really? Ouch. Which shelf?'

She pointed. 'The ones under the cliffs, with the rock pools we were in yesterday.'

Finn frowned. 'It doesn't look dangerous there.'

'It is on a king tide. And his timing was off if you ask him. They lifted him out with a chopper but the good news was his son met Ellie, my boss, when he came to locum while his father was away, and they married and are having a baby. That's why I'm doing Ellie's job for the next year—hence the change from night duty.'

'Happy ending.' His voice held only a trace of bitterness. She got that. But she'd moved on herself, thankfully.

She wondered if he'd heard his own subtext because his voice came out warmer than before. 'So were they all the people in the restaurant on Friday?'

She'd forgotten. 'Yes, that's right—you were there. With Piper and your sister.' She thought back over those present. 'They were celebrating Ellie's leave and my promotion.'

'Congratulations.'

She laughed. 'Thanks. First day tomorrow. We'll see.'

She thought back to Friday and the pleasant lunch. Her own surprise to see Finn there. With another woman. Felt just a little embarrassed now she knew it was his sister. Hurried on in case it showed on her face. 'The other older lady at the table is the one who makes the most divine cakes—Dr Southwell's wife, Myra.'

'I guess I'll get to know them all. Dr Southwell's offered me a place in his practice. I'll start as soon as I can find day care for Piper.'

She raised her brows. 'Do you have a specialty?'

'I started in general practice. Then I went on and studied paediatrics. I thought everyone knew?' Then he shook his head. 'I guess I haven't really spoken to many people. I have my Diploma of Obstetrics from my GP days, but no real experience in that. Just the antenatal side of it. Not the delivery part.'

He didn't look old enough to have done all that. Catrina smiled at him, decided she wouldn't share that thought and shook her head mockingly. 'We don't say delivery any more. Especially in Lighthouse Bay. We're Midwifery Group Practice.'

He put his hands up. 'Midwifery Group Practice. And I said *delivery*. My bad.'

'Very.' She smiled at him. 'Everything is midwifery-led and woman-centred. The antenatal clinic is drop-in and popular. When the mother births, we support her choice to stay or go, and she's visited at home within the day after if that's what she wants or she can stay for a few days in the hospital. Either way, we don't call a doctor unless someone is sick.'

He put out his hands helplessly and pretended to sigh. 'I'm defunct and I haven't even started.'

She laughed. 'You'll get used to it. You should meet Ellie and her husband. Sam's the Director of Obstetrics at the base hospital and fell in love with Lighthouse Bay too. And Ellie, of course.' She smiled at the thought. 'Sam moved here from a big Brisbane Hospital so we're lucky to have him as an unofficial back-up in real emergencies when he's not on-call at the base hospital.'

She looked at him thoughtfully. 'I've thought of someone who could mind Piper, if you're interested.'

His face went blank and she hesitated. Maybe he wasn't ready yet.

'I'll need to find someone eventually,' he managed but she could see it cost him. She wished she hadn't mentioned it now.

Then he said more firmly, 'Sure. That would be great. I need to start looking.'

Trina thought about Marni. She didn't regret mentioning her, though. 'She's a doll. A natural mother. Her twins are six months old and she's just registered for day care status.'

CHAPTER NINE

Finn

FINN FELT HIS stomach drop. He wasn't seeing the path or the ocean or the sky overhead. He shouldn't have asked about day care. But something inside had dared him to. Something that wanted him to move on, as if he'd known he'd be catapulted into a decision if he put it out there. All his instincts wanted to draw back. Stop her telling him. Say he'd ask if he decided it was time. She'd understand. Not sure how he knew that but he believed in the truth of it.

Instead he said, 'Would you recommend her?'

She looked at him thoughtfully. Kindly. 'That's tough because it's not about me,' she said gently, as if she could read his distress. Then she looked at Piper. 'Marni could mind my child, if I had one.' The tone was almost joking. He saw something that looked like pain flit across her face and remembered again there were people out there who did suffer as much as he did. People like Catrina. Left alone by the love of their life—without choice and unintentionally. Loss of love and no baby to hold like he did. Imagine life without Piper.

Catrina's voice wasn't quite steady but he could hear the struggle to make it so. It had been a very brave thing to say and he wanted to tell her that. Wanted to tell her that he understood. But still the coward inside him shied away from so much emotion.

Catrina said, 'Maybe you could see if Piper likes her before you commit to work and see how she goes? Just an hour or two?'

'That's a good idea. Tell me about her.'

He saw her gaze into the distance, a soft smile on her face and a glimmer of distress, though this time he didn't think it was for herself. 'She's a younger mum. Early twenties. She and her husband own the dry-cleaners in town but she's a stay-at-home mum. Marni's Mother Earth and the boys are six months old. Bundles of energy, healthy as all get-out, which is great because she nearly lost them at twenty-three weeks, and she spent a lot of time in hospital. As far as the midwives of Lighthouse Bay think, she's a hero to us.'

He had to smile at that. '*The Midwives of Light-house Bay*. Sounds like a serial on TV.'

She laughed a little self-consciously and he regretted making light of the one stable thing she had in her life, hadn't meant to embarrass her. 'Don't get me wrong. It's another good ending to a story.'

Catrina seemed to relax. 'It really was. Ellie's husband, Sam, had been involved in research into preventing extreme premature birth in Brisbane, and thankfully he was here when she went into labour.

Marni and Bob are a lovely couple who'd already lost an extremely premature baby daughter.'

Finn wasn't so sure. She already had twins and he wanted someone who could concentrate on Piper. 'How could she care for Piper as well?' Finn was more uncertain now. 'Sounds a bit hectic. She has twins and she's doing day care?'

He caught Trina's encouraging smile and suddenly saw how she could be a good midwife. Her empathy shone warm—he felt she understood and was reassuring him that he would conquer his fear of letting Piper out of his sight. All without putting on pressure. Encouraging him to test his own strength without expectations. Treating him like a woman in labour battling her own fear. *Wow*. She had it down pat.

Then she said, 'She loves minding babies. And babies love her. Usually she's minding them for free. We keep telling her she should become a midwife and I wouldn't be surprised when the boys go to school if she'll look at it. But, for now, she's just starting up official day care.'

Absently he bent and stroked Piper's leg at his side. 'Maybe I could meet her before I talk to Dr Southwell? It's a good idea to see if Piper likes her before I commit to work, though. You'll have to give me her number.'

'Or we could visit her. Meet her and her husband. See their house. They're a lovely couple and live only a few doors up from you. In the blue pastel cottage.'

It was all happening too quickly. He could feel the panic build and squashed it down again. He could do this. Just not today.

Catrina touched his arm—the first time she had physically connected with him of her own volition—and again that frisson of awareness hummed where they touched. He glanced at her but her expression still showed only compassionate support. 'It's something to think about. Marni is just the one I know. There will be others when you're ready.'

His relief made his shoulders sag. She must have seen it on his face. Was he that transparent? He'd have to work on his game face before he went back to work or his patients' parents would run a mile.

He tried to make light of it. 'I imagine every parent must feel like this when they have to go back to work. Torn.'

'Absolutely. We see mums that can't stay in hospital for one night after birth because they hate leaving the other child or children too much.' She looked towards Piper and smiled. 'I'd find it hard to leave Piper if she were mine.'

His face tightened. He could feel it. Some women could. Piper's mother had no problem. And he'd be the one who had to break his daughter's heart when the time came to tell the truth.

Catrina opened her mouth—he didn't want to talk about Clancy—but all she said was, 'The cave's just around this next headland.' He was glad she'd changed the subject.

The cave, when they arrived, curved back into the cliff and created an overhang half the size of his house. A few round boulders acted as seats for looking out over the ocean out of the sun. Or rain. Plenty of evidence suggested people had camped and made campfires there but on the whole it had stayed clean and cool, and dim towards the back. The sort of place young boys would love to go with their mates.

He could stand up in the cave easily and they stomped around in it for a few minutes before Catrina suggested they go the small distance further to the glade so Piper could be released from the backpack.

The glade, when they arrived, had a park bench and table at the edge of the slope down into the bowl-shaped dip of grass. The bright sunshine made the grass lime cordial-coloured and the thick bed of ki-kuyu and daisies felt softer and springier than he expected when he put Piper down to crawl. Because of the sloping sides of the bowl Piper tended to end up back in the lowest point in the middle even when she climbed the sides and he could feel his mouth twitching as she furrowed her brows and tried to work out what was happening.

He pulled a bright saucer-sized ball from her backpack and tossed it in the centre of the glade while Catrina set their picnic bag on the table and spread the cloth. Piper crawled to the ball and batted it. Of course it rolled back down the side to her again. She pushed it again and crowed when it rolled back again.

'Clever girl,' he said to his daughter, and 'Clever girl,' to Catrina, who grinned at him as she finished laying out their treats and came to sit next to him on the side of the grass hill. 'I can't remember when I last had a picnic,' he said as he passed an arrowroot biscuit to Piper and took one of the apples for himself.

'I know. Me either.' She handed him the can of

drink and took a sip of her own. Then he heard her sigh blissfully.

'We couldn't have had more beautiful weather this afternoon.'

'A bit different to this morning.'

'That's the beauty of Lighthouse Bay. We're temperate. Not too hot for long or too cold for long. Always leaning towards perfect weather.'

'Always?'

Catrina laughed. 'Well, no. We do have wild storms sometimes. That's why I have shutters on my windows and doors. But not often.'

The afternoon passed in a desultory fashion and once, when Piper dozed off in his arms, he and Catrina lay side by side watching the clouds pass overhead in companionable silence. He'd never met anyone as restful as she was. It would have been so simple to slide closer and take her hand but the man who could have done that had broken a year ago.

An hour later, on the way home from their walk, he asked again about the exact location of the day care mum.

'I could come with you to knock on the door? Maybe meeting the family would help?'

'Just drop in?' Despite his initial reluctance, he could see that an impromptu visit could be less orchestrated than one when they expected him. And he had Catrina to come with him to break the ice.

It made sense. Not fair perhaps, but this was his baby he was considering leaving in their care, and he wanted a true representation of the feeling of the household.

When the door opened to answer his knock, a smiling red-haired man answered. Past him they could hear the sound of a child squealing and the smell of a roast dinner drifted out to tantalise his nose. He hadn't had an old-fashioned roast for years. His mouth watered.

'Can I help you?' Then the man saw Catrina and smiled beatifically. 'Trina!'

'Hello, Bob. How are you?' The man stepped forward and hugged her and Finn was surprised.

When they stepped back from each other she said, 'Something smells divine. Lucky you—Sunday roast.'

'You're welcome any time, Trina.' He grinned and looked at her companion.

'This is Finn Foley. He's a friend and I told him about Marni offering childcare and—' she indicated Piper '—he and Piper have just started looking.' Finn glanced at Catrina. Took a second to savour that she'd claimed friendship. She really was his only friend here.

She still spoke to Bob. 'I wondered if he could have a chat with Marni?'

'Absolutely. Any friend of yours and all that.' Bob grinned at Finn. 'Come in. Marni? There's a dad here looking for information about childcare.'

Finn liked the way he said that. To his wife, with deference, and that he wasn't committing to anything. Just asking. His nerves settled a fraction as he followed Catrina, with Piper on his back, in the door.

The room had been divided into two, with a kitchen and lounge on one side and a wall with doors on the other. Bedrooms, he guessed, unlike his one-room cottage. An extension had been built out the back with a big play room that overlooked the tiny fenced garden. Everything sparkled; even the toys strewn on the floor in the play room caught the sunlight and looked new and well cared for. The family warmth in the little abode made the tension drop from his shoulders and his eyes met Trina's in acknowledgement.

A young woman crossed to them, drying her hands on a tea towel. She too hugged Catrina, and her shy smile eased the tension in Finn's stomach like magic. 'Trina. Great to see you.'

'This is Finn, Marni.' She turned to help Finn extricate Piper from the backpack—which he was pretty darn good at, but he had to admit it was quicker with help. And he liked her touching him.

'Nice to meet you, Finn. You live a few doors down, don't you?' she said as she held out her hand. They shook briefly and he liked that her fingers were cool and dry, her grip confident.

'Welcome.' She smiled at Piper, who now sat on his hip, then turned around and pointed to two boys as if introducing her to them not Finn. 'The one on the left is Olly, and the cheekier one is Mikey.' She looked at Piper. 'And what is your name, beautiful?'

Previously fascinated by the smaller humans, Piper looked back at the lady's face, realised everyone was looking at her and then she clutched at his neck and buried her face.

Finn rubbed her back. 'Piper can be shy.'

'Of course she can.' Marni indicated the rear of the cottage. 'Come and sit out on the deck at the back and we'll show you the play area and I can answer your questions.

'So Catrina told you I've started doing childcare?' The smile Marni gave Catrina lit up her face. 'The midwives are my cheer squad. They're all champions up there. If it wasn't for them and the younger Dr Southwell, we wouldn't have our gorgeous boys.'

Finn looked at the two chubby-faced little boys, one sitting in a blue tub of a chair kicking his feet and the other lying on his back on the patterned play carpet with a red spiral rattle. The little boy—Finn thought it was Olly—began to screw his face up, dropped the rattle and began to rock until he rolled over and lay on his stomach. The mischievous chortle he let out at the feat made Finn smile.

'Clever boy, Mikey,' his dad said. So he'd got that wrong, Finn thought. And then Bob gestured to his wife. 'I'll finish the potatoes. You take our guests and Piper out and have a chat.'

Finn liked that too. He could see they were a team and, despite having two babies, the air of serenity as Marni smiled made his trepidations settle. This sort of calm atmosphere looked perfect for Piper to learn about other babies and new adults.

A heck of a lot different to the busy, efficient childcare he'd had her in before. But Piper still clung to him like one of the stripy shells on the side of a rock pool and he remembered the hard times at the big kindergarten when he'd tried to leave.

Marni pointed to a scrubbed wooden table and four sturdy chairs. Two highchairs took up the other spaces. They all sat down and Marni put a soft-sided squeaky farm book on the table in front of Piper without making a fuss of it.

'I am looking for two more toddlers. That will give me enough to cover the wage of the girl working with my husband at the dry-cleaners and then there's no rush for me to go back to work. I'm hoping to stay home for the next year at least. In a perfect world, I won't go back to work until the boys go to school.'

She smiled calmly at Finn. 'But we'll see what happens.'

So a stable place, Finn was thinking, and he wondered, if he offered to pay twice the rate, would Marni consider having Piper by herself, at least at the beginning so the young mum wasn't pushed by the demands of four children? Piper would benefit and money wasn't a problem. Finding someone caring and kind for Piper would be priceless.

He tried to think of a question. 'Catrina said you've just been registered. Having two babies seems intense to me. Piper can keep me busy and there's only one of her.'

She glanced lovingly towards the two gurgling on the floor and then across at her husband. 'I mind lots of children. Have always loved them and thought for a while we'd never be able to have any. But then the boys came along, though I spent a couple of months in hospital hanging onto them, so they are beyond precious.'

She shrugged ruefully. 'I'm worried I might spoil them and want them to learn to share, not just with each other but with other children. Some extra income would help and my husband and I are both the eldest from big families. Our families are in West-ern Australia so we miss having lots of kids around.'

'I guess childminding makes sense in that case.'

Piper reached out and picked up the book. Scrunched it with her inquisitive fingers. Barely audi-ble squeaks erupted when she squeezed and a crooked smile tipped her mouth as she battled between shy-ness and delight.

All the adults looked at her fondly. 'So, information-wise, what sort of minding were you looking for?'

'I've been offered a position three days a week, Monday, Tuesday and Wednesday.'

Marni nodded. 'Three is better than five for Piper. Especially in the beginning. Has she been in care before?'

'Yes, poor baby, most of her life, when I worked. About fifty hours a week. But not for the last six weeks and she was becoming unhappy before that. I was thinking to start a half-day, as a trial, just until Piper gets used to it. If she gets too upset I'd prob-ably not go back to work for a while.' He shrugged his apology.

Apparently she didn't need it. That serene smile drifted across her face. 'Being adaptable is good around kids. One of the secrets. She'll miss you if she's had you to herself for six weeks.' A quirked brow made that question.

'I'm not even sure it's what I'm ready to do.'

'That's fine. You're fact-finding, which is very sensible.'

Well, he'd better glean some facts. This was harder

than he'd thought it would be. He glanced at Catrina and she sat tranquilly beside him, lending moral support, not interrupting. Just there. It felt good not to be on his own through this. 'What hours do you have available?'

Marni laughed. 'As I haven't started yet it's hard to say. Big picture—Monday to Friday, no more than forty hours, but the hours are flexible. And I get to keep the weekends for the boys and Bob.'

'Where would she sleep in the daytime?'

'We've a little room next to the boys' room. Bob put two new folding cots in there and I think it'll work well. And I'll supply all the food. No hardship to make for one more and that way nobody wants what others have.'

It all sounded too good to be true. Plus they lived a few doors away from his own house. Even in this short time Piper seemed relaxed here. He gently swung her off his lap, book still in her hands, and rested her bottom on the floor. Just to see if she'd go.

As soon as she hit the floor she dropped the book and crawled curiously towards the two little boys. Stopped about a body's length away and sat up. The three tiny people all looked at each other.

The adults smiled and Finn felt the tension leave his shoulders. The gods, or Catrina, had saved him again.

'What about if I go and talk to my prospective employer tomorrow? Perhaps leave Piper here just for an hour and see how she goes while I negotiate? Then we'll all know more.'

'Why don't you make it two hours? That will be

a quarter of the time of her next visit, if you decide to go ahead. Just to give her time to settle. And take the rush out of your appointment. She'll be fine. It will give us all a chance to trial the fit.'

'I think that sounds like a plan. Yes, please.' Finn stood up. Blew out a breath. 'Phew. Thank you. I do feel better for asking and talking to you. That would be great.' He glanced at Catrina, who stood as well. She smiled at him as if he'd just done an excellent job. It felt good. Reassuring.

Marni went across to the dresser and picked up a business card. 'Here's our phone number, and it's got my mobile on it as well. You can ring or drop in when you know your time. The sheet has information about my business.' She handed him a sheet of paper with her numbers and the payment rates. Easy.

'That's great.' He picked up Piper, who had crawled over to him as soon as he stood up. She didn't cling, more curious than panicked he'd leave her. 'I'll leave one of my own cards when I bring Piper. Then you can contact me any time.'

'Give yourself ten extra minutes before you leave her tomorrow. To help her settle.'

He nodded. Then Bob came and shook his hand. Then they were outside and the door closed.

He felt like sagging against it. He'd done it. Another step towards a new life.

'You didn't say much.'

Catrina laughed. 'I didn't have to. You're all made for each other.'

CHAPTER TEN

Trina

TRINA'S FIRST MORNING as Midwifery Unit Manager, and her first day shift for a long time, proved too busy to worry about a man she'd met on the beach and declared her friend. Though she had spent a fair time mulling over all the things she'd learnt about Finn the night before.

This morning, in her new world, the midwife coming off shift had celebrated a birth at five a.m., so still lots of settling of mother and baby for Trina to help with before mother left at lunchtime to go home. Another mother who preferred to rest at home, not separated from her toddler, and it made her think of her conversation with Finn yesterday. Finn again. She pushed those thoughts away and concentrated on the new tasks.

There were Monday pharmacy orders and sterile stock orders, and a hospital meeting and a visit from Myra, her neighbour, which lightened a busy time with a quick break.

'Hello there, new midwife in charge.' Myra's serene face peered around the corner of the nurses' station, where Trina typed efficiently into the discharged mother's electronic medical records.

'Hello, Mrs Southwell, what have you got there?' Myra had a steaming cup and a white paper bag tucked under her arm. Ellie had said that Myra always brought something when the place got busy.

'A long black with extra water, the way you like it.' She smiled mischievously. 'And a savoury tart with spring onion in case you haven't had lunch.'

Trina glanced at the clock, the hour hand resting on the two. 'An angel. That's what you are.' Though she would pack lunch tomorrow to make sure she had something. She hadn't realised how hard it could be to get away from the ward to the cafeteria. She'd expected that on night duty but not through the day.

Myra tilted her head to scrutinise her. 'Have you had time to stop for a few minutes?'

Trina sat back and gestured to the chair beside her. 'Not yet. But I do now. And I will.' She took the china mug Myra carried and took a sip before she put it down on the desk beside her. 'Ah!' She smiled at the older lady. 'I seriously needed that.' She looked at the mug again and picked it up. Took another sip and closed her eyes. 'The world won't stop turning if I don't achieve everything today.'

Myra laughed. 'Something I've learnt since I came here. So how is it going? Is it strange to be on the ward in the daytime?'

Trina glanced around the sunlit reception area. The windows that showed the gardens. The sunlight slanting across the polished wooden floors. 'It is. And there are so many people I need to talk to.' She pretended to shudder. 'Business requirements have given me interaction overload. Present company excluded, of course.'

'I won't be offended.' Myra looked at her with concern. 'Are you sure you wouldn't prefer sitting in the tea room and I could answer the phone for you while you finish your tart?'

Trina laughed. 'No. This is a social conversation. Much more fun. Besides, I haven't seen you for days. How are you? How is married life? Any adventurous plans?'

'I'm well. Ridiculously content, and I'm trying to talk Reg into coming away with me on a cruising holiday. There's a last-minute deal that's breaking my heart not to take.'

Trina could see Myra at a Captain's Cocktail Party, dressed to the nines in those stunning vintage outfits she seemed to source at will. Trina could never find anything when she looked in the pre-loved section. Or if she did she looked ridiculous. But Myra looked soft and elegant and stunningly stylish. She sighed and let the envy go. She hadn't really thought much of clothes since Ed. 'That sounds fun. Does he like the idea?'

'More than I thought he would. But it all depends if he finds locum relief for the practice. I'm a little keen for him to scale right back but he's become immersed in the bay and the hospital.'

Trina could see why Myra wanted to play. 'I haven't seen him out on his surfboard lately.'

'He still goes out every Sunday with his son. It's

lovely to see. Says he doesn't have the need to get out of bed at the crack of dawn now—especially with me in it.' Myra smiled with just a hint of pink in her cheeks and Trina smiled back.

'Understandable.' She thought of Finn. Her own cheeks heated and she dipped her head and took a sip from her mug to hide it. Of course he was the locum Myra hoped for, and of course she wasn't blushing just because of Myra's mention of mornings in bed. 'Is he hopeful of the locum situation?'

Myra sighed. 'There's a young doctor in town he's had a chat with. Some family issue that's keeping him from starting, but hopefully that will sort soon. If not, I think he should advertise.'

'I met the one I think he's talking about. Finlay Foley. He's a single dad. Has a delightful little one-year-old.'

Myra unwrapped the tart from its white paper bag and pushed it towards Trina. 'That's the one. That's right—Reg said he had a daughter. What's he like?'

'He's an amazing dad. Anyone can see that. It's a wonder you haven't seen him walking along the beach with his little girl on his back.'

Myra's eyes brightened. She lifted her head in delight and glanced towards the general direction of the beach way below, though she wouldn't be able to see it. 'Oh. I have seen him. Younger than I expected. I didn't think of him as a doctor. Looks too young.' She lowered her voice and said suggestively, 'And handsome.'

Trina laughed. 'I used to see them in the mornings after work when I walked. Been here for a month but

I've only really talked to him this weekend.' Funny how it felt as if she'd known Finn for ages. What was that? 'His little girl turned one yesterday. And I did mention Marni as a suggestion for childminding. He's thinking about it.'

'Oh, that's marvellous news. And a really good idea. Marni is the perfect mother to those tiny boys. I might get Reg to give him a nudge—not a big nudger is my Reg. But I would like to catch that sailing if possible.'

Trina laughed. 'You might have a surprise when you get home, then.' She picked up the tart and bit into the buttery pastry with slow enjoyment. The tang of Parmesan cheese, fresh spring onions and cream made her eyes roll. She took another bite and savoured. Before she knew, the tart was gone. 'Goodness, Myra. I should have a standing order for those.'

Myra laughed. 'My man is a bit pleased with my cooking.'

Trina picked up her coffee and then paused as a thought intruded. If Finn took over Dr Southwell's practice while he was away, he'd be working in the hospital. And he'd probably walk through Maternity. Might even seek her out as a friendly face. Not that everyone wasn't friendly at Lighthouse Bay. Maybe he'd even come over if they needed a third for a tricky birth. Their own personal paediatrician.

Her belly seemed to warm and it had nothing to do with food and hot coffee, though they had been good. She finished the last of the coffee not quite in the present moment. It was all positive because he was a paediatrician. Good for those babies that didn't breathe as well as you expected them to. *Oh, my.*

'You look much better for stopping and eating,' Myra said with some satisfaction. She stood up. 'I won't bother you any longer and let you get on before your afternoon midwives come on.'

'You're never a bother. More of a life-saver. Thank you.' She glanced down at the empty crumpled white bag. 'You've made my day.' In more ways than one.

Trina finished work at five-thirty that evening and decided to walk quickly down the breakwall and blow the stress of the day away. The administration side of the maternity unit would take a little time to get used to but she'd mastered most of the things that had slowed her up. The joy of finishing work and not having to worry about sleep until it was dark felt like a sweet novelty. Especially when, on her way back, she saw that Finn and Piper, wrapped in scarves, were walking too. Finn swung along effortlessly, the bundle on his back wriggling when she saw Catrina.

Finn raised his hand and changed direction and she sat on the breakwall and waited for him to reach her. As they approached she couldn't help watching his stride as his strong thighs closed the distance between them. His broad shoulders were silhouetted against the ocean and his eyes crinkled with delight as he came up to her.

The smile he gave her made the waiting even more worth it. She realised she'd been staring and spoke first. 'Hello. How did Piper go today?'

He patted Piper's leg. 'She didn't want to leave when I went to pick her up.'

Trina tried to hide her smile behind a sympathetic look but it didn't stick.

He pretended to scowl at her. 'You think that's amusing?'

She straightened her face. 'I'm pretty sure you were relieved too.'

He dropped his mock-injured façade. 'Absolutely. It felt good to see her so comfortable in another setting. And I owe that to you.' A genuine heartfelt smile which she might just snapshot and pull out later when she got home. 'Thank you, Catrina.'

She'd done nothing. He seemed so serious. And he seemed to expect some comment. 'For the little I did you're very welcome, Finn.'

'I'm serious.' Had he read her mind? 'In fact, Piper and I would like to invite you to our house to share dinner on Thursday night. In celebration of her finding childcare and me starting work next Monday. If you don't have a previous engagement?' There was a tiny hesitation at the last comment and she wondered why he thought she would.

'No previous engagement.'

Was that relief on his face? 'Just our usual slap-up meal. So you don't have to cook when you get home.' He hurried on. 'It will be early and if you needed to you could still be home by dark.'

She laughed. It would certainly be an early dinner as night fell about seven. 'I finish at five-thirty so can be there by six. Though sometimes the wheels fall off at work and that could slow me down or make me cancel.'

He shrugged. 'Been there. We'll take that as we have to.'

Trina smiled. Of course. A paed would know that. 'In that case, lovely. Thank you.' She tweaked the baby toes at Finn's chest. 'Thank you for the invitation, Piper.' The little girl gurgled and said, 'Mum, Mum, Mum.'

Trina pretended she didn't see Finn's wince. 'I bet she was saying that all the time at Marni's house. The boys will come ahead on their speaking with her there.'

He still looked subdued so she went on. 'Soon they'll be able to say *fiss*.'

Finn seemed to shake himself. She saw him cast his mind back and his smile grew. Could see when he remembered the rock pool. Saw the relief for the change of focus.

His smile dipped to rueful. 'You're right.' Then he straightened and gave her his full attention again. 'How was your first day as the boss?'

'Administrative. Hats off to Ellie for never complaining about all the paperwork and ordering. But it's well worth it to have finished work at this time and still get a full night's sleep. It will be amazing when Daylight Saving comes back in and it doesn't get dark till after eight at night.'

CHAPTER ELEVEN

Finn

FINN SHIFTED ON the hard boardwalk, listened, but inside he thought, *Yes, she's coming on Thursday.* He felt like dancing a jig. Didn't want to think about why. The tension that had been building slowly released. She made him feel like a teenager which, though disconcerting, made a good change from feeling like an old man most of the time.

He'd considered the invitation from every angle because it had become increasingly important he didn't scare Catrina away and he still remembered her warnings when they'd first met. Enjoying her company had lifted his life from survival to anticipation. And he anticipated that Catrina could be great company for the foreseeable future if he stayed careful.

But she'd said she didn't want a relationship. It suited him fine, he kept telling himself that, and it had nothing to do with the fact that every time he saw her he noticed something new about her.

Like that especially golden strand of hair that fell across her forehead and made him want to move it out of her eyes. Or the way the soft skin on the curve of her long neck made him want to stroke that vulnerable spot with one finger. Just to assess if it felt like the velvet it resembled.

Of course it was all about Piper—she needed to have a female figure in her life who didn't demand anything—but Catrina gave so much warmth he could feel himself thawing more each day. Or maybe it was the fact he'd told himself he'd change now that Piper's first birthday had passed.

He tamped down the suspicion it could be selfish to blow so persistently on the flame of their friendship when he didn't have much to offer, was still married in fact, but he could feel the restoration of his soul and sensibilities. And the better he was in himself the better he was for Piper.

So he'd considered all the barriers she might have had to agreeing to a first dinner date and had methodically worked on arranging for them to disappear. To make it easy for both of them.

It would be a celebration—Piper's care with Marni and his new job.

She started work early the first four days of the week—so he'd invited her on Thursday—she had to eat, so no reason not to grab a free meal from him on the way home.

Plus he was hoping to set up some connections with her over the coming weekend and that would seem more impromptu if he mentioned those on Thursday.

And the big card—Catrina had to be curious to see his house. It had all paid off.

'Did you like the Southwells' surgery?' Her voice startled him back into the present moment. He thought back to earlier in the day. To the white cottage that held Dr Southwell's medical rooms.

'It's quaint. Not as strange as it could have been. A small practice, one receptionist, and I'd have my own room to settle into, which is always better than using someone else's. I'll have all my equipment sent ASAP.' Or he could drive back and get it, but the idea made him shudder.

Catrina's voice grounded him. 'That's good. Did you see any patients?'

'You mean behave like a real doctor?' He smiled at her. 'Not yet. But I will start with those with urgent needs and Reg seems to think I could concentrate on children, which would suit me very well, and meet a need for the community.'

Catrina nodded slowly as she thought about it. 'I know at the base hospital it takes a few weeks for the paediatrician to see new patients. Perhaps you would even have some of those mums driving their children over this way, like the Lighthouse Bay mums go to the base for the service. Certainly easier for people like Marni to take the boys for their premmie check-ups.'

'Plus I'd be available for general patients when it was busy, but it seemed pretty sleepy today. Perfect hours of work for a dad with a little girl to consider.'

'Did he talk about you covering the general patients in the hospital when he goes away?'

'He did say that. Which is fine with me. It's not a big hospital and I can read up on who's in there when the time comes.'

Catrina stifled a laugh and he glanced at her. 'Dr Southwell's wife is keen on a cruise that leaves soon. Don't be surprised if it happens faster than you think.'

He raised his brows in question. 'Inside information?'

'I saw Myra today and she did mention she hoped Reg would find someone soon and that she had a boat she didn't want to miss.'

'Thanks for the heads-up. I'm sure I'd manage. That's what locums do, after all.' But everything seemed to be happening very fast. 'Do they get called out at night much?'

'Rarely. And it's shared call. So no more than three nights a week as a twenty-four-hour cover.' He watched her expression change as she realised that leaving Piper could be a problem on those nights.

'Hmm.' He could tell they were both thinking of Marni's flexibility as a day care mum.

'Something to think about,' Catrina said with massive understatement. 'And it won't be a problem unless Dr Southwell takes Myra away.'

'Which apparently might be sooner rather than later.' Had he started work too soon? Would his boss have an idea? Was it too much to ask the babysitter for Piper to sleep over those nights? As long as he didn't go over the forty hours, maybe it would be okay? His feeling that everything had fallen into place shifted again and he sighed. He wondered, not for the first time, how single parents managed to work at all.

Thursday arrived and Finn had been cooking, creating and carving in the kitchen. Something his mother had tried to instil in his sister but she'd found more fertile ground with Finn. He'd loved the times he and his mother had spent cooking, and in his short marriage the kitchen had been his domain at the weekend. It felt good to make something apart from nutritious finger food for Piper.

So, tonight a roast dinner. Something his wife had scoffed at but something he loved and missed— possibly because when they'd called at Marni's house the smell had reminded him how much he'd enjoyed a roast dinner as a child. And when Catrina had shared their lunch that first weekend they'd started talking— was it only a week ago?—she'd chosen a roast beef sandwich so she must like meat.

He'd slow roasted the beef and it lay, carved and foil-covered, in the oven with a veggie dish of potatoes, sweet potato, pumpkin and whole small onions. A side of fresh beans, carrots and broccoli would have Piper in seventh heaven. His jug of gravy was reheating and fresh bread rolls were on the table with real butter waiting.

He glanced around. The house remained a little spartan in his areas and cluttered in Piper's. She lay on her side in the playpen talking to her bunny. She'd had her bath and was dressed in her pyjamas, now looking a little sleepy, and he wondered if he should give her dinner early in case Catrina was late.

But it would be hard to dish up Piper's and not pick for himself. His belly rumbled. Just then a knock sounded on the door and he put the oven mitt back on the bench. He felt an unaccustomed eagerness as he crossed the room and tried to damp it down. They were just friends.

Then he opened the door and there she stood, the afternoon sunlight a glow around her and an almost shy smile on her beautiful lips. Her eyes were clear and bright and her lovely dark auburn hair swung loose in the sea breeze with glints of gold dancing like ribbons.

She'd changed out of her work clothes. Stood calmly clad in a pretty sundress and a cream cardigan, her bare legs brown and long with painted toes peeping out of coral-coloured sandals. Finn admonished himself not to feel too special because she'd taken the time to change for him.

He couldn't believe how good she looked. Needed to remind himself he barely knew this woman, but it was as if he'd been waiting a long time for this moment. Found himself saying softly, 'You truly are a picture.'

Catrina blushed but lifted her head. He liked the way she did that. No false modesty that she hadn't put in any effort. 'Thank you.' She lifted her chin higher and sniffed slowly. 'And you have a divine aroma floating out of your house.'

He laughed. 'I'll be glad when we can eat. It's been teasing me for hours now.' Not the only sensation that had been teasing him but he was trying not to think about Catrina's mouth.

She laughed then, her lips curving enticingly, but, unlike another woman, this one held no expectations to use her beauty and the tension stayed behind in the swirl of salt and sunshine outside as he invited her in and shut the door.

CHAPTER TWELVE

Trina

TRINA STEPPED INTO Finn's house, still feeling a little mentally fragile at the tiny handprints she'd seen on the step. There was something so heart-wrenchingly adorable about a dad doing cement prints with his baby daughter. If she wasn't careful she'd end up falling for this guy so hard she'd be vulnerable again to loss.

It was a sobering thought.

Then, to make matters more serious, when Finn had opened the door her heart had lifted at the sight of him. Two steps up, he'd towered over her, but his quick movement sideways as if he couldn't wait for her to come in had softened the impression of feeling small into a feeling of being very much appreciated.

She couldn't miss the approval and delight on his face as his gaze had run over her. So, yes, she was glad she'd spent the extra fifteen minutes changing and refreshing her make-up. Brushing her hair loose—not something she did often but it did feel freeing, and apparently it met with Finn's approval.

She felt the warmth of his body as she squeezed past him into the bright and airy room, and more warmth when she saw the way Piper pulled herself up and smiled at her. She bent down and blew a kiss at the little girl, who clutched her bunny and smiled back. Then to be enveloped in the warmth of expectation with a table set and meal prepared for her—well, it did seem a little too good to be true.

She turned back to look at Finn—Dr Finn— lounging against the closed door as if savouring the sight of her. His strong arms were crossed against his chest as if taking the time to watch her reaction. She was getting a little heady here. She licked unexpectedly dry lips. 'I'm feeling special.'

'Good. You are special. Piper and I can thank you for the help you've given us.'

She hadn't done much. But her grandmother had said, *Always answer a compliment with gratitude and don't correct the giver.* 'Thank you.' But she could change the subject. 'It looks great in here. So light and airy and fresh. I love the wood grain in the floor.'

He crossed said floorboards towards her and pulled out her chair. 'Silky oak. It was under the carpet. Feels nice underfoot and I can hear Piper coming up behind me when I'm not looking. Though I had a polisher come and help me rub it back and polish it by hand. Hardest day's work I'd done all year.' He grinned at her and she could see he'd enjoyed the challenge.

'And what did Miss Piper do while you were playing around on the floor?'

'Luckily it was a typical Lighthouse Bay day—

sunny—and we put up a little pergola. She stayed just outside the door in her playpen and kept us hard at it.'

Lucky her. To watch two men rubbing polish into wood for a few hours. Something very nice about that thought, Trina mused as she took the seat he held out for her.

Finn crossed to pick up Piper and poked her toes into her high chair and she snaked her way in like a little otter. Then he clipped a pink rubber bib around her neck. Piper did look excited at the thought of food.

'Can I help?' Trina asked, feeling a tad useless.

'It's a tiny kitchen nook, so you girls sit here while I produce my masterpiece and wait on you.' Then he glanced at his fidgety daughter. 'But you could hand Piper that crust on the plastic plate. She can chew on that while she waits for her veggies to cool.' He cast a sideways glance at Trina. 'I learnt it's better to give her something to chew on when she's in the chair or she starts to climb around when I'm not looking.'

'Ah—' Trina hurriedly passed the crust to Piper '—there you go, madam. Diversion tactics.'

Piper held out her hand and gleefully accepted the morsel and Finn strode the few steps to the kitchen bench and back across with the first plate and a jug of gravy.

'Roast veggies. Gravy.' He deposited his load and spun away, then was back in moments with a heaped plate of carved roast beef, the barest hint of pink at the centre of each slice. 'If you don't like it rare the more well-done pieces are at the edge.'

Trina's mouth had begun watering as the food began to arrive. 'I think I'm in heaven. It was busy today and I missed lunch. Plus I haven't had a roast for two years.' Not since before Ed's illness. Guilt and regret swamped her and she tried to keep it from her face.

Finn took a swift glance at her and said smoothly, 'It's all Marni's fault. That first day we visited. The way her house smelled of roast dinner did me in.' She decided he was very determined that they would enjoy the meal. Good thing too.

Trina pulled herself together and asked, 'So is this Piper's first roast dinner?'

'Indeed. More cause for celebration.' He leaned and poured them both a glass of cold water from the carafe on the table. The water glasses looked like crystal to Trina. 'Let's drink to that.' Then he raised his hand to hers and they touched glasses with a tell-tale perfect *ching* and her melancholy fell away as they sipped. Life was pretty darn good.

He indicated the food. 'You serve yours and I'll fix Piper.' Finn dished some veggies and meat onto Piper's cartoon-illustrated plastic plate and swiftly cut them into bite-sized pieces.

This was all done so efficiently that Trina found herself smiling. Such a maternal thing to do but this dad had it covered.

She arranged her own plate, finishing with a generous serve of gravy, and sat back to wait for Finn.

He wasn't far behind. He topped his meal off with his gravy and then looked up to meet her eyes. *'Bon appétit.'*

They didn't talk much as they ate, neither did they rush, and Trina glanced around as she savoured the subtle and not so subtle flavours of a well-cooked roast dinner. Marvelled at the decorating touches that showed this man's love for his daughter. A mobile of seashells over the cot, a run of circus animals in a wallpaper panel behind her bed. An alphabet mat on the floor with a Piper-sized chair on it. A row of small dolls in bright dresses.

She indicated the dolls with her fork. 'So these are the ladies you talk to?'

'All the time. Especially the brunette on the end. Remarkable conversationalist, really.'

'I can imagine.' She smiled at the dark-haired doll which, at a stretch, could look a little like Trina herself.

'Do you like our home?' Needy? Keen for her approval? But there was something endearing about that.

She nodded sagely. 'I think Piper will be a famous decorator one day.'

She was teasing him but it must have been the right thing to say because his pleasure was almost palpable. 'Remind me to show you the shower. We have very nice tiles.'

'I'll make sure I do that.' And she allowed herself to consider the possibility of a future here. With this man and his daughter. At the very least as friends and with a potential for more…but she wouldn't rush. Couldn't rush. And neither could he.

The thought crashed in. Who knew where his wife was? The thought brought a deluge of dampness to her sunny spirits and she looked down at her food, which suddenly didn't taste as good as it had.

'So tell me about the rest of your week. Did Piper still want to stay at Marni's when you went to pick her up after a full day or did she miss you?'

'Both. Marni is wonderful with her. And your Myra has booked her drop-and-go cruise. A five-nighter to Tasmania. They leave Sunday. So call and three-day rosters at the hospital. Piper will have to stay over when I'm on call. Though they've managed to give me only the one night call, which I appreciate.'

'Wow. You've dived into work with a vengeance.'

'I should have done it earlier. I'm feeling more connected to humanity every day.' He glanced up at her with definite warmth. 'Though that could have been you.'

Glad he thought she was human. But that wasn't what he meant and she knew it. Her face heated and she looked down at her almost empty plate. 'Thank you, kind sir.' She lifted her head and shook the hair away from her face. It was getting hot in here. 'One night seems like the perfect answer. That's not too bad as a start. When did you say that night was?'

'Next Thursday. We'll see how she goes. Marni's not worried.'

She could have offered for a Thursday night but she was glad he hadn't asked. She wasn't ready for that much commitment. 'Well, good luck.' She lifted her glass of water. 'And here's to your first week at the hospital. I'll look forward to your smiling face.'

'I'll try to remember to smile.'

CHAPTER THIRTEEN

Finn

BY MONDAY MORNING, his first day in the hospital, Catrina continued to seep into Finn's thoughts with alarming regularity and he was feeling just as strange about that as he was about the new work model he'd slipped into. A general GP, admittedly with extra specialist paediatric consults on the side, and a rural hospital generalist as well. With maternity cover? Never thought he'd see the day.

Over the weekend he and Catrina had met a lot, each meeting better than the last, plus they'd talked about the hospital and the patients he'd probably find come Monday. About how the medical input had changed since the new midwifery model had started, even some of the times that Dr Southwell had been called away from the main hospital to provide back-up in Maternity.

He could see Catrina enjoyed their discussions and, to be truthful, he was a little curious to see how it all worked. They'd bumped into each other often.

Intentionally on his part and, he suspected glumly, unintentionally on hers.

He'd managed the Friday morning beach bump into when, after his own walk, he'd offered to share the breakwall with Catrina, Piper on his back, and they'd spent more than an hour together talking non-stop.

Saturday morning, after Catrina's scuba lesson, he and Piper had been back in their rock pool at just the right time for her to walk past them again and fortuitously share an early lunch as Catrina offered to return last week's lunch shout at the beach café.

Saturday night he and Piper had been invited to a barbecue dinner at Ellie and Sam's and, of course, Catrina had been there as she lived next door.

Naturally he'd spoken to other people but they'd spent most of the time standing together. He'd had an excellent conversation with Sam on the strangeness of working in a cottage hospital after coming from a tertiary health facility and Myra had shaken his hand and thanked him for making it possible to drag her husband away on a cruise. But the stand-out moments were those watching Catrina's quiet rapport with the other dinner guests.

His eyes had drifted in her direction way too often.

The best had been on Sunday when Catrina had asked if Piper—and Finn—could come and help her choose colours for her new carpet and cushions and they'd had a hilarious day at the nearest large town choosing colours via a one-year-old in a stroller.

A huge weekend, in fact, but one that had passed

without kissing her once. And that also was something he couldn't get out of his mind.

Her mouth. So mobile, always smiling and doing that soft chortling thing when he said something to amuse her—a new skill he seemed to have acquired that did more to heal his soul than anything else.

Or that unconscious, but luscious, lip-pursing she did when she seriously considered something he said. Or just her mouth looking downright kissable when he didn't expect it, and he was having a hard time not drifting off and staring at the lift of a corner or the flash of white teeth.

He didn't remember being this fixated on Piper's mother when he'd met her. There had certainly been attraction, almost a forest fire of heat and lust culminating in a headlong rush into marriage when their contraception had failed. More his idea than hers and he had certainly paid the price for that.

But he was coming to the conclusion that he must have been meant to be Piper's daddy because he couldn't imagine life without his baby girl so he thanked Clancy for that. There was a bit of healing in there somewhere and he wasn't sure he didn't owe Catrina for that thought too.

But Catrina? Well? He needed to slow down and not lose the plot, but Catrina made him want to be better at being himself, a better person, even a better partner since he'd obviously fallen short on that last time.

His attraction to Catrina had been exquisitely stoked by want and need, and he feared—or was that dared to hope?—she might be coming to care for him too.

This morning, as he climbed the hill to the little white hospital sitting on a cliff, he hoped that very much. He glanced at the cottage garden as he approached for his first day as visiting medical officer and could feel his spirits soar as he strode towards a new perspective of Catrina at work.

The ocean glittered a sapphire blue today, brighter and more jewel-like than he could remember seeing. Piper had been as lively as a grig being handed over to Marni and the boys. And he, well, he was back at work, feeling almost comfortable already in Reg's practice, like a normal human being. It had taken a year of shadow. And a week. And Catrina.

Except for the colour of the ocean, Catrina had a lot to do with most of his forward progress. Though maybe all the colours were appearing brighter this week because of her as well.

Reg had suggested he call into Maternity first— 'Around eight, my boy!'—to see if any women were in labour—'Just so you can be aware.' And then attend to his hospital round on the other side of the small white building.

He suspected that the midwives didn't need the visit but Reg clearly felt paternal in his concern for them. Finn thought it prudent not to share that insight with Catrina.

But what a gift of an excuse, he thought as he stepped through the automatic front door to Maternity and glanced around for her.

Instead, a nurse he'd met on his orientation round

with Reg on Friday came in through the side door from the main hospital at a run and her relief at seeing him alerted his instincts faster than her voice. 'Dr Foley—please follow me through to the birthing suite. Urgently!'

The smile slipped from Finn's face and he nodded and followed.

When he entered, he saw Catrina standing over a neonatal resuscitation trolley, her fingers encircling the little chest with her thumb pressing cardiac massage over the baby's sternum in a rhythmic count.

Another nurse held the tiny face mask over the baby's face, inflating the chest with intermittent positive pressure ventilations after every third compression.

Finn stopped beside them, glanced at the seconds ticking past on the trolley clock that indicated time since birth. It showed ninety seconds.

Catrina looked up and the concentrated expression on her face faltered for the briefest moment and he saw the concern and the relief on her face. Then she looked at the clock as well. Her voice remained calm but crisp.

'Rhiannon's baby was born two minutes ago, short cord snapped during delivery so probable neonatal blood loss. Baby is just not getting the hang of this breathing business.' Her voice came out remarkably steady and he filed that away to tell her later.

'Heart rate less than sixty for the last thirty seconds so we added cardiac compression to the IPPV and it's just come back to eighty.' She loosened her fingers around the baby's chest and turned down the oxygen to keep the levels similar to where a two-minute-old baby would normally be. Too much oxygen held as many risks as not enough oxygen for babies.

'This is the paediatrician, Dr Foley, Rhiannon,' she called across to the mum, who was holding the hand of an older woman, concern etched on their faces.

Finn lifted his hand and smiled reassuringly. Because the fact the baby had picked up his heartbeat was an excellent sign. 'Give us a few minutes and I'll come across and explain.'

He glanced at the pulse oximeter someone had strapped to the flaccid pale wrist. 'You're keeping the oxygen levels perfect. Umbilical catheter then,' Finn said calmly. 'I'll top up the fluids and the rest should stabilise.'

'The set-up is in the second drawer. There's a diagram on the lid because we don't use it often.'

He retrieved the transparent plastic box and put it on the nearby bench, squirted antiseptic on his hands and began to assemble the intravenous line that would be inserted a little way into the baby's umbilical cord stump and give a ready-made large bore venous entry point to replace the fluids lost.

He glanced at Catrina. 'Warmed fluids?'

'Cupboard outside the door.' The nurse he'd arrived with handed Catrina the clipboard she'd taken to jot observations on and slipped out to get the fluids. By the time he had all the syringes and tubing set she was back and they primed the line with the warmed fluids and set it aside.

Finn squirted the antiseptic on his hands again and donned the sterile gloves to wipe the baby's belly around the cord with an antiseptic swab, and wiped the cord stump liberally with the solution.

After placing a towel on the baby's belly to give himself a sterile field he could work from, he tied the soft sterile tape around the base of the finger-thick umbilical cord. The tape was a safety measure, so that when they removed the cord clamp Catrina had fastened at birth, he could pull the tape tight around the umbilical cord to control any further blood loss.

Once the tape was in place and fastened firmly, Catrina looked at Finn, who smiled reassuringly because he doubted it was something she did on a newly cut cord very often, and watched her remove the cord clamp with only a trace of anxiety.

Finn nodded to himself, satisfied—no bleeding— then sliced off the nerveless ragged edge of the snapped cord closer to the baby's belly with a scalpel blade, the white tape preventing any further blood loss. Now he could easily see the vessels inside where he wanted to put the tubing.

Using fine artery forceps, he captured one edge of the cord and then offered the forceps to Catrina to hold to free up his other hand.

With the cord now pulled upright, Finn lifted the catheter and another pair of forceps to insert the end into the gaping vessel of the vein in the umbilical cord. He glimpsed the nurse from the main hospital looking wide-eyed and said quietly, 'It's easy to tell which is the vein, being the largest and softest vessel of the three in the cord. That's the one that leads to the heart.'

Catrina asked, 'Do you have to turn the catheter to insert it? Aren't the vessels spiral?'

'Yes, spiral so when the cord is pulled in utero there's give and spring, the longer the cut cord the more spiral you have to traverse until you get to the bloodstream. That's why I cut this fairly short. Not too short that you don't leave yourself a back-up plan, though.'

The fine clear intravenous tubing disappeared just below the baby's abdominal skin. A sudden swirl of blood mixed with the warmed fluid Finn had primed the tubing with.

'And we're in,' Finn said with satisfaction. He adjusted the three-way tap on the line with one hand and slowly injected the warmed saline fluid with a fat syringe into the baby's bloodstream. 'Ten mils per kilo will do it, and I'd say this little tyke is about three kilos.'

He glanced at Catrina, who watched the monitor to see the baby's heart rate slowly increasing. She nodded. He then glanced at her colleague, still calmly applying intermittent puffs of air into the baby's lungs, and then watched as the tiny flaccid hand slowly clenched as tone returned to the baby's body and he began to flex and twitch.

Finn looked over at the mum. 'Not long now.'

'Get ready to tighten the cord again, Catrina,' he said softly and, once the full amount of fluid had been injected and Catrina was ready, he turned the tap on the infusion and removed the syringe.

'We'll just wait a few minutes before we remove it in case we need to give any drugs, but I think that will do the trick.'

CHAPTER FOURTEEN

Trina

TRINA'S GALLOPING PULSE slowed as the baby's heart rate began to rise above eighty. Her hand loosened on the resuscitation trolley she seemed to have gripped as Finn did his thing. After what had seemed like forever the baby's heart rate hit a hundred and ten and finally the baby blinked and struggled, grimaced against the mask and, in the most beautiful screech in the world, he began to cry. The tension in the room fluttered and fell like a diving bird and she watched Finn slowly withdraw the tubing from the vein. She tightened the cord as it came clear and then snapped on a new umbilical clamp close to the end of the stump. Done.

Baby threw his hands and kicked his feet and they pushed the resuscitation trolley closer to the mum's bed so he could be handed across with the pulse oximeter still strapped to his wrist.

Trina considered removing it as he'd become so vigorous with the replacement of fluid but it would be easier to monitor instead of listening with a stethoscope so, despite the tangle of wires, she left him connected and pressed his bare skin to his mother's naked breasts.

Once baby was settled on his mother, his breathing clear and unobstructed, she could relax a little more. A blanket covered them both, and she glanced at Finn, standing at the side of the trolley, his beautiful mouth soft as he watched the baby and mother finally together. His eyes shone with pleasure and he gave a little nod just before he saw Trina looking at him.

The smile he gave her, one of warmth and pride and appreciation, made her clutch her throat and heat surged into her cheeks. She'd done nothing.

When she looked back at him he was watching the mum again, his eyes still soft as he spoke to her.

'Hello there. Congratulations. As Trina said, I'm Dr Foley, the paediatrician, and your little boy looks great now. Snapped cords are fairly rare, but if a baby grows in utero with a short umbilical cord…' he smiled that warm and reassuring smile that seemed to seep right down to the soles of Trina's feet and he wasn't even looking at her '…which he is perfectly entitled to do.' He shrugged. 'Not surprisingly, though it *is* always a surprise, they can run out of stretch at birth and the cord can pull too tight.'

Rhiannon nodded and her own mother sat back with relief to see her grandchild safely snuggled into Rhiannon's arms.

Finn went on. 'Babies don't have a lot of blood to spare so some extra fluid through that intravenous line allowed his heart to get back into the faster rhythm it needs. As you saw, it's usually a fairly dramatic improvement. We'll do some blood tests and if we need to we'll talk about a blood transfusion. But he looks good.'

'Too much drama for me,' Rhiannon said, as she cuddled her baby close to her chest. Trina could agree with that. Now that she had time to think about it, she had to admit that Finn's appearance had been a miracle she'd very much needed. But there wasn't time for that yet as she began to attend to all the things that needed doing in the immediate time after a baby had been born.

Two and a half hours later Trina had settled Rhiannon and baby Jackson into their room, and the myriad of paperwork, forms and data entry had been sorted. The nurse from the hospital had stayed to help Trina tidy the ward because Faith, the midwife from night duty, had already stayed later than normal. Trina glanced at the clock, just ten-thirty, so, on top of the tasks still waiting to be done, she did need a moment to sit back in the chair and consider the excitement of the morning.

It had been a little too exciting but thankfully Finn had appeared at exactly the right moment without needing to be called. An opportune thing.

Like he did at that moment. Striding through the doors from the main hospital as if he owned the place.

She felt a smile stretch her face. 'I was just thinking about you.'

His laughing eyes made her belly flip-flop and caution flooded her. He had a wife. Somewhere.

'Good things, I hope?' he said.

She shook her head. Pretended to think about it.

'How I didn't need you this morning and you just pushed in.' Teasing him.

His face froze for a second and she slid her hand over her mouth in horror, saying quickly, 'Joke. A very mean joke. Especially when you were so good. I'm sorry.' But she could feel the creases in her cheeks as she smiled because his shock had been palpable when the statement had been totally ridiculous. He must have known she'd needed him desperately. She had no idea why she'd said such a crazy thing except to startle him. Or maybe because she'd been trying to hide how absolutely thrilled she was that he'd come back to see her when she'd thought he would have been long gone from the hospital.

This man brought out very strange urges in her. At least she wasn't giggling like a twit. She was saying bizarre things instead.

He laughed a little sheepishly. 'I was worried for a minute there.'

She looked up at him. Seriously? 'Don't be. Sorry. I was never so glad to see anybody in my life. My pulse was about a hundred and sixty.' And it wasn't far from that now with him standing so close, which would not do.

He studied her. That didn't help the galloping heart rate. 'Well, you looked as cool as a cucumber.'

'On the outside. Good to know.' Hopefully she looked that way now as well—especially with her brain telling her to do stupid things in fight and flight mode. 'But, seriously, you were very slick with inserting that umbi line. Most impressive.'

And she had no doubt her eyes were telling him

a tad more than she was saying because he smiled back at her with a lot more warmth than she deserved after what she'd just done to him. He sat down beside her at the desk.

To hide the heat in her cheeks she looked past his shoulder towards Rhiannon's room and murmured, 'It would have been very tense to keep resuscitating a baby who didn't improve as we expected. He really needed that fluid in his system to get him circulating properly.'

He didn't say anything so she looked at him. He was studying her intently again and her face grew hotter. 'What?'

'We were lucky. That was all it was. I'm wondering if you could call me for the next couple of births through the day while Piper is in care, just so I can sneak in a refresher course on normal birth. It's a long time since my term in Obstetrics working towards my OB Diploma and I want to be up to speed if an emergency occurs.'

His diffidence surprised her. 'Of course, you're welcome. I call in a nurse from the hospital as my second but I can easily call you instead if we have time. Or as well. I don't mind. And I can run a simulation through the latest changes in post-partum haemorrhage and prem labour if you like.'

'Excellent. I've been doing some reading but things aren't always the same when you get to the different hospital sites.'

'We're a birth centre not a hospital, even though we're joined by an external corridor. So all of our women are low risk.' But things still happened. Not with the regularity you saw in a major hospital but they did deal with first line emergencies until a woman or her baby could be transferred to higher care.

He nodded. 'Is that your first snapped cord?'

'My first here.' She shook her head, still a little shocked. 'We've had them tear and bleed but to actually just break like that was a shock.'

'It's rare. Had probably torn already and when the last stretch happened at birth it broke—but you handled it well, getting the clamp on so quickly. I've seen some much worse situations.'

'I kept expecting him to get better, like nearly all babies do when you give them a puff or two, but by the time you arrived I was getting worried.'

He nodded. 'Hypovolemia will do that. How's Mum?'

'Taken it in her stride. Said her angels were looking after her and baby Jackson.' She thought he'd laugh.

'Useful things, angels.' Then, in an aside, 'My mother was a medium. I should have listened to her.'

He shrugged and Trina tried not to gape. His turn to say something off the wall, maybe, or he could be pulling her leg because he grinned at her surprise.

He changed the subject before she could ask. 'Today Jackson also had the midwives and doctor.' He grinned. 'Shall I go down and see if she has any more questions now she's had a chance to think about it?'

Trina stood up as well. Off balance by his throwaway comment about his mother...and his proximity. Moving to a new location sounded like a great idea, she thought, still mentally shaking her head to clear it. That had been the last thing she'd expected him to say. But she'd ask more later. This moment, here at work, wasn't the time. Angel medium? Seriously, she was dying to find out.

'Great idea. Thank you.' She stood up and followed him. Finn was thoughtful, kind and darn slick as a paediatrician. Lighthouse Bay might just have to count its blessings to have another fabulous doctor in the wings when they needed him. Speaking of wings... Angels? Her head spun as she followed him down the hallway.

Over the next four days while Finn covered the hospital, he shared three births with Trina between breakfast and morning tea. It was almost as if the mothers were on a timetable of morning births to make it easy for him to be able to watch and even catch one.

She could tell he was enjoying himself. Basking in the magic that was birth. But the busyness meant she didn't get a chance to ask about him. About his mother's angels. About his childhood. About his marriage—not that she would! The woman who had given birth to Piper and what had happened to her.

Trina hoped they were at the stage of friendship where she could ask about at least some of those things soon. But then again, she hadn't shared anything of her past either. Maybe they should just leave it all in the past and keep talking about Lighthouse Bay nineteen to the dozen like they had been. Share the past slowly because she was probably reading too much into his interest.

Lighthouse Bay Maternity must have decided to draw in the babies for Dr Finn, because they just kept coming. The overdue ones arrived, the early ones came early, and the more time they spent together with new babies and new families the more her curiosity about Finn's world before he came here grew.

He left soon after each birth to continue his appointments at the surgery but returned at late lunchtime with his sandwiches to talk about the morning's events.

On Thursday, his last hospital shift before Dr Southwell returned, Finn entered the birthing room quietly after the soft knock Trina had trained him in. She'd left a message with his secretary to say they were having a water birth, and even though he'd not long gone he'd been very keen to see the way water and birth 'mixed'.

Trina had given him a scolding glance at his wording, but she had immense faith that once he'd seen the beauty of the way the bath environment welcomed babies into the world he'd be converted. She was glad he could make it.

Sara, the birthing mum, was having her second baby and had come in late in the labour. She'd phoned ahead to ensure the bath had been filled, mentioned she wanted lots of photos of her daughter's birth because she had lots from her son's birth.

They arrived almost ready for second stage and Trina had the bath prepared. At Finn's knock her head lifted and Sara frowned at the sound.

Trina worried. Maybe things had changed. 'Are you still okay if the doctor sits in on your birth, Sara?'

'As long as he stays out of the bath, I'm fine,' Sara said with unexpected humour considering the glare at the door and the contraction that had begun to swell and widen her eyes.

Trina turned to hide her grin and motioned for Finn to enter the room. She liked the way he always waited for permission. Though she might have mentioned it a few times and she had no doubt her eyes betrayed her amusement at his docility. No, not docility—respect. Her amusement faded. As he should.

Finn said a brief thanks to Sara and her husband and settled back into the corner on the porcelain throne, making himself as inconspicuous as a six foot tank could be. Once he was seated Trina tried to forget about him.

She suspected by the way Sara was breathing out deeply and slowly that she'd felt the urge to bear down. Second stage. Time to up the monitoring. When the final louder breath had been released Sara lay back with her eyes closed.

Trina murmured, 'Is baby moving down and through, Sara?'

'Yes.'

'Can I listen to the heartbeat between those outward breaths?'

'Yes.' Bare minimum. She had more important things to concentrate on than answering questions and Trina understood that.

Sara arched her belly up until it broke the surface of the bath water and Trina leaned forward and slid the Doppler low on Sara's belly. The sound of a happy clopping heartbeat filled the room. With her eyes closed, Sara smiled.

After a minute Trina moved the Doppler away and Sara sank back below the water, causing ripples to splash the edge of the bath. She didn't open her eyes when another minute passed and her heavy outward sighs started again.

It took fifteen minutes, and five cycles of breathing, listening, smiling and sinking below the surface of the water and then they could see the baby's head below the surface.

Sara's breathing didn't change, nobody spoke. Below, in the water, the small shoulders appeared. Trina hovered, but Sara reached down, waiting, as an expelled breath larger than the rest released a flurry of movement. The movement heralded the rest of the baby's body had been born. Sara clasped her baby firmly between her hands below the water level and lifted her smoothly to the surface to rest on her belly. The little face rose above the water, blue and gaping, and then the baby's eyes opened and she began to breathe in as the air hit her face.

Everyone else breathed out. The father photographing constantly and the glance the couple shared between clicks made tears sting Trina's eyes. So beautiful.

The birth left Finn sitting thoughtfully at her desk as he replayed the scene.

Finally, he said, 'That was amazing. The mum was so in control, lifting the baby after birth out of the water like that.' He quirked one brow at her. 'How could you stop yourself reaching in to do it for her?'

Trina smiled. 'If she'd hesitated or if she'd needed me to, I would have. But Sara had it covered. That's her second water birth so she knew what she wanted and what would happen.'

He rolled a pen between his fingers thoughtfully. 'I have to admit to scepticism. Why add water to the list of things that could go wrong for a baby at birth?' He tapped the pen on the desk. 'I could see Mum looked super-relaxed—baby just appeared with the breathing, not even pushing, and slowly birthed. Hands off. A very relaxed baby though a little bluer than normal in the first few minutes.'

That was true, Trina thought. 'We find the colour can take a minute or two longer to pink up, mainly because the babies may not cry.'

She shrugged. 'People need to remember no analgesia was needed for Mum because of the thirty-seven-degree heat and relaxation of the bath, so babies aren't affected by drugs for the next twenty-four hours like some are. That helps breastfeeding and bonding. She didn't have an epidural so no drip or urinary catheter either.' And no stitches. Trina always felt relieved when that happened—and it was usually when a mother advanced second stage at her own pace. Something they prided themselves on at Lighthouse Bay—but then they had all the well mums and babies to start with.

It had been a beautiful birth and Trina still glowed from the experience, even after all the tidying up and paperwork had been done.

She glanced at the clock. Finn would go soon. Lunchtime seemed to fly when he came to talk about the births and she could feel their rapport and their friendship, the ease she fell into with their conversations, had all grown this week with his shifts.

Finn stroked the cover of the book Trina had lent him to read on water birth. 'I'm intrigued how you managed to sell the idea here to the board of directors. I know water birth was vetoed at my last hospital.'

It had been easier than expected. One of the board member's daughter had had a water birth at another hospital. But they'd covered their bases. 'Our statistics are meticulous. Ellie has always been firm on keeping good records and it shows we have excellent outcomes on land and water birth. I'm doing the same.' She thought about how smoothly their transition to a midwife-led unit had been in the end. 'Of course it helped with Sam as back-up. Ellie's husband has such high standing in the area now. The local authorities consider us backed by experts even though Sam's not technically here. So water birth with the midwives at Mum's request is the norm here and proved to be very safe. Just remember we start with well mums and well babies.'

'Good job. Everyone.' He stood up. Looking down at her with that crooked smile that seemed to make everything shine so bright it fuddled her brain. 'Well, you've converted me. Which is lucky as tonight is my all-night on-call.'

He gathered up his lunch wrap from the kiosk meal he'd bought. 'I'd better get back to the surgery; my afternoon patients will start to arrive at two. Then my first night without Piper for a year.'

She knew plenty of mums who would love to have a night where their babies slept overnight with someone else. 'How does that make you feel?'

He shrugged. Apparently not overjoyed. 'Very strange, I have to admit. I think I'm going to be lonely. Don't suppose you'd like to join me?'

'If you get forlorn give me a call.' As soon as she said it Trina began to blush. What on earth had got into her? Practically throwing herself at the man at the first opportunity. But she'd been thinking he'd looked sad when he'd said it.

She soldiered on. 'What I meant was, unlike Piper, I can go home if you get called out.' That sounded even worse.

His blue eyes sparkled. Mischievously. Suddenly he looked less like an assured paediatrician and more like a little boy offered a treat. 'Now that's an offer I'd like to take you up on. We could get takeaway.'

'Now I feel like I've invited myself.'

He laughed. 'Thank goodness. We could both die of old age before I had the nerve to ask you properly and I've been wanting to since Marni agreed to have Piper overnight.'

He flashed her a smile. 'It's a date. You can't back out now. I'll see you at mine at six p.m.'

She couldn't have him cooking for her after work. 'I finish at five. So why don't you come to my house? I can make us dinner or order in and your mobile will go off anywhere. Do on-call from there.'

'If that's okay, then great. I'll appear at six.' He waved and smiled and…left.

Good grief. He'd been wanting to ask her. Then reason marched in. Wanted what? What could happen if she wasn't careful? It was a small town and she needed her reputation and her just healing, skin-grafted heart needed protection. Was she getting too close to this guy—a guy with a cloud of unresolved questions that even he didn't know the answers to?

Well, yes. She was getting too close.

Did it feel right?

Um, yes. So why couldn't she spend the evening, or the night if that came up, with a man she was very, very attracted to?

Because he was married. His wife was missing, alive or dead, he was still married—and she didn't sleep with married men.

CHAPTER FIFTEEN

Finn

FINN KNOCKED ON Catrina's solid timber door and his heart thumped almost as loudly as his knuckles on the wood. He couldn't believe he was back in the game. Taking risks. Making a play. With his twelve-month-old daughter asleep at a babysitter's and his wife still missing.

He wasn't a villain to do this. He was on-call. Calling on Catrina beat the heck out of sitting at home alone, waiting for his mobile phone to ring for work. And Catrina made his world a more rounded place. A warm and wonderful place.

Different to the walls he normally pulled around himself and Piper. Guilt from the past had become less cloying over the last few weeks, the cloud still there but it had gone from dense and choking to thin and drifting away like ocean mist. Like a new day awakening. Thanks to Catrina.

The door opened and she stood there, with that gorgeous smile of hers that lifted his heart and made him want to reach forward and, quite naturally, kiss her. Which, to the surprise of both of them, he did. As if he'd done it every time she opened the door to him—when in fact it hadn't happened before—and, despite the widening of her eyes in surprise, she kissed him back. *Ah, so good.*

So he moved closer and savoured that her mouth melded soft and tentative against his. Luscious and sweet and…

He stepped right in, pulled the door shut behind him, locking the world away from them, because he needed her in his arms, hidden from prying eyes.

She didn't push him away—far from it, her hands crept up to his neck and encircled him as she leaned into his chest. The kiss deepening into a question from him, an answering need from her that made his heart pound again and he tightened his arms even more around her. Their lips pressed, tongues tangled, hands gripping each other until his head swam with the scent and the taste of her. Time passed but, as in all things, slowly reality returned.

He lifted her briefly off her feet and spun her, suddenly exuberant from all the promise in that kiss, then put her down as their mouths broke apart. Both of them were flushed and laughing. He raised his fingers to draw her hold from his neck and kissed the backs of them. 'Such beautiful hands.' He kissed them again.

In turn, she created some sensible space in the heat between them and turned away.

But not before he saw the glow in her eyes that he had no doubt was reflected in his. They could take their time. The first barrier had passed—they'd kissed, and what a kiss. The first since heartache and they'd both survived. Not just survived—they'd thrived! Finn felt like a drooping plant, desperate for water, and he'd just had the first sip. You could tell a lot from a first kiss, and Catrina had blown his socks off.

Finn slowed to watch her cross the room, mostly because she fascinated him—she walked, brisk and swinging, out through the open door of the veranda overlooking the sea, the backdrop of sapphire blue a perfect foil for her dark hair as distance widened between them.

He tried hard not to look at the bed in the corner of the big room as he passed but his quick glance imprinted cushions and the floral quilt they'd bought on Sunday which she said she'd needed to brighten the place. He pulled his eyes away but he could feel the tightening in his groin he couldn't help and imagined carrying Catrina to that corner.

'Come on,' she called from the little covered porch and he quickened his step. Almost guilty now his body had leapt ahead after one kiss but the cheeky smile she'd flung over her shoulder at him eased that dilemma. She was thinking about the bed too. But not today. He needed to make sure she knew it all. Before he tarnished something beautiful and new with ghosts from the past.

He'd never seen her so bubbly—as if she were glowing from the inside—and he watched her, a little dazed, that he'd done this to her. Lit her up. With a kiss as if she were a sleeping princess. But he was no prince. And it was a long time since he'd lit anyone up like this—just Clancy in the beginning—and look how that ended. He pushed that thought away.

She'd set the table with bright place mats and put out salad and pasta and cheese. Orange juice in a pitcher stood beside glasses and the sunlight bathed it all in golden lights and reflections as the day drew to a jewelled close above the sea.

Like a moth to the light, he closed in on her where she'd paused against the rail overlooking the sea. Her silhouette was willowy yet curved in all the right places, her dark hair, sun-kissed in streaks, blowing in the ocean breeze. He came up behind her and put his hands on the rail each side, capturing her. Leant ever so lightly against her curved back, the length of his body warming against her softness, feeling the give against his thighs.

Then he leant down and kissed the soft pearly skin under her ear and she shivered beneath him; her breath caught as she pushed back, into him. His hands left the rail and encircled her hips from behind, spreading low across her stomach and pelvis. 'You're like a sea sprite up here.' His voice came out low and deeper than normal. 'A siren high on her vantage point overlooking the sea.'

She turned her head and, with a slow wicked smile, tilted her face to look at him. 'Does that make you a pirate?'

He lifted his brows. 'I could be?'

'Not today, me hearty,' she said and pushed him back more firmly with her bottom to suggest he give her space and he let his hands slide down the outer curve of her thighs, savouring the feminine shape of her, and then away.

'Right then,' he said and stepped back. 'Do your hostess thing, sea sprite.'

She spun and pulled out a chair at the table. 'Yes, you should eat in case you get called away. It's Thursday and I know there's a buck's party on tonight before the wedding on Saturday. You might be needed if things get silly.'

She indicated the food in bowls. 'Start now, please. Don't wait for me.' She avoided his eyes and he saw the exuberance had passed. There was no rush and this wasn't just about him—it was about this brave, beautiful widow finding her way to exposing her heart again. He reminded himself he knew how that felt though his circumstances were far different. He wanted to do this right. Right for Catrina. Right for him. And right for Piper. He needed to remember Piper. And try not to forget he had Clancy in the wings.

Though how could he do this right with a missing wife God knew where and this woman bruised from her own past? He forced a smile to his mouth. 'The pasta looks amazing.'

He saw the relief as he changed the subject and knew he'd been right to give her space.

She gestured vaguely to the hedge that separated her house from the one next door. 'Herbs make the difference. We share a herb garden. Myra does the tending and Ellie and I share the eating.'

She smiled with her mouth but not her eyes and he wondered what she was thinking while she was talking trivia about herb gardens. Had he been too full-on? Yes, he had—they both had—but that had been some kiss. Like a steam train carrying them both along at great speed and only just finding the brakes.

'But it works for us.'

What works for us? Then he realised she was still talking about the herb garden. He had it bad. Just wasn't so sure about her. He stuffed some pasta in his mouth. A taste explosion rioted there and he groaned in delight. And she could cook. His gaze strayed to her.

Time. *It all takes time*, he reassured himself. Took another scrumptious bite and prayed the phone wouldn't ring at least until he finished his food. Preferably not at all.

She poured him some juice, then sat opposite him, her hair falling to hide her face, but something about the hesitant way she tilted her face as if she were weighing her words before she spoke. He swallowed more divine food and slowed down. Then asked, 'Question?'

'I'm wondering if it's too early to ask you about your mother. You said something on Monday that's been driving me a little wild with curiosity.'

His head came up. More because the idea of her being driven a little wild stirred his interest rather than any concern about her prying into his past. 'A little wild, eh?' He speared a pasta curl.

She looked at him and shook her head. 'You're a dark horse, Dr Foley. One bit of encouragement and I can see where that leads you.'

He grinned at her. Spread his fork hand innocently. 'I'm just happy.'

She laughed. 'I'm happy too. So, now that I've made you happy, can I ask you about your mother?'

'Go ahead.'

'What did you mean she was a medium? It's the last thing I expected.'

He'd come to terms with it years ago. Funny how women harped on about it. His sister. And Clancy. Both had hated it. Funny he hadn't thought Catrina would be like that. He'd always thought of his mum's beliefs like a choice. Believe in angels or not. Be a vegetarian or not. Take up ballroom dancing or tarot cards.

'What's to expect? She was a psychologist then became fascinated by the cards and became a medium. I loved her. My sister couldn't have been more horrified if my mother had taken six lovers instead of a sudden attraction to talking to the angels.'

Catrina leaned forward earnestly. 'It doesn't repel me. I'm not sure what fascinates me about it. It's just different. That's all. And a bit out there for a paediatrician to have a medium in his family.'

He'd heard that before. 'That's what my sister said. But it made Mum happy and when she went she went with peace. She died not long after I fell for Clancy.' He shrugged but heard the grief shadowed in his voice. Tried to lighten the tone. 'She said that Clancy had sadness wrapped around her like a cloak and she worried about me.'

Catrina opened her eyes wide.

He sighed. 'I didn't listen.'

CHAPTER SIXTEEN

Trina

TRINA GLANCED OVER the rail to the wide ocean in front of them. Sought the point where the ocean met the sky and sighed too. Of all the things she wanted to ask Finn, she wasn't sure why she'd chosen to ask about his mother. And now that she knew she'd never meet her it made her sad. Another mother gone. It had been a ridiculous question.

Or maybe it was about her because she couldn't remember her own mum, could only remember an ethereal figure tucking her in and singing a lullaby she couldn't remember the words to. But she knew mothers were special. She'd always wanted one and Finn's had sounded magical. Someone who talked to angels.

For Trina there'd been a succession of foster homes in her childhood, the quiet child, the plain one with her hair pulled back tightly, the one people were briskly kind to but nobody became interested in, except the younger children she seemed to gather around her every time she ended back in the home.

Many kids had it a lot worse, and she'd come to a stage where she'd asked not to be fostered, not to raise her hopes that she'd find a mother to love, and she'd stayed and helped in the home until she could leave. Had worked for a scholarship, always determined to do her nursing.

A nice sensible profession followed by her glimpse into midwifery—and that was when she'd seen it.

The families. Starting from the glory of birth, the connection to the child, the true beginning of a mother's love. The journey she'd make one day because she knew in her bones this was her destiny and then she'd be home. She had so much love to give.

'I'm sorry your mother died. I would have liked to meet her.'

He looked at her thoughtfully and then nodded. 'She would have liked you too.'

The thought warmed her melancholy and she appreciated his kindness. 'Thank you.'

He was the one with the questioning look now. Weighing the difference of needing to know and being too forward. 'Where did you meet your husband?'

So they'd reached that stage. She'd started it. Gingerly she began to unpack it a little. 'Edward was a nurse like me. At uni. We both worked at a restaurant waiting on tables and we laughed a lot. Then we both graduated and went to work at the same Sydney hospital. We married just before I started my transition to midwifery year. He was my knight in shining armour, my soulmate, an orphan like me and a man who understood my need for family.'

She had to admit Finn looked less happy. 'He sounds a great guy.'

She breathed in slowly. To control the tickle of sadness in her throat. 'He was.' Gone now. They'd been so full of plans. 'We were saving up for our family that never came. Because Ed died. Killed by a fast brain tumour that robbed him of speech before we could say much, and his life before we could properly say goodbye.'

She saw the empathy for her sudden loss. Not as sudden as his. But worse.

Finn said, 'That must have been devastating.'

'It was. I sold our flat and came here. Watching the sea helped.' She'd been adrift, swamped by the withdrawal of a future again, the loss of her love and her husband. She'd sworn she would not risk broken dreams again. But then she'd stumbled into Lighthouse Bay and the warmth of her midwifery family had helped her begin the long, slow journey to heal.

'But it seems I'm resilient. Maybe all those foster families in the past made me tough. Because now I'm scuba diving and I've even had lunch and dinner with a man and his daughter. It took two years but I'm becoming braver.' She looked at him. 'But I'm still wary.'

'I understand that.' He grimaced. 'I'm a little wary myself.'

One more question then, Trina thought as Finn put the last of the pasta into his mouth. She waited for him to swallow. 'So how did you meet Clancy?'

CHAPTER SEVENTEEN

Finn

FINN GUESSED HE owed Catrina that. He remembered the day vividly. Puffy white clouds. Brilliant blue sky. Painted ponies and unicorns. 'At a fairground, of all places. She was riding the merry-go-round with a little girl my sister had taken there. A distant relative she'd asked my help to mind for the day. We were introduced by a five-year-old. Clancy knocked me sideways. Her hair—' he shook his head '—just like Piper's, a daffodil cloud around her head.'

He saw Catrina's wince and mentally smacked himself up-side the head. *Idiot. Don't tell one woman another is beautiful.* He moved on quickly. 'I should never have married her. She wasn't that young but she was a child, not a wife.'

'Do you think Clancy knew what she was doing when she ran away? That she planned to stay hidden?'

'I hope so. That has kept me sane. She ran away for a couple of days twice during the pregnancy. I was frantic. Then she reappeared as if she'd never been away and I told myself to stop making a big deal of it. That nobody owns anybody. But to leave straight after the birth?' He shrugged. 'It was a quick labour, but physically it was still a labour. So why would she leave her recovery time and make life hard on herself?'

'What happened?' He heard the gentleness in her voice, the understanding, and, despite his reluctance to talk about a time he wanted to forget, Catrina was a midwife and understood women, plus—he'd kissed her. Planned on doing more. She needed to know.

'Clancy stayed very focused during the birth. Distant, when I look back on it. As if she'd already pulled back from me. Even when Piper was born Clancy pushed her to me and of course I was over the moon. I scooped her up whenever she wanted. Clancy said no to breastfeeding so I gave Piper her first bottle.'

He remembered those first precious moments with his daughter in his arms. 'I've wondered how long she'd known that she was leaving.' He shook his head. Felt Catrina's eyes on him and was glad she didn't interrupt. He just wanted it out. 'So I changed the first nappy, gave Piper her first bath. And when I came back in on the second day to take them home she'd already gone. She'd left Piper with the nurses.'

He saw Catrina's hand cover her mouth but now he was there—in the past—remembered the incomprehension and disbelief. The beginnings of anger and how he'd expected her to walk back in at any moment.

How could Clancy possibly leave her day-old baby? How could she leave him when they were just starting as a family? And the worst. Selfish really.

The innuendo that he had been impossible to live with and for what dark reason had she left?

Finn found himself opening his mouth to let those words out too. Ones he'd never shared with anyone else. 'I could feel the sidelong glances from the midwives—domestic violence must have run through their minds. Why would a new mother leave her baby? Was I the sort of man who looked loving on the outside yet was evil on the inside? What had I done to her to make her do this?'

'I don't think so,' Catrina said softly. 'If that were the case, I imagine the mother would take the baby and not leave a child at risk. The staff would have seen how you cared for Piper.' She reached out and laid her fingers on his arm. 'I see how you care for Piper.'

He appreciated that. He really did. But maybe he had done something Clancy couldn't live with. He'd rehashed their short marriage but couldn't see anything. If only he knew why she'd left. 'I don't want the guilt if something happened to her. But I'm well over waiting for her to turn up every morning. My biggest regret, and it still rips out my heart thinking about it—is how am I going to explain to Piper that her mother walked away from her? That's what makes me angry. I can survive but how does a young girl understand her mother doesn't care enough to at least ask how she is going?'

'Every child needs a mother. But Piper has you. I guess Clancy knew you would make Piper your world. You're a paediatrician so you must love kids. Could keep her safe.'

'Maybe. But to have no contact? Just disappear?'

'You don't know why?'

He shook his head.

'Then you may never know. And it's no wonder you wanted to hide and start again.'

Start again. The words repeated in his head. Yes. He wanted to start again with Catrina. Instead he said, 'Moving here helped with that. Living in our house was pure hell. She wanted the big house, but it wasn't as much fun as she thought it would be. She didn't want a baby, just wanted to enjoy life without worries. She didn't want to be a doctor's wife or a stay-at-home mum. She wanted to be seen with a man on her arm. And I was busy. I guess I did let her down.'

CHAPTER EIGHTEEN

Trina

TRINA LISTENED TO Finn and tried not to judge Piper's mother. Tried not to hear the reverence in his voice when he spoke of her hair. He was right. Of course people would ask why she had left. Would wonder if he'd been the monster to force her into such a desperate act. Would harbour suspicions that somehow he had harmed her. She wondered if Finn knew how lucky he was she'd left the hospital and not when she'd got home, when the innuendos could have been worse. At least he hadn't been the last person to see her.

She tried to comprehend a mental imbalance, or a strange delusion, or just plain selfishness that had made it possible for a woman to leave her day-old baby. To leave without warning, or explanation except for a brief note, but no assurance of her well-being and expect her husband not to suffer with doubts and worry and loss of the family dream all under a cloud of suspicion. It proved difficult to imagine. Poor Finn.

'You said you tried to find her. The police?'

'The police agreed the note was real, didn't find

anything and then other cases took precedence. They didn't have the resources for runaway wives.'

'You said you hired a detective?'

Finn waved his hand. 'The detective finally tracked down her last known contact before I met her, an older man, an uncle, but he'd gone overseas recently. The trail stopped there.'

Trina couldn't imagine how hard that must have been. 'She never wrote? Or phoned you?'

'Her phone went straight to message bank and eventually even message bank disconnected. Her credit cards or bank accounts that I knew she had were never touched. She didn't drive so they couldn't trace her through her driver's licence.'

Poor Finn. 'How can someone just disappear?'

'I've asked myself that question many times.'

'Do you think she went with her uncle? Overseas?'

He grimaced. 'It's possible. Or he set her up somewhere. I never met him. Didn't know of his existence until the detective told me.'

'What about your wedding?'

'She wanted the register office. My mother was in her last month and very ill. Half a dozen people came on my side. None on hers.'

It all sounded very sterile and unromantic. Quite horrible really. Not in keeping with this man who adored his daughter and made cupcakes and sand-castles.

She wanted to ask if Finn still loved Clancy. Started to. 'Can I ask…'

Finn's phone rang and they both looked at it vaguely and then reality hit. He was on call.

Finn dug it from his shirt pocket and said, 'I did not plan that.' Then he stood up to listen. Trina tried not to strain her own ears.

Finn left a minute later. 'One of your buck's night boys has cut himself on oysters.' He kissed her cheek. 'Thanks for dinner. And for listening. My turn next time.'

He said *next time*. So she hadn't scared him away. And, despite that harrowing story of his wife's disappearance, he hadn't scared her away either. And he kissed her before he left. Trina hugged herself briefly and began to clear the dishes away. There were lots of reasons not to rush this.

Friday morning Finn met her on her walk and invited her down to his cottage backyard for a barbecue. Despite her need to prepare for the next week of work—washing, sorting, a little shopping—the day dragged until it was time to go over, and her stomach was knotted with excitement when she arrived. This was not being wary.

He looked so good when he opened the door.

He bowed her in. Then he kissed her. Twice. Piper was toddling across the room stark naked and put her arms up to Trina. *Wow.* She scooped her up and hugged her.

'Well, that's a hello anyone would be happy to get.' She met Finn's eyes over the top of Piper's head and her cheeks warmed at the smile Finn sent her. She hoped he didn't think she wanted him naked to greet her at the door. Her face grew warmer.

'Welcome,' Finn said softly. Then changed the subject away from the charged atmosphere of how fast this was all going. 'It's fresh-caught fish tonight. As soon as I bath Piper.'

'Let me.' Trina laughed as the little girl played peek-a-boo around her neck at her father. 'You go ahead. I'll bath her.'

Piper wriggled to be free and Trina put her down. The little girl toddled towards the bathroom. Finn laughed. 'She's getting smarter and faster.' Then he gestured with his hand. 'Her clothes are on my bed.'

So Trina bathed Piper in the little shower tub Finn had made. The enchantment of ceramic tiles with starfish, animals, moon and flowers around the walls of the shower cubicle, a mishmash of words that Piper tried to say when Trina pointed them out.

She loved that Finn had created the novelty for his daughter. Loved the way Piper watched her father with sometimes wise eyes. Loved them both. She sighed.

She was in trouble and she knew it. She'd fallen for him and he was still married. Fallen for the idea of joining their family as pseudo mother and she had no right.

Somewhere there was a woman who did have the right and until that dilemma was sorted she should be spending less time with him, not more—but she couldn't seem to say no. She didn't even want to ask if he still loved Clancy. She didn't want to know.

On Saturday morning she met Piper and Finn at the rock pools on her way back from her scuba lesson. 'What a surprise!'

Finn laughed when she teased him about being predictable and they bickered pleasantly about who was paying for lunch this week after a pleasant half an hour splashing.

After lunch Finn took Piper home for her sleep and Trina went home to make a cheesecake.

She'd been invited to Myra and Reg's for another barbecue; they'd arrived home from their cruise excited about the fun they'd had and eager to talk about the adventure.

Reg was impressed when Trina told him of Finn's assistance during Rhiannon's baby's birth and patted himself on the back for finding such a useful fellow. He rubbed his hands and winked at Myra and then Finn arrived and the story was repeated.

Finn came to stand beside Trina with Piper on his hip. Piper leaned towards Trina so naturally she put her hands out and took her from Finn.

'It's a great unit. I was glad to help,' Finn said as Piper's soft little hands reached up and touched Trina's hair on her cheek. Pulled it experimentally. Absently Trina lifted her fingers to free herself and caught Ellie's raised brows as she adjusted the child on her hip more comfortably. It was clear Piper felt at home with Trina and, judging by Ellie's expression, she was wondering why.

Finn went on, oblivious to the unspoken conversation between the two women. 'Catrina was as calm as a cucumber, as was Faith, of course.' She saw him glance around and was glad he'd mentioned Faith. Faith, Trina and Ellie had been the original three midwives and Faith wasn't there to hear. But it was nice to be mentioned. His gaze settled on Ellie. 'You have great midwives.'

Ellie's questioning gaze finally shifted off Trina, who gave a little sigh of relief. 'I know. Though it's the first time we've actually had to give fluids by a UVC in our unit.'

'Happens a couple of times a year where I worked,' Finn said and took a ginger ale from Ellie's husband. 'What about you, Sam? Seen many babies need IV fluids at birth?'

'Nope. And don't want to. That's one of the benefits of working at the base hospital. Paeds do all that stuff. Give me a nice straightforward obstetric emergency every time and leave babies for the paeds.'

Finn laughed. 'Each to their own. I'm the opposite. Though Catrina's been letting me sit in on births for the week as a refresher and we even had a water birth.' He smiled at her and she felt her cheeks heat. Ellie winked at her and she tried unsuccessfully not to blush.

Quickly she decided she might as well join the conversation and try to look normal. 'He's converted. It was Sara and you know how calm she is.'

Ellie nodded. 'I was there for her last baby. Gorgeous. I'm hoping to have a water birth,' she told Finn. Then glanced at Sam, who pretended to sigh.

'I'm just the father. But, as an obstetrician, I'd like to go to the base hospital and feel like I have every conceivable back-up plan in place—but I've been outvoted.' He didn't look too worried.

'When's your baby due?' Finn asked Sam and, seeing the expression on his face, Trina wondered if he was remembering the feeling of being a father and knowing too much—but not wanting to say it.

'Three weeks.' Sam grimaced. 'I'm more nervous than Ellie.'

His wife took his hand and kissed it. 'You're excited, dear, not nervous, and it could take five weeks if I go overdue.'

Sam looked at her, his face softened and he squeezed her hand back. 'I'm very excited.'

Trina decided he was manfully suppressing the *and nervous* addition to that sentence and she remembered that Sam's first wife had miscarried many times. Everyone had their past and their crosses to bear. She should be thankful that she had good friends, wonderful support around her, and now she had Finn. *Be thankful. And stop worrying.*

The night held lots of laughs, tall stories and excitement from Myra and Reg about their cruise. And a few hints that they'd go again soon if Finn was happy to take Reg's on-call roster.

Myra and Trina had shared a bottle of lovely champagne they'd brought back from Tasmania and Trina glowed with good food, good wine and the joy of having a male dinner partner who fancied her for the first time in two years and didn't mind letting others know.

Finn and Trina left the party at the same time. Trina ignored the arch looks. As they stopped at Trina's gate she pointed to her door. 'You're welcome to come in if you like and have coffee.'

'I'd like that but Piper is drooping and she'll go to sleep soon.'

Trina's previous reservations were muted by the delightful fizz of the pleasant evening and she didn't want the night to end. She could sleep in tomorrow. 'I do have a folding cot in the cupboard. Sometimes Faith's daughter sleeps over if her aunt has to go away. She could sleep in there until you go.'

Finn looked surprised. 'I didn't realise Faith had a daughter.'

'We all have life stories. Her daughter's a real doll. We should introduce her to Piper.'

He looked down at his dozing daughter. Pretended to panic. 'I don't think I'm ready to cope with play dates.'

Trina laughed. 'You're funny.' Then glanced at the door. 'Come in or go?'

'If you have a cot, I'll come in. Thank you.'

Trina led the way, pushed open the door and gestured to her bed in an airy fashion. 'You could change her there and I'll make up the cot.'

Finn nodded and carried his daughter across the room and undid the nappy bag while Trina happily poked around in the cupboard and pulled out the bag with the folding cot in it. She had it out in minutes, grinning a little when it proved difficult to stand upright and kept sagging in the middle.

'I think you're tipsy,' Finn said, laughing. 'Here.' He reached forward with one hand and clicked the last lever into place to make the folding cot stand straight.

'Who, me?' Trina laughed. 'Maybe slightly but this cot is tricky.' She smiled at him a little dreamily. 'It was a lovely night.'

Trina laid the two quilts she'd taken from the bag

down on the cot mattress—one as a bottom quilt and one to put over Piper as Finn laid her down in the cot. He put her cuddle bunny beside her head and Piper took it, rolled over and put her thumb in her mouth. She closed her eyes, secure that she was safe, even though the bed was different.

Trina gazed at the little girl for a moment and then sighed softly as she turned away. 'I'll put the kettle on.'

'Wait.' Finn's voice was low, gentle. His hand on her arm stopped her. 'What was that sigh for?'

'Just because.'

'Because what?'

She sighed again. 'Because you're a great dad. Because you have a beautiful daughter who doesn't seem to give you a moment's bother.' She paused, then finished the thought. 'And I want that too.' Trina felt herself sobering fast when she realised that she'd actually said that out loud.

She pulled away. 'Must be tipsy. Sorry.'

'Don't be sorry. I wish Piper had a loving mummy like you would be. But that's for the future.' Then he turned her and drew her into his arms. 'It was a lovely night. You looked beautiful and happy and I'd really like to just sit and talk and maybe canoodle a bit. What do you think?'

'Define canoodle?'

He stroked her cheek. 'I really, really want to kiss you.'

And she melted. He drew her to the sofa and as he sat he pulled her towards his lap. She wasn't fighting him. In fact she did a bit of climbing on herself.

They both laughed. 'So beautiful. So sweet,' he said and then his mouth touched hers and she lost herself in the joy of being cherished.

CHAPTER NINETEEN

Finn

FINN WOKE TO moonbeams spilling across the bed and despite the silver threads of light a feeling of foreboding crept over him. He didn't like it. Splashes of brightness fell on the gently rounded form of a naked Catrina in his arms and he could hear the little snuffles of Piper asleep in the cot they'd moved close to his side of the bed.

They should have waited. His fault. They should have talked about worst-case scenarios if Clancy came back. Should have put in a plan to protect Catrina, but his resistance had been tempted beyond sense once Catrina had climbed onto his lap.

He thought about waking her. Telling her that he would start looking again so he could end his marriage. Protect Catrina from gossip. Gossip that if he stayed would follow her from tomorrow morning when he was seen leaving her croft.

He whispered, 'It might not happen but there's a chance…' But she was asleep. Sound asleep.

Finn slid his arm out gently from beneath Catrina

and paused to look down at her in the moonlight. How had he been so lucky to have found this woman—how could he have been so careless to fall in love when he didn't have the right?

He should never have slept with her, should never have let her fall in love with him, with everything still unsettled, and he knew she did love him enough to be vulnerable to hurt, knew she trusted him now, knew he had to fix this if she was ever to forgive him for such carelessness.

He considered waking her then. He'd always intended warning her there was still a chance but the time had never been right to say it again. What they had nurtured between them had seemed so fragile, so new, had happened so fast, he'd feared to destroy it before it began.

Impossible. Fraught with danger. To lose what they'd just found was unthinkable. He needed to work out tonight how they could move forward with Clancy still out there. But for the moment he could prevent some of the gossip. He'd come back tomorrow.

He wrote a quick note on the back of one of his business cards, then gathered up his sleeping baby, felt her snuggle into his shoulder with complete trust. Like Catrina had. He winced. Slung the nappy bag over his other shoulder and let himself out.

The moon was up, full and bright like daylight, which was lucky as he had no hand free for a torch. Suitable really—he'd been baying at the moon like an idiot, following the siren's lure. Impulsive fool, risking Catrina's happiness.

In minutes he was home, had tucked his daughter

into her cot and sat on his own empty bed to stare at his feet.

He should never have slept with Catrina with his wife still out there somewhere.

CHAPTER TWENTY

Trina

SUNLIGHT PEEPED AROUND the curtains in Trina's croft as she stretched her toes luxuriously and remembered Finn's arms. She could almost feel the warmth and strength around her that she'd missed so much and couldn't believe she'd found again. Found again but different. Fairy tales did come true.

It was as if she'd turned into someone other than the broken-hearted woman she'd been for the last two years; she even had a new name. She was Finn's Catrina. Not Ed's Trina. Or maybe both.

She squashed down the piercing guilt and sent love to her departed husband. Yes, she would always love him, but now, after these last few weeks, she knew she loved Finn too. Needed to love Finn. In a different way. But in a real way. Not the ethereal way she loved and always would love Ed. And then there was Piper. Sweet, motherless Piper. She loved Piper too. And, my goodness, she loved life!

How had she been so lucky? She stretched again

and wondered what Finn was thinking this morning. She'd found his note.

Spare the gossips—we need to get this sorted.
Finn Xx

Her thoughts took a sensuous turn down the hill towards his house and she was tempted to sneak down there and snuggle into his bed. And him. But apparently, until they told people, they should be discreet. For her sake, he said. But he was the new doctor. For his sake as well. She got that. But what a whirlwind these last two weeks had been.

Maybe a six a.m. break and enter wasn't discreet.

She took her time. Showered in a leisurely fashion. Washed and dried her hair. Applied light make-up though—she stared into the glass with a small curve of her mouth—her well-kissed lips needed no colour this morning. The heat surged into her cheeks. Nor did her face need blusher either. She smiled at herself—a cat-that-ate-the-cream smile—and turned away from the blushing woman in the mirror.

She'd never been that uninhibited with Ed. Their lovemaking had been wonderful but there was something about Finn that drove her a little wild. Or a lot wild. Apparently, she did the same to him. She smiled again.

Her chin lifted. Life was too damned fickle not to take advantage of that fact and she wouldn't be ashamed, and she never, ever wanted to be cold in the night again.

She could grow used to being driven wild in bed.

She drew the gaily coloured scarf that Finn had said he liked from the drawer and flung it around her neck. She looked like an excited schoolgirl.

She tried to think of an excuse to turn up that wasn't purely, *Let me into your bed.*

Maybe she could make a breakfast picnic and they could take it down to the beach and eat it on the breakwall? Piper would like that. She could just knock on his door like a neighbour and invite him to join her. Her stomach flipped at the thought of the light in his eyes. That special smile he seemed to find when she appeared.

She took off the scarf again and made bacon and egg sandwiches, the delicious scent swirling and teasing and making her belly rumble. She was hungry for everything this morning. Even the coffee smelt divine as she made up the Thermos, and extravagantly tucked in a small bottle of orange juice as well. She packed her checked rug and tucked her little picnic bag under her arm as she closed the door.

Then she stopped. Leaned back against the cool wood and sucked in a breath as if someone had thrown a bucket of cold water over her. Finn would be there for her.

For ever? The words trickled through her brain like rivulets of pain on her mind. Questioning. Prodding scarred memories. Undermining her belief in their future.

What if he couldn't? It hit her. What if he wasn't there? What if she fell more and more and more in love with Finn until it was too late? What if something happened to Finn and she'd given the last half of her heart, all that was left of her own self, to him and it got smashed and broken and buried in a coffin like the half she'd given to Ed? What if the worst happened and Finn died and left her for ever? She had said she'd never allow herself to feel that pain again. Piper would go to her aunt and Trina would be alone again. Smashed to smithereens like the broken shells pounded by the surf on the beach below.

She sucked in a burning breath and clutched the ball of pain in her chest. It was too easy to remember the ripping pain of loss. Too devastating to imagine her empty bed now tainted with Finn's imprint so it would always be there. *No!* Nobody could be that unlucky!

She reached out to lay her hand against the wood of the door. Seeking support. Felt the hard wood as a solid force and drew strength from it. Drew another deep breath as if she were one of her mothers and she needed to be coached through a tough contraction. *Okay then.* Breathed again. That wasn't going to happen.

She sagged against the door. Beat it. She'd beaten it. But the voice inside her mind wasn't finished yet.

So, you don't want to imagine that? The voice in her head tried another tack. What if the almost as bad happened and his wife came back and Finn chose her as Piper's mother over Trina? She'd never asked if he still loved Clancy. Had she?

Of course Piper's needs would outweigh hers, maybe even outweigh Finn's, to be fair to him. Either way, she would lose.

Of course Piper needed her mother. If Finn had Clancy he wouldn't need Trina either.

No! They were going to talk about that. Make plans. She straightened her spine. Thought back to the gentle way Finn had cradled her through the night. The whispered promises. The closeness. Finn was a worthy man and she trusted him. And she needed to trust in the future.

Catrina tweaked her scarf reassuringly, lifted her head and a little less jauntily set off down the hill. Felt the promise of the day fill the void. She stopped and closed her eyes and welcomed the sunshine in. Felt it flooding through her body, healing the fear that had gripped her moments before. Opened her eyes and began walking again. A panic attack. She'd had a panic attack. That was what it was. *Silly girl.* Everything would be fine. She clutched the picnic bag and lifted her face again. Smiled.

The sun seemed to be shining with extra brightness today—what was that? Overhead, gulls soared and swooped and she could feel the rocks scatter and pop with exuberance under her every step. The salty breeze brushed her hair across her cheek and it tickled, making her smile. Like Piper had tickled her cheek with her hair. It began to seep back into her. The joy she'd woken with, the excited thrum of blood in her veins. It had been so long since she'd felt this way—excited, alive and happy, yes, happy. Too long. She'd just been frightened for a moment but she was fine now. One night in Finn's arms and she was a goner. But what a night!

Life had certainly taken a turn for the good. New

job, new man friend—she shied away from the word *lover* as she glanced down through the trees to where she could see Finn's front door.

There was an unfamiliar car in the driveway and she slowed her steps. Then she remembered Finn telling her about his sister's new car. A red convertible. That was who it would be. *Darn it.* She couldn't be neighbourly when he had a visitor.

Her footsteps slowed. The door opened and Trina stopped in the lee of a telegraph pole, not wanting to intrude on goodbyes. Three people stepped out. One was Finn with Piper on his hip, clinging like a limpet. Trina smiled fondly.

One was the woman Trina had seen at the restaurant that day that seemed so long ago but was only weeks—Finn's sister. She'd been right. She had a look of Finn.

And the other… Well, the other had a mist of fine flyaway hair the colour of sun-kissed corn, the exact hue of daffodils, just like Piper's. Finn and the woman stood together and only Finn's sister got into the car. Trina felt as if her heart stopped when Finn's sister was the only one who drove away.

Finn and the golden-haired woman turned and went back into the house. The door closed slowly, like the happiness draining from Trina's heart. An icy wind swirled around her shoulders as she stared at the closed door. *Who was that?* But she knew with a cold certainty who it was. Felt the knowledge excising the joy from her day like an assassin's knife. A killing blow. She turned around and climbed the hill like an old woman to her lonely croft.

Once inside she closed the door and locked it. Before she could shut the curtains and climb into bed the phone rang.

It wasn't Finn.

They needed her at work.

CHAPTER TWENTY-ONE

Finn

IN THE MORNING someone knocked on Finn's door. Surely only minutes after he'd fallen asleep just before daybreak. Groggily he sat up, pushed the covers away and automatically glanced at Piper.

Bright inquisitive eyes sparkled at him and she bounced up and down on the balls of her feet, holding onto the top of the cot rail. 'Mum, Mum, Mum,' Piper said gleefully.

'It better not be,' he muttered for the first time but he had to smile. It probably was Catrina. It was good she was here. Though he smiled to himself at her lack of discretion. To think he'd sneaked away to stop the gossips and she'd come at sparrow call anyway. Today he would throw himself on the mercy of the court and find out how to file for divorce. He wanted that new beginning.

Except when he opened the door it wasn't Catrina. It was his sister. Looking shell-shocked and pale. She opened her mouth and closed it again.

'Frances? What's wrong?' Finn reached out to draw her inside but she pulled back. Glanced at her car.

'She's here.'

'Who's here?' He looked at the car. Saw the cloud of floating golden hair and knew. Felt the world slam into him with the weight of a sledgehammer, driving the breath from his body. He leant his hand on the door frame to support himself for a second and then straightened.

Licked his dry lips and managed to say, 'Where did you find her?'

'She found me. Saw your house was for sale in the paper and recognised it. The real estate agent rang me.'

Finn's mind had shut down. He couldn't think. Piper was clinging to him and the door was closing his wife and his daughter inside his house.

One year late.

And—absolute worst—one day late.

Finn shut the front door and turned around to lean against it, the weight of Piper on his hip grounding him like she had done so many times before, and he stared unbelievingly at the woman he'd given up on seeing again.

And, after last night, hadn't wanted to see again. Or not like this.

She was talking. He could see her lips move, though she was looking at the ground as she spoke, so that didn't help the comprehension. Her hair was that floating cloud of daffodil yellow that he'd noticed when they'd first met. Beautiful, he thought clinically, as if he had nothing to do with the scene about to unfold, but too fine; her hair was a golden mist around her head, like Piper's.

She was still talking but his ears were ringing and seemed to echo with the weight of his emotion. She wasn't dead. That was a good thing. That was good for Piper. For the future. Maybe they would have some connection in the future. Not so good for him. He was married. And he'd just slept with another woman. Her timing could not have been worse.

He cut across her long-winded explanations that he hadn't heard a word of. 'Wait. Sit down. I can't understand you when you talk to the floor like that.'

She glanced around a little wildly, her hair a drift of golden cotton in the breeze of her movement, so fine and light it swayed with her like yellow seaweed under the ocean.

He sat down too. Piper stayed stuck to his hip with her head buried into his shoulder. He wished he could bury his head too. 'Why are you here?'

She spoke softly. Hesitantly. 'To talk to you. Talk to Piper.'

He could feel the scowl on his face. Tried to smooth it out. To listen with empathy as if she were a tiresome patient who refused to take necessary advice. But she wasn't. She was his wife who had abandoned them. Remember his oath to treat the ill to the best of his ability. He'd always known she wasn't one hundred per cent well. It didn't help a lot. 'You're a year late.'

'I'm sorry.'

Well, that didn't cut it, but he hadn't heard the reasons yet. He fought the panic that engulfed him. His brain had seized. His chest felt tight. And he had to keep from squeezing Piper too tightly against him. How could she be here? And—the most frightening of all—was he even glad?

He stood again. Turned his back on his wife and moved across to put Piper down in her playpen, but she clung to him. He kissed the top of her head and reached for the fruit sticks he kept in a jar in the fridge.

'Here you go, sweetheart. A bit cold but you don't mind, do you?' Then he put her in the playpen and she sat quietly with her big eyes watching him as she began to chew the fruity sticks.

He heard Clancy's soft voice. 'You're very good with her.'

He stamped down the anger. 'We are family. Plus...' he looked at her steadily '...someone had to be.'

She flushed. 'I made a mistake.'

Really? he thought. *Just one?* But didn't say it. *And it took a year for you to tell us that?* Instead he tried to make his voice neutral and said, 'I don't understand why you would drop out of nowhere like this. What are you hoping to get out of this?'

'Just to talk. At first.'

He winced at 'at first'.

She went on hesitantly. 'See what happens. If what happens is good then maybe—' she drew a long breath and squared her shoulders for a second '—I'm hoping that we could start again.'

Finn sucked in a breath, stunned she could even

contemplate that, but then he was in shock. His thought processes were not good. He needed to be calm.

Her shoulders drooped again. 'I could learn to be a mother.' She looked up at him and her eyes were shiny with tears. 'Maybe even a wife.'

CHAPTER TWENTY-TWO

Trina

TRINA PUSHED OPEN the door to Maternity and from down the hallway she could hear quiet moans from the closed doors of the birthing units. Someone sounded very close to having a baby.

In the other birthing room it sounded as if someone else was also very close to having a baby. It happened sometimes. Not often, but when it did at change of shift a third midwife was needed. Technically she didn't start her Sunday call until after eight a.m. but the other midwife had plans for today and Trina was pathetically grateful to be doing something.

She tucked her bag into her locker and washed her hands. The fine tremor of distress was barely noticeable but still she glared at her quivering digits. *Stop it.* She liked and trusted Finn. She would just have to leave it there, parked, until she finished work.

But, deep inside, a crack of loss began to tear and rip and widen. Too soon for loss. She should have stayed safe from pain for a lot longer. Healed more solidly before ripping at the wound.

The woman down the hall moaned louder and Trina drew a deep breath and shut the world outside the doors far away. This was her world. Inside this unit. This was where she needed to concentrate.

The called-in midwife appeared beside her and spoke very quietly. 'I'm in room one with Bonnie. She won't be long. All going well and I have a nurse with me. Jill has Jemma. It's been a long hard labour and slow second stage. Will you take her?'

Catrina was one hundred per cent there. 'Absolutely.'

She turned and knocked gently and pushed open the door.

Jill, the midwife on night shift, looked up with wordless relief. 'Here's Trina, come in to help,' she said to the woman with a brightness that didn't quite ring true. 'You know Jemma and Pierce, don't you, Trina?'

'Yes, I do. Hello there, Jemma.' She nodded to the usually jolly Pierce as well, but his face had strained into taut lines. Some dynamic wasn't working or there was a problem. 'You both look to be doing an amazing job here.'

Then she looked back to Jill as she reached for the handheld Doppler to check the baby's heart rate. 'I always like to say good morning to babies too, so is it okay if I have a listen to yours, please, Jemma?'

'Sure,' Jemma sighed as the last of the contraction ebbed away, and Trina put the dome-shaped Doppler on Jemma's large rounded stomach. Instantly the clop-clop of the foetal heart-rate filled the room. The contraction ended and no slowing of beats indicated the baby had become tired or stressed, and the rate sat jauntily around one-forty. There was even a small acceleration of rate as baby shifted under Trina's pressure, which told her that baby still had reserves of energy, despite what she guessed had been a long labour.

She stared at the large shiny belly and guessed the baby's size to be larger than average. Acknowledged that position for birth would be important to optimise pelvic size.

'He/she sounds great,' she said after a minute of staring at the clock. 'Magnificent belly there, Jemma.' The tension in the room eased another fraction.

'Can I check the position, please?' Jemma nodded and Trina ran her hands quickly over Jemma's abdomen. Confirmed the baby was in a good position and head too far down to palpate. That was good. 'So, catch me up on Jemma's progress, Jill?'

Jill glanced at the couple and smiled wearily. 'It's been a long night and they've been amazing. Jemma's due tomorrow; this is her first baby and her waters broke about four p.m. yesterday. The contractions started pretty much straight away and they came in here about five p.m.'

She glanced at the clock that now pointed to almost seven a.m. 'The contractions have been strong and regular since six p.m. so she's been working all night to get to this point. Her observations have stayed normal, and she's been in the shower and the bath, has tried the gas but didn't like it much. We've walked a fair way and at five she felt the urge to push. I checked and she'd reached that stage already.'

Two hours of pushing and head well down. *Good, not great*, Trina thought. 'Wow, that's a hard and long labour,' she said gently and Pierce nodded worriedly.

'So,' Jill went on, 'Jemma's been pushing for just under two hours now; she's tired and we almost have head on view but it hasn't been easy for the last few pushes. We've been in the bathroom for most of that time, but she wanted to lie down so she's just come back to the bed.'

Trina looked at the night midwife and nodded. In bed on her back was the last place any midwife wanted Jemma if she had a big baby on board. Jill wasn't happy with the progress which, on the surface, seemed timely and acceptable so there must be more.

Jemma moaned as the next wave of contraction began to build and Trina tuned to see why Jill would be worried as the team went to work to support Jemma in the expulsive stage.

Tantalisingly close, the baby's head seemed to be hovering but not advancing that last little bit to birth and Trina kept the smile on her face as she suspected Jill's concern.

Trina moved in with the Doppler again to listen to the baby after each contraction. 'How about you give the doctor a ring and he can be here at the birth? Then he can do his round early and leave early. He'll like that. I'll stay with Jemma and Pierce for this last little bit. You can write up your handover notes here in the room, and that way you'll be ready to go as soon as we have this determined little passenger in his mother's arms.'

Gratefully, Jill nodded and they changed places.

When Jill had finished the phone call, she settled herself on the stool in the corner at the side desk and they all rested as they waited for the next contraction.

Trina looked into Jemma's tired face. 'After this next one, I'd like you to think about changing position.'

Jemma sighed and Trina smiled. 'I know.'

Jemma grumbled, 'I just want this over.'

Trina nodded and glanced at Pierce. 'I'm thinking Pierce wants to see this baby snuggled up between you both too. Your baby probably has his father's shoulders, so I'm suggesting turning around and kneeling on the bed or even down on the floor, because that position gives you an extra centimetre of room in your pelvis. That tiny amount can make all the difference at this stage when it feels hard to budge.' She smiled at them both. 'It's a good position for making even more room if we need it after baby's head is born.'

'Is there a problem?' Pierce had straightened and looked down at his wife.

'No. But sometimes when second stage slows this much it means there might be less room than expected. We have set body positions a mum can go into that create extra space in her pelvis. I'd rather have Jemma ready to do that, even if we don't need it, than try to awkwardly scramble into position if we have a more urgent need.'

Pierce nodded. 'What do you think, Jem?'

'I think I'd do anything to get this baby here.'

After the next long contraction a weary Jemma rolled over in the bed onto her knees and rested her head on her forearms on the high pillows that had been behind her. Trina settled the thin top sheet over her and gently rubbed the small of her back. Pierce offered her a sip of water from the straw at Trina's silent prompting.

In the new position baby made progress and the first of the head began to appear on view. There was a soft noise at the door and, instead of old Dr Southwell, it was his son, Sam, and Trina could have kissed him.

Reg was good, but there was nothing like an obstetrician when you needed one. 'This is Dr Southwell, Jemma. Pierce, this is Sam.'

The men shook hands quickly as Trina went on. 'We've some second stage progress since Jill spoke to you, after moving to all fours. There's better descent with the last contraction.'

She moved her hand and placed the ultrasound Doppler awkwardly upwards against Jemma's now hanging belly. It wasn't as clear as before in this position but they could hear the steady clopping from the baby on board.

Sam nodded at the sound. 'Baby sounds good. I'm here as extra hands if position changes are needed.' He went to the sink, washed and put gloves on.

Pierce looked at him. He glanced at his wife and seemed to change his mind about asking more. The next contraction rolled over Jemma and she groaned and strained and very slowly the baby's forehead, eyes and nose birthed. But that was all.

'Keep pushing through,' Trina said with a touch of urgency and Sam nodded. But no further descent of baby occurred. Trina found the foetal heart again with the Doppler and it was marginally slower but still okay.

'We'll try putting your head down. Move the pillows, Trina,' Sam said quietly. Jill appeared at their side and Sam said, 'Phone Finn. Tell him I want him up here to stand by.'

Trina looked up as Jill disappeared and her heart sank. Sam must think it was going to be more difficult than expected.

She removed the pillows and encouraged Jemma to put her head on the bed and stretch her knees up towards her chest with her bottom in the air. It would straighten out her sacrum and, hopefully, give them a tiny bit more room in her pelvis.

The head came down another centimetre and the face cleared the birth canal but then the chin seemed to squeeze back inside like a frightened turtle's head against his shell.

Trina listened to the heart rate again and this time they all heard the difference in rate. Much slower. The cord must be squeezed up between the body and the mother's pelvis. That would dramatically reduce the oxygen the baby was getting.

'It looks like your little one has jammed his anterior shoulder against your pubic bone, Jemma. Not letting his body come down, even though his head is out. I'm going to have to try to sweep baby's arm out so the shoulder collapses to make room.'

'Do it,' Jemma panted.

'Try not to push as I slide my hand in.' From where she stood, Trina saw Pierce fall back in his chair and put his hand over his face.

Jemma stared at the ceiling and breathed slowly, striving for the calm that was so important, and Trina felt her eyes prickle with admiration for the mother in crisis as she squeezed her shoulder and spoke reassuring words in Jemma's ear.

She watched Sam's eyes narrow as mentally he followed his hand past the baby's head and reached deeply to slide along the upper arm to the elbow. Trina saw the moment he found the baby's elbow and swept it slowly past the baby's chest and face; she saw the relief and determination and wished Ellie was here to see her amazing husband, saw the muscles on Sam's arm contract and watched the slow easing of the limp arm out of the jammed space and suddenly there was movement.

The arm was out, the head shifted. 'Push, Jemma,' Trina urged, and then the baby's flaccid body slid slowly into Sam's hands.

'I'll take him,' a voice said behind Sam and Trina looked up to see Finn there. The relief that swamped her was so great she didn't care that his wife had arrived. Didn't care her heart was broken. No space for that. She wanted this baby with the best paediatric care and she didn't doubt that was Finn.

Sam cut the cord quickly. Trina saw Jill's worried eyes and knew she'd be better at the resus than Jill without sleep.

'Swap, Jill.'

Jill looked up, relief clear on her face. She nodded and hurried over to change places with Trina beside the mother.

CHAPTER TWENTY-THREE

Finn

FINN HEARD CATRINA say, 'Swap, Jill…' as he carried the silent and limp baby to the resuscitation trolley that Jill had set up. The lights and heater were on and Finn rubbed the wet baby firmly. Catrina handed him the next warmed dry towel and he did it again.

She spun the dial on the air and handed the tiny mask to Finn, who started the intermittent positive pressure breaths while she placed the pulse oximeter lead on the lifeless white wrist.

After thirty seconds, the heart rate was still too slow. 'Cardiac massage.' Finn said briefly.

Catrina circled the baby's chest and Finn wondered if this had happened twice in a fortnight before for her. It was unusual. For a low-risk unit this was too much.

He watched as she began compressing the baby's chest by a third in depth. He intoned, 'One, two, three, breathe. One, two, three, breathe.' For another thirty seconds.

Catrina said, very calmly—too calmly, 'Still heart rate below sixty.'

He glanced at her face and saw the fear she held back. 'Thinking about adrenaline after the next thirty seconds,' Finn said quietly, and then Sam appeared.

'I'll take over the cardiac massage, Trina.' He'd be thinking that, as the midwife, she could find their equipment faster.

Trina nodded and Sam slipped in with barely a pause in the rhythm. She reached down and pulled open the drawer, removed the umbilical catheter set he recognised and pulled out the adrenaline. Once you needed adrenaline things didn't look so good.

Good idea about the umbi catheter. He prayed it wouldn't get to that. Finn hoped this baby would breathe before then. Then the big adrenaline ampoule appeared in his vision; the sound of her snapping off the glass top was reassuring. She was slick and he heard her muttering as she began to draw it up. 'The new guidelines say point five of a mil standard; is that what you want, Finn?'

'Yes, thanks. ARC Guidelines.'

He glanced at the clock. 'Next thirty seconds. Heart rate still fifty. Slightly better. Keep going.' He looked at Catrina and nodded at the box.

Thirty seconds later and Catrina had dashed out for the warmed fluid for the umbilical catheter box.

'Seventy.' He saw her sag with relief. He felt a bit that way himself. *Thank goodness.* No adrenaline needed. No umbi catheter needed. If the heart rate kept going up.

Sam stopped compression and Finn continued on

with the breathing. The baby wasn't white any more. Streaks of pinkish blue were coming. The blue on the face stayed but that would be compression of the head causing congestion and that might take hours to go. The body was pink. *Excellent.*

He heard Trina breathe out as the baby's hands flexed, as did his little blue feet. Then the neonate struggled and gasped. And cried. Finn sighed and let the mask lift off his face for a second to see what he did. The baby roared.

He glanced at Trina, saw the tears she was trying to hold back. He didn't blame her. That had been a little too close.

'Good job,' Sam said quietly and Finn looked at him. All in all, it had been an emotional day.

'You too.'

Catrina had gone. Over to the mother to explain her baby was coming over soon. Reassure, like she always did. Being the midwife. To help Jill with settling the woman more comfortably when her baby came across. The baby that was crying vigorously now. Finn felt the muscles in his shoulders release.

Sam said, 'It was in good condition before the cord was occluded by the body. So he had some reserves.'

'They'll have to keep an eye on his blood sugars after that resus.'

'Does he need transfer?'

'See what the glucometer says. Not if his sugars stay good.'

They both knew it wasn't good if a baby had no reserves and got into that kind of bother. Shoulder dystocia was a mongrel. Not common, but fifty per cent of the time there were no risk factors when it happened. At least this baby had been strong enough to come back with a little help.

Sam had lived up to the glowing praise he'd heard. Catrina had been amazing again. They all were. He could grow to be a part of this team.

Then the real world crashed in. If his wife went away and left him to it. And he still hadn't told Catrina that Clancy had arrived.

He stepped back as Catrina lifted the baby to take across to the mum.

Sam was leaving; he'd go too, as soon as he'd spoken to the parents, explained what had happened, that baby had been fine by five-minute Apgar and he didn't expect any sequelae. Then he'd go, but he cast one glance at Catrina. She was busy. Too busy for his drama. It would have to wait. He just hoped he got to her before she found out.

CHAPTER TWENTY-FOUR

Trina

TRINA SAW FINN leave the room after he'd spoken to the parents. *Good.* She didn't have the head space. He'd come to help when he'd been needed. And gone as well. She'd needed him to go.

She didn't think Finn had known his sister would bring his wife. She wasn't that blindly jealous. She even still had faith that he'd come eventually to explain and thanked him mentally for not attempting that now in the midst of the birthing centre drama. But then again, he didn't know that she had seen his visitor. Guest. Whatever.

Her heart cracked a little more and she forced a smile onto her face. 'Let's get you into the shower, Jemma. Then into bed with your little man for a well-earned rest.'

Jemma had physically fared well. Apart from some grazes, she hadn't needed stitches, her bleeding had been normal not excessive, which could happen after a shoulder dystocia, and her baby had recovered to the stage where he'd fed very calmly, had excellent blood sugar readings and gone to sleep in his father's arms after an hour on his mother's skin.

Finn had explained everything very slowly and calmly and both Jemma and Pierce seemed to have come to an understanding of what had happened. And, without being told, what could have happened. They kept thanking everyone. It was after such a harrowing experience that things replayed in a mother's mind—and a father's. So it was very important the information was given and the chance to ask questions was given.

Trina reassured her again. 'It's one of those things that we practice for. Do drills and prepare for because when it happens we need to have a plan.' *We also had two very experienced doctors available*, Trina thought and thanked her lucky stars they hadn't had a tragedy. For a minute she thought how good it would be to talk to Finn about what had happened, then remembered she couldn't. Maybe never would be able to. Pain sliced through her and she hugged it to herself to stop the heartbreak showing on her face. He'd probably leave now and she'd never see him again.

Four hours later the second birthing mother had gone home with her baby and the morning midwife could take over the care of Jemma and baby. Trina could go home. Not that she wanted to but she wasn't needed here now.

She had time to think. Maybe that was for the best. But damned if she was going to regret the fact she had shown Finn she cared. A lot. And he'd cared about her. There was nothing sleazy in their making love last night. Not a lot of sense either. But mostly the fact they hadn't waited showed a whole lot of bad timing.

It would probably be better if she didn't see him again.

Except that when she got home he was leaning against her front door.

Her heart rate thumped into overdrive and suddenly she felt like crying. She forced the words past the thickness in her throat, looking at a spot beyond his left shoulder. 'I didn't expect to see you here.' Understatement of the year.

'I asked the morning midwife to ring me when you left,' he said. His voice came to her low and strained. 'Clancy turned up.'

'I know.' When she glanced at his face she saw his shock. And, if she wasn't mistaken, his distress that she had found out on her own. The thought brought some comfort. At least he cared about that.

'When did you find out?'

She sighed and shrugged. Pushed past him to open her door. 'I saw your sister drive away. Saw a woman with the same hair as Piper go back inside with you. It wasn't hard.' She felt him come in behind her and didn't know if she wanted that or not. Might as well get the whole embarrassing mistake out in the open. But in private. Her face heated a little and she hoped her hair hid it. She'd let it down when she left the ward, needing the screen of it blowing around her face. Even more now. 'I was bringing breakfast.'

His hand touched her shoulder, the barest skim of his fingers, as if he thought she might shy away from him. 'I'm sorry, Catrina. I wouldn't have had you find out like that.'

What was the optimal way to find out your lover's wife had moved back in? She turned to face him. Saw the sincerity in his face, the pain, and spared a moment to think about just how much his world had been turned upside down by the unexpected return of his wife into his house. If she was Superwoman she'd feel sorry for him. Couldn't quite achieve that yet. 'Where's Piper?'

His face twisted. 'With her mother. Who has no idea what to do with her. Thinks she's a doll to play with.'

And that hurt too. And there was the crux of the matter. Trina had grown up without her mother and, even if Clancy was ditzy, like Finn had given her the impression she was, she was still Piper's real mother. Trina would have given anything to have an imperfect mother over no mother. One who was her very own. There was no way she could go anywhere near taking Piper's mother away from her or Piper away from the woman who'd given birth to her.

She forced the words out. 'I'm glad for Piper. Every little girl needs her mother.'

He sighed. Pulled his fingers through his hair as if he wanted to yank it out. 'Surprisingly, so am I. And yes, a little girl does need her mother. But don't get me wrong. Or get Piper's mother wrong. This is why I need to be here now. Tell you now. Clancy doesn't want to be a full-time mother. She has that "deer in the headlights" look in her eyes. I can see that already and I can't even stay here long in case she runs.'

If he was worried about that, despite the fact she needed to hear this, he should go. 'Should you even be here?'

He sighed. 'I phoned my sister. When the hospital rang earlier. She turned around and came straight back. She's with them at the moment. But I had to come. I need to tell you three things.'

She almost laughed. Tried not to let the bitterness out. The loss that she was only just holding back like the little boy with his finger in the dyke. The whole dam was going to swamp her soon and she didn't think she could hold back the disaster from drowning her for much longer. Her voice cracked. 'Only three?'

He stepped closer. His voice softened. 'They're important. Because you are important to me. Just listen. That's all I ask.'

She nodded mutely. She could listen. Just don't ask her to talk. She was totally unable to articulate the words through her closed throat.

He lifted his chin. Stared into her eyes. And his voice rang very firm. 'One, I'm sorry that you've been hurt by this.'

Yes, she'd been hurt, but she knew it was partly her own fault for falling in love with a man she knew wasn't free. She'd known right from the beginning and still she'd sailed along blithely, ignoring the impending disaster that had come just like she deserved.

He put up a second finger. 'Two. The good part of Clancy being here is that I can ask her for a divorce. Start all the paperwork that was impossible while she was missing. That is a huge thing for us. For you and me. And arranging when and how and the logistics of Clancy's access to Piper so that she and Piper can find the bonds that work for them. To create a relationship that is wonderful for both of them too. Piper will have two mothers.' He smiled like a man with a huge load lifted off his shoulders. 'You and I and Piper can look to the future. But that's where it is. In the future. It will take time and I may have to leave for a while as I sort it all out.'

She nodded dumbly, her head spinning.

He stroked her cheek. 'When it's sorted I will come back and ask you to be my wife properly. Romantically. Like you deserve and like I want too. Like I need to because you deserve everything to be perfect.' He shrugged those wonderful shoulders ruefully. 'Perfection can take a little while, with me. I'm sorry you have to wait for that.'

Trina sagged a little, relief bringing the dam closer to cracking. But the words swirled in her head, glimmers of light beginning to penetrate the weight of the wall hanging over her. He still wanted a future with her. Wanted her to be a part of the big picture. Part of his and Piper's future. Was it too good to be true?

'Three.' He paused. Stepped closer to her and tipped her chin up with his finger ever so gently. Wiped the tears that she hadn't realised were running down her face. 'I love you, Catrina Thomas. Fell in love with you weeks ago. And it's real love. Not the infatuation I had for Clancy. This is I-will-die-for-you love.' He sucked in a deep breath as if preparing for battle. 'We will conquer all the obstacles, my love.' He pulled back to see her face. 'Will you accept my apology and wait, dearest beautiful Catrina, while I sort this mess I made? Please.'

Trina drew her breath in with a shudder, trying not to sob with the relief of it all. The incredible wonder of Finn declaring his love when she'd thought it all lost. The unbelievable reprieve from having to rebuild her shattered heart. She moistened dry lips with her tongue and whispered very, very softly, 'Yes, Finn. I'll wait.'

His strong arms closed around her and she buried her face in his beautiful chest and sobbed while Finn leaned into her hair and whispered over and over again that he loved her so much.

EPILOGUE

A FULL YEAR later in a little pink cottage on the fore-shore of Lighthouse Bay, Finlay Foley woke with anticipation and wonder at the change in his life. His two-year-old daughter, Piper, bounced in her cot. She'd thrown out all her toys and demanded to be allowed up to start this most special day.

'Cat. Want Cat. Where's Cat?' She bounced and searched with her eyes. Finn had to smile as he picked her up and swung her through the air.

'Try Mum, Mum, Mum, Mum, baby. You can't call your new mummy by her first name. And your other mummy wants to be called Clancy.'

'Mum, Mum, Mum, Cat,' Piper chanted and turned her head this way and that as if Catrina would appear from behind a chair in the tiny house.

'She's not here. It's bad luck for Daddy to see his bride on the day of their wedding.'

Her little face crumpled. 'Want Cat. Now!'

'I know, baby. Daddy wants her too. I can't wait either. But the girls will be here soon to pick you up and take you to Cat. Then you can put on your pretty dress and watch your daddy become the happiest man in the world.' He hugged the small body to him, feeling her warmth, and wondered again how he had been so blessed to have Piper and Catrina in his world.

The village church at Lighthouse Bay stood with the open arms of two white-columned verandas overlooking the sea. The slender throat of the small bell tower and the skirts of soft and springy green grass that surrounded it had begun to fill with milling guests who had arrived before the groom.

The day shone clear and bright, freshly washed by an early morning shower as if the extra sparkle of purity was a gift from the sky to help celebrate their day.

Finn drank in the serenity, the warmth of those who smiled at him as he crossed the iridescent grass with his best man, Sam, and the rightness of Catrina's wish to sanctify their union in front of the townspeople and inside the church. He couldn't wait.

The journey of the last few months had taught him to look forward, and that something good—or, in this case, someone amazing—always came out of struggle. He'd learnt to accept that every day held promise, despite the ups and downs, and now his days with Catrina held an ocean of promise that he couldn't wait to venture into.

The minister moved determinedly to greet them as they reached the porch, his kind eyes and outstretched hand reassuring in appreciation of Finn's nerves.

But Finn's nervousness had left—had departed the day Catrina said yes. Eagerness was more the word he was thinking of.

Ten minutes later he was standing at the front of

the wooden church in his morning suit, surrounded by smiling townspeople, with row upon row of well-wishers jammed into the little church. All fidgeting and excited and smiling with enthusiasm for the event about to begin. Finn was pretty certain that, despite their enthusiasm, no one was more impatient than he was.

Sam by his side fidgeted too. Probably waiting to see Ellie. He saw Myra, looking particularly stylish in old lace, with Sam and Ellie's one-year-old daughter, Emily, in her arms. He'd been there when Emily was born. Waited outside the birthing room door just in case, to allay Sam's worries, and his own, and been a part of the joy and celebration of their beautiful birth. He couldn't help thinking of that post-birth hour, how such a magic time was one he wanted to share with Catrina when their time came. And Sam would wait outside the door for them. He'd never seen or been a part of such a place that offered so much solid friend-ship as Lighthouse Bay. And it had all started with the woman who would walk through that door for him any moment now.

The music soared and finally there was movement at the entrance. His eyes strained to see her. Catrina?

Faith, one of the midwives and Catrina's brides-maid, appeared with his darling Piper in her arms, framed in the doorway. Faith and Piper's deep fran-gipani pink dresses matched frangipanis in their hair, and Piper was wriggling to be put down. As soon as she was free she toddled swiftly towards him, draw-ing gasps of delight from the onlookers as she waved a pink sign on a thin stick that read, *Here comes Mummy, Daddy.*

With Faith sedately bringing up the rear, Piper ran full pelt into his legs and he picked her up and hugged her. His throat was tight, his heart thumped, and then Sam's wife Ellie appeared. He heard Sam's appreciative sigh beside him but Finn was waiting, waiting... And then she was there.

Catrina. His Catrina. Shining in the doorway. Resting her hand on Sam's dad's arm, her beautiful coffee-brown eyes looking straight at him with a world of promise and an ocean of love. Finn wanted her beside him now, but he also wanted everyone to see, admire her, as she stood there in her beautiful ivory gown—looking at him with such joy and wonder. Incredibly beautiful. Incredibly his.

Faith reached across and took Piper from him, and everyone turned to savour the sight of the star, Catrina, his beautiful bride, as she stepped firmly towards him with so much happiness in her face he could feel his eyes sting with the emotion of the moment. How had he been so fortunate to win this woman's love? He didn't know if he deserved her but he would hold her and nurture her and protect their love and his darling wife for the rest of his life.

Catrina walked on a cloud towards Finn.

Her husband-to-be. Tall, incredibly debonair and handsome in his formal suit, his ivory necktie crisp against his strong throat. Emotion swelled but she lifted her chin and savoured it. She loved Finn so much, had been blessed, finding him when she had never thought she could possibly feel this way again. The music swelled to draw her forward. She needed no coaxing, couldn't wait, couldn't smile enough, feel enough, be thankful enough as she walked towards the man gazing at her with so much love her feet barely touched the ground.

'Cat, Cat, Dad,' Piper said. Then she looked at her father. Frowned and then chortled. 'Mum, Mum, Mumcat. Mumcat!' she crowed, as if she'd found the perfect word.

The congregation laughed as her parents touched hands and held on.

Much later, in the cavernous surf club hall, the best party Lighthouse Bay had seen for a year had begun winding down. They'd turned the sand-encrusted, silvered-by-the-sun clubhouse into a flower-filled bower of fragrant frangipanis and greenery. Tables and chairs and a small dais for the bride and groom all glowed under ropes of hanging lanterns and people milled and laughed and slapped Finn on the back as he stood surrounded by friends. Waiting.

In a screened alcove at the back of the hall the midwives of Lighthouse Bay gathered to help the bride change from her beautiful ivory wedding gown into her travel clothes, a trousseau created by her friends. The laughter and smiles filled Catrina's heart to bursting as she looked around and soaked in the affection and happiness that radiated from her friends. Her family.

There was Ellie, with Emily on her hip, taking back the reins of the maternity ward full-time for only as long as Catrina and Finn were away. Then the two friends would share the duties, two mothers who had been blessed with a career they loved, and a workplace that could still leave plenty of time for family. It suited them both.

Ellie held out the gorgeous floral skirt found by Myra that had once belonged to a French princess. It felt like a caress against her skin as she drew it on.

Myra held the hand-embroidered cream blouse made by Faith's aunt especially for the occasion, and Faith clapped her hands as she began to slide it on.

She had two families now in her full life. In the main hall she had her new handsome and adoring husband, Finn, and her gorgeous Piper, soon to be her adopted daughter, and Finn's sister Frances and her husband, and, of course, Clancy—her unexpected almost sister.

Catrina had grown to care for flighty Clancy, saw that she had not a mean bone in her body, just a little foolishness and a wanderer's heart, underscored by an adventurer's gleam in her eye. Clancy would never be happy for too long in one place. But now, because of Piper and the growing relationship that made Catrina's orphan's heart swell with joy, Clancy could come and share family time with Piper, where she could have the best of both worlds without the responsibility that made her run. With Finn's new family she had people who loved her and people who waved goodbye and let her go.

Catrina noted that Faith, kind Faith, stood alone as she watched them all, watching her daughter chasing after a determined to escape Piper, a whimsical half-smile on her pretty face as she dreamed.

Catrina took a moment to suggest to Finn's mother's angels that Faith should find her own second family and happiness, like she and Ellie had, in the very near future. *Please!*

But then Ellie straightened her collar and she returned to the moment. She was ready and Ellie spun her slowly to ensure she was perfect and the oohs and ahhs of her friends suggested the outfit lived up to expectations. She felt like a princess herself, the beautiful skirt restored to its former glory by Myra, as she floated out from behind the screens to where her husband waited, his eyes lit up.

Finn's eyes found hers, darkened with approval, and she felt a flutter in her stomach at his expression. A look that said she shone like his princess too.

They stepped towards each other and he took her hand and that frisson of awareness ran all the way to her shoulder with the promise of magic to come. Watching her, his beautiful mouth curved and he raised her hand to his lips and pressed his mouth against her palm.

'I've spent too much time away from you today,' he said quietly as the room swelled with excitement at their impending departure.

'Soon.' She leaned up and kissed him and breathed in the wonderful manly scent of him. She loved him and she couldn't wait until they were alone. 'I wonder how Frances and Clancy will manage with Piper tonight?'

He shrugged. 'One night. They'll be fine. She'll

be in her own bed and Marni is on call for them and dropping in tomorrow before we come home, just to check. Then we all go on our honeymoon.'

'We could have taken her.'

'One night isn't too much to ask. I've been talking to Marni. She suggested we should go away every month for one night in the future.' He waggled his brows at her. 'I'm thinking that's a wonderful idea.'

Catrina would take as many nights in her husband's arms as he offered and she had no doubt he felt the same about her. She placed her hand on the crook of his and he captured it there with his other hand.

'Let's go,' he said and, heads high, they walked out into their future.

* * * * *

REUNITED BY
THEIR BABY

JENNIFER TAYLOR

MILLS & BOON

For the other members of the earring club:
Charlotte, Janet and Ruth. With thanks
for all the fun and laughter.

Special thanks must go to Ruth for her 'research'.
Above and beyond, is all I can say!

CHAPTER ONE

HE WAS LATE. Almost a year late by his reckoning, although, by rights, he should have been here from the very beginning.

Callum O'Neill's mouth thinned as he paid off the cab and turned to face the cottage that had once been his home. He had sworn when he had left that he would never come back here again. This place held too many bad memories and he had promised himself that he would do his best to forget what had gone on. However, that had been before he had received that letter. Before everything had changed.

Callum could feel his heart thumping as he walked up the path. He knocked on the door, wondering what sort of reception he would receive. He wasn't expecting red carpet treatment but he was hoping that things would improve once he explained what had happened. It had taken months for the letter to reach him. He had been moving around such a lot as he had helped to set up the programme he had been working on. It was vital to roll it out to as many communities as possible as Malaria was endemic over much of sub-Saharan Africa. It was little wonder the letter hadn't reached

him for such a long time but would Beth understand
that? He hoped so. He couldn't bear to think that they
would end up arguing again. They had done enough
of that in the past and he, for one, couldn't bear to go
down that route again.

'If you're wanting Dr Andrews then she isn't there.'

Callum swung round. 'Oh, right. Do you know
where she is, by any chance?' he asked, recognising
the elderly woman who had spoken to him as a patient from the surgery. He had worked at The Larches
Surgery for almost a year, filling in as a locum GP
so he could be with Beth. Their relationship had already been under a lot of strain by then and it hadn't
helped that they were living so far apart—he based
in London and Beth in the Yorkshire Dales—so he
had made the decision to relocate. Sadly, it hadn't
helped their marriage as much as he had hoped it
would. Things had gone too far by that stage and so
instead they had split up, which made what had happened later all the more poignant…

'Why, she's in the church, of course! Where else
would she be?' The woman frowned. 'You're Dr
O'Neill, aren't you? I thought I recognised you. We've
not seen you around here for a while. Funny that you
should turn up today, although maybe you've been
invited.'

'Invited?' Callum repeated uncertainly. 'Invited
to what?'

'The wedding.' She sniffed. 'Although if you ask
me it's far too soon for them to be getting married. I
mean, they barely know each other. Still, fools rush
in, as my old mum used to say.'

With that, she went on her way. Callum stared after her, feeling shock reverberating throughout his entire body. Beth was getting married again? She was getting married *today*! His feet were already moving before the thought had sunk in. He raced across the road, taking the path that led to Beesdale Parish Church. He could hear the church bells ringing and put on a spurt. He had to make Beth see that she couldn't go ahead and marry someone else, not now, not ever! It was as though his mind was crystal clear all of a sudden and for the first time in ages he knew what he wanted, and that was Beth.

The bells had stopped ringing by the time Callum reached the church and his panic increased to epic proportions. The service must have started and he had no idea how long it took to reach the part where the minister declared the couple man and wife. When he and Beth had married it was in a registry office, a no-frills affair that had been over in minutes. Neither of them had cared about the ceremony. The only thing that had mattered was that they could make their vows to love and cherish each other for the rest of their lives. They had been so sure that their love would last for ever, he thought sadly, but it hadn't worked out that way. As he had discovered, all the promises in the world couldn't guarantee that.

The thought lent wings to his feet as he raced up the path. The heavy oak doors were closed and he wasted valuable seconds, wrestling them open. He almost fell into the church when they finally gave way and he saw people turn to look at him but he had eyes for no one except the woman in white standing before the altar. She was the only person who hadn't turned around and his heart ached with a searing pain when it struck him that she was oblivious to his presence. She was too busy looking at the man she was about to marry to notice him.

Callum felt the coldness of defeat sweep over him. In that moment, he realised that he had no right to stop what was happening. He turned to leave, knowing it was the only thing he could do. He'd had his chance and blown it; it wasn't fair to expect Beth to take him back. Maybe he hadn't known the truth until that letter had reached him but he had still left her, hadn't he? Why would she want him back when she had found someone else?

'Callum? What are you *doing* here?'

He recognised her voice immediately, heaven knew, he should do when he heard it every night in his dreams. Each time he fell asleep he heard her speaking to him, saw her, touched her, held her, loved her, felt her love him in return. The only difference was that she wouldn't be looking at him with love in her eyes now. Her love was reserved for another man, the man who was going to do his best to make her happy, as he had failed to do.

'I asked you a question, Callum. At least have the decency to answer it!'

There was no welcome in her voice, no hint of warmth. That she didn't want him there was obvious. Callum turned slowly around because what else could he do? Just for a moment his vision blurred before he managed to focus and he blinked as he took stock of the pale pink dress she was wearing and the jaunty little hat with its swirl of purple feathers on the crown…

His gaze flew to the couple standing in front of the altar and he felt the blood drain from his head when he realised that the bride was Polly. He didn't recognise the groom; he had never seen him before, but it didn't matter. The only thing that mattered was that Beth wasn't getting married today. It meant that he still had a chance, one precious chance to win her back! His heart was in his mouth as he turned to face her. This was the most important moment of his life and he had to get it right.

'I came to see you, Beth. You and our baby.'

Beth could feel her legs trembling and clutched hold of a nearby pew. She could hear the murmur of voices as the congregation started whispering together. Were they as shocked as she was to see Callum? Were they wondering why he was here and what he wanted? In a small town like Beesdale, it was hard to keep anything secret—everyone knew that he had run out on her and left her pregnant. Now the thought of her daughter helped to steady her. No way was she going to allow Callum to destroy Beatrix's life the way he had destroyed hers!

She turned cold hazel eyes on him. 'Come outside. We can't talk in here.'

She didn't wait to see if he was following as she led the way out of the church. It was up to Callum what he did and she had no intention of trying to influence him in any way. She walked down the path, only pausing when she reached the lich gate. There

was very little traffic about as most of the townspeople were in the church. Polly was the local midwife and greatly loved; everyone wanted to help her
celebrate her special day. Tears suddenly pricked her
eyes but Beth blinked them away. She wasn't going
to think about the dreams she'd had when she and
Callum had married. That was all in the past and too
much had happened since. Their divorce had been difficult enough, but the fact that he hadn't even bothered to acknowledge their child until today was so
much worse.

'I'm sorry. I know it isn't enough but I am truly
sorry, Beth.'

There was a note in his deep voice that tugged at
her heart strings before she pulled herself together. If
she gave in and allowed her emotions free rein then
she would regret it. She had to focus on the facts,
highlight them in neon-bright letters so she would
never forget them. Callum had left her. He had left her
because he hadn't loved her any more. He had been
so desperate to be rid of her that he hadn't even contacted her when she had written to tell him that she
was pregnant. He could apologise all he liked, but it
wouldn't change anything.

'It's too late for apologies, Callum. I'm not interested. The only thing I want to know is what you're
doing here.'

'Surely that's obvious,' he shot back. 'I came to
see you and the baby.'

'I see. And it's taken you—what?—over a year
to get round to it?' She gave a little laugh, hoping
he couldn't hear the bitterness it held. There must

be no displays of emotion, no hint of any feelings that might make him think that she still cared. 'You didn't exactly rush to get here, did you? But there again, I doubt if Beatrix and I were your number one priority—'

'Beatrix? You mean that we have a daughter?'

'Yes,' Beth replied curtly, closing her mind to the shock she could hear in his voice. If she refused to admit to her own feelings then she certainly didn't want to wonder how Callum felt!

Callum felt his head reel. Ever since he had read Beth's letter he had wondered about the sex of their baby. To be honest, it had been difficult to believe that he was finally about to become a father after everything they had been through, yet all of a sudden finding out that they had a little girl made it seem real. His breath caught as he was swamped by a whole host of emotions ranging from shock to sheer elation. He had a daughter. A little girl called Beatrix. The thought seemed to rock his whole world so that it was hard to speak. 'H-how old is she?'

'Almost ten months,' Beth replied tightly. 'Although if you hadn't been so busy saving the world then you wouldn't need to ask that, Callum.'

'That isn't true!' He ran his hands through his thick dark brown hair, feeling them trembling as he tried to picture what Beatrix looked like. Was she dark like him or fair like Beth? It was impossible to guess and before he could ask, Beth carried on.

'Oh, I think it is true, but you just don't want to admit it.' She stared back at him, unwilling to give him the benefit of the doubt. Even though he understood why she refused to accept that he was telling the truth, it still hurt. 'If you'd cared back then, you would have contacted me. Even a text message would have been better than nothing, but you couldn't even spare the time for that. The fact that I was expecting our child meant nothing to you, did it, Callum?'

'Of course it did!' He grasped hold of her hands, his fingers biting into hers as he willed her to believe him. 'It was what we'd wanted for so long, Beth. What we'd struggled to achieve...'

He broke off, obviously recalling what a struggle it had been, Beth thought sadly. She had always wanted a family. Coming from a close and loving family herself, she had never even considered the idea that conceiving a child of her own might prove to be a problem. With two older sisters, who both had children, she had simply assumed that she would have them too. However, as the months had passed, and she had failed to get pregnant, it had seemed increasingly unlikely that she would ever achieve her dream of becoming a mother.

Callum had never been as keen on the idea of them having a child, however. Although he had gone along with her desire to have a baby, she knew it had been more to please her than out of a genuine need to have a family of his own. She had told herself that it didn't matter, that he would love their child every bit as much as she did when it arrived. She had been so sure it was the right thing for them to do that she had set aside her doubts when the consultant had suggested they try fertility treatment.

Had she been wrong to do so? she wondered suddenly. Wrong to force him into a course of action that he had been reluctant to take? There was no doubt that the strain of keeping to the gruelling regime had put intense pressure on their relationship. Lovemaking had changed from being an expression of their feelings for each other to a duty, passion no longer dictated by their mutual desire but by the readings on a thermometer.

Was it any wonder that Callum had resented it? That they had argued? With the benefit of hindsight, Beth could see that there had been faults on both sides, but it didn't alter the fact that it had been Callum who had called a halt, Callum who had decided that he didn't want to be with her any more, Callum who had asked her for a divorce. If he had loved her, *really* loved her, then he would never have left her. He would have stayed.

CHAPTER TWO

CALLUM COULD FEEL his insides quivering. First there was the shock of thinking that Beth was getting married again and now this. Her hostility was palpable even though he could tell that she was doing her best not to show how angry she felt. That in itself hurt because she had never hidden her feelings before. Whatever Beth had felt, she had been completely open about it.

When she had fallen in love with him, she hadn't tried to hide it, the same as she hadn't tried to hide her distress when their marriage had ended. To know that he was responsible for such a change in her was incredibly painful but he couldn't allow himself to be sidetracked. He had come here for a specific purpose and he had to focus on that. Beth wasn't going to believe a word he said unless he managed to convince her that he was telling the truth.

'Look, Beth, I know how it must appear but the situation isn't as straightforward as you think,' he began.

'Save it, Callum. I've already told you that I'm not interested.' Her tone was cold, indifferent even, and something inside him died a little. Even anger was preferable to this total lack of interest. 'You've had months to contact me and never bothered. So why should I listen to you now just because you've suddenly decided it's time we talked?'

'Because you don't understand!'

He let go of her hands, feeling the pain of her rejection biting deep into his soul. Heaven knew, he had enough experience of being rejected to recognise it. His parents had never really wanted him. They had both been high-flyers, dedicated to their work, and his unscheduled arrival had been viewed as a disruption to their busy lives.

He had been brought up by a succession of nannies until he was old enough to be sent away to boarding school. Holidays had been a nightmare; both his mother and his father had made it clear that they resented having to waste time entertaining him. It had been a relief to them all when he had been old enough to go away on his own. Skiing trips, diving holidays—he'd done the lot and enjoyed them too. At least he hadn't felt like a burden. People were being paid to look after him and that made it easier.

The ties had been completely severed by the time he went to university. Apart from the obligatory birthday and Christmas cards, he had no contact with them these days. He didn't miss them; it was impossible to miss something he had never had.

However, they had taught him a valuable lesson, which was that no one should have a child unless they were prepared to put it first. That was why he'd had reservations when Beth had suggested they should have a baby. He had been afraid that he wouldn't measure up as a parent, that the genes he had inherited would affect his ability to be a proper father to their child, but he had allowed himself to be persuaded because it was what Beth had wanted so desperately.

Would he have agreed if he'd had any idea how hard it would be? he wondered suddenly. How agonising it would be to watch her suffer such terrible disappointment, month after month, when she had failed to get pregnant? Of course he wouldn't! He had loved her to distraction and it was unthinkable that he would have allowed her to go through that kind of torment.

That was why he had called a halt and asked her for a divorce. Maybe Beth believed that he had done it for his own sake but it wasn't true. He simply couldn't bear to see her torturing herself any longer. How ironic that after all they had been through, she should have fallen pregnant that last night they had slept together.

'What is there to understand? I wrote to tell you I was pregnant and you didn't reply. That says it all.' She shrugged, her expression so cold when Callum forced his mind back to the present that he felt chilled to the bone. It was hard to believe that Beth could look at him that way.

'But I never received your letter!' he protested.

'Then why are you here?' she shot back and he felt relief surge through him when he heard the stirrings of anger in her voice. It was better to be upbraided than be treated with such indifference.

'What I meant was that I never received it for months. I was in Africa, travelling around while I

helped set up a new malaria programme, and somehow it never caught up with me.' He looked deep into
her eyes, willing her to believe him. 'It only reached
me last month and as soon as I read it, I made arrangements to fly back to England. I got here as fast
as I could, Beth—I swear.'

Beth wanted to believe him, she wanted it with a
desperation that defied all logic. She had sworn that
she would never allow herself to be swayed by anything Callum said but, staring into his deep brown
eyes, it was so very tempting... The sound of bells
ringing broke the spell. Beth stepped back, her breath
coming in fast little spurts as she realised how close
she had come to breaking her own promise. Surely
she had learned her lesson after what had happened
between them? Learned never to believe a word Callum said? If he could tell her that he loved her and
then leave her, it proved beyond any doubt how un-
trustworthy he was.

She swung round, ignoring him when he called
her name. She didn't want to listen to him any more,
didn't want to see him, to be tempted in any way at
all. She had to think about Beatrix and the effect it
would have on her in the future if she found out that
her father was a liar.

She re-joined the wedding party, nodding when
Polly asked her if she was all right. She wasn't all
right, by any means, but she wouldn't say so, wouldn't
ruin her friend's special day. Polly deserved this after
everything she had been through. She deserved every
second of happiness that came her way. She had found
the man she loved and he loved her too—their fu-

ture was rosy and golden and would be filled with joy. Just as hers should have been if Callum hadn't stopped loving her.

The tears came then, hot and bitter as they streamed down her face, but she wasn't the only one crying. Weddings were an emotional time and a lot of the guests were shedding a tear or two. Beth dried her eyes then took her place on the church steps while the photographs were taken, smiling and pretending to be full of joy on this happy day while inside she felt devastated and angry and so very alone.

She glanced towards the lich gate but there was no sign of Callum. Whether he would seek her out again, she had no idea. It didn't really matter. Nothing he said could make up for what he had done, no excuses about letters taking months to reach him would change things. The fact was that he had left her, left her when she had needed him most of all. And that was the only thing that counted.

Callum had managed to book himself a room in the local pub. He carried his bag up the narrow staircase and opened the bedroom door. The room was small and rather cramped with double dormer roofs taking up most of the ceiling space but he didn't care. It was somewhere to sleep tonight because one thing was certain: he wouldn't be sleeping in Beth's bed!

Frustration ate away at him as he tossed his bag onto the bed. Maybe he hadn't expected red carpet treatment but he had hoped for a better reception than that. It was obvious that Beth wasn't going to forgive him in a hurry and it made him see how foolish he'd been to hope that she would. He sighed wearily. Had he really thought that he could win her round with a few well-chosen words? That he could tell Beth what had happened and that she would just accept it? He must have been living in cloud cuckoo land if he had!

No way was this going to be easy. He would have to work at it, gain her trust, make her understand that he hadn't ignored her or their baby, and *then* convince her that he wanted to be involved in their lives.

Fear trickled coldly down his spine at the thought. He knew nothing about what it took to be a father, did he? Most people learned the art from their own father but he certainly wasn't going to use his as a role model. He would be batting in the dark, striking out this way and that in the hope that he would somehow discover how to be a good parent. What if he failed? What if he tried his best but still couldn't measure up to the role? He couldn't bear to imagine the harm it might cause his daughter if he flunked it. His heart caught. He couldn't bear to imagine Beth's contempt either if that happened.

Beth collected Beatrix from the childminder's house and took her home. Polly had wanted her to take the baby to the church but Beth had decided not to risk it. At almost ten months old Beatrix was attempting to walk and soon became frustrated if she was made to sit still for any length of time. The thought of her daughter creating a fuss during the service had made Beth decide to leave her with Alison, the childminder. Now she was doubly glad that she had. She still wasn't sure if she was going to allow Callum to see her. After all, if he had been that interested in his daughter then he would have been in touch before now, although, according to Callum, it hadn't been his fault, had it?

The thought nagged away at her as she got Beatrix ready for bed. The little girl loved water and Beth let her splash away in the bath for longer than usual. She rarely spent any time apart from her and she had missed her that day, although she would have to get used to being without her. She was due to return to work in a couple of weeks' time now that her maternity leave was coming to an end and Beatrix would be looked after by Alison. While Beth knew the other woman would take good care of her, it would be a wrench to leave her. Still, it was what she had to do if she was to provide for her daughter. Maybe Beatrix was destined to have only one parent but Beth didn't intend that she would miss out, financially *or* emotionally.

Her mouth thinned as she lifted Beatrix out of the bath and wrapped her in a towel. One loving parent was more than enough and far better than having someone unreliable in her life like Callum!

The pub served food so Callum had something to eat then went back up to his room. He had spent almost thirty-six hours on the go and he was bone-tired. He desperately needed to sleep and lay down on the bed, fully clothed, but he couldn't settle. He kept thinking about what had happened with Beth and knew that he wouldn't be able to rest until he had resolved at least some of the issues with her.

In the end, he got up and left the pub, taking his time as he walked to the cottage. He had no idea what he was going to say to her when he got there but he needed to convince Beth that he had been telling the truth about her letter failing to reach him for so long. At least, it would be a start if he could do that, a small step towards convincing her about all the rest. Despite what she thought, he *did* care about their daughter. He cared a lot, far more than he would have expected, in fact. He had a child and even though he had never really wanted a family of his own, he intended to do his very best for her…

If only Beth would let him.

The thought felt like a lead weight inside him. Callum was very aware that Beth would have the deciding vote when it came to a decision about his input into their daughter's life. Bearing in mind how she had reacted earlier, it seemed unlikely that she would let him have anything to do with her, and he was devastated at the thought that he might not be able to play any part in his child's life.

He stopped outside the cottage, wondering how best to approach this. He might only get this one chance and he couldn't afford to waste it. Maybe it had hurt to be treated so coldly by Beth before but his feelings didn't matter. It was his daughter who mattered, the child he and Beth had conceived against all the odds that last night.

Callum found his thoughts winging back to that night and he shuddered. He had only gone to see Beth because the papers finalising their divorce had come through that morning. For some reason he still couldn't explain, he had felt that he'd had to acknowledge the ending of their marriage in person. What he had never expected was that they would end up in bed together. He had honestly thought that their desire for one another had died, but that night it had felt just like it had in the beginning. The feel of her hands on his skin, the brush of her lips against his, had transformed their lovemaking into something magical. Special. Something he had never felt before and knew he wouldn't feel again.

His heart ached with a sudden searing pain. He had loved her so much and knew that she had loved him too—how could they have lost sight of that?

Beth tiptoed to the nursery window. Beatrix had fallen asleep and she didn't want to wake her. Reaching up, she went to draw the curtains then paused when she caught sight of Callum standing outside. Her heart leapt even though she'd half expected that he would seek her out again. All of a sudden, she wasn't sure what to do. If she let him in then he would only repeat what he had said earlier and she couldn't see any point in that. He had claimed that it had taken months for her letter to reach him but did she believe him? If he could lie about loving her then he could lie about that too!

Beth felt a wave of anger wash over her as she drew the curtains then made her way downstairs. Opening the front door, she stared, stony-faced, at the man standing outside on the step. He had his hand raised in readiness to knock and she glared at him. 'Beatrix is asleep and I'd appreciate it if you didn't wake her up.'

'Oh. Right.'

He looked momentarily disconcerted, which was rare for him. Callum's confidence was one of the things that had attracted her to him when they had first met. They had both been invited to a mutual friend's birthday party in London, a noisy affair that had grown rowdier as the evening had worn on. Although most of the people there had been similar in age to her, Beth had found their behaviour childish. Their main aim seemed to be to drink as much as they could but getting drunk wasn't something she planned to do.

She was due in work the following day and had no intention of turning up with a hangover, so when one of the men had tried to persuade her to take part in their drinking game, she had refused. The situation had turned ugly then. Beth had felt really frightened when he had grabbed hold of her and forced the glass to her lips, and that's when Callum had stepped in.

He hadn't said a word as he'd removed the glass from the other man's hand and placed it on a table, but his expression had said it all. The man had immediately let her go and hurried away. Only then had Callum spoken and all he'd done was ask her if she was ready to leave. They had left the party and found an all-night café down by the docks. The time had flown past as they had talked about their lives over mugs of tea.

Callum had explained that he worked for an aid agency and that he had only recently returned from India. It was very different from the career path Beth had chosen and she was intrigued to hear more, not that the conversation was in any way one-sided when he'd seemed equally fascinated by what she had done. She had never met anyone who was as easy to talk to as Callum and she'd found herself telling him things she had told no one else. By the time they left the café, she was already half in love with him…

'Look, Beth, I know you said before that you didn't want to hear what I had to say but it's important that we sort this out.'

The urgency in his voice brought her back to the present, although it was hard to rid her mind of the memories. They had been so good together, true soul mates, totally attuned to one another, until she had decided that she wanted them to have a baby. Would their relationship have lasted if she hadn't made that decision? She had no idea. However, it was that thought that made her step back so Callum could come in. If she was even partly responsible for ruining what they'd had then she owed him this at least.

'Come into the sitting room,' she said shortly, leading the way.

Callum followed her in, smiling when he saw the basket of toys tucked under the coffee table. 'I see our daughter's into cars rather than dolls.'

'She loves anything that has wheels.' Beth sat down on the chair, leaving Callum to have the sofa. It would have been too hard to sit next to him and recall all the other times they had sat there, cuddled up together. It was something else she didn't want to dwell on and she sprang to her feet. 'I'll put the kettle on. What d'you want—tea or coffee?'

'Neither, thanks.' He grimaced. 'I drank so much

tea and coffee on the journey back here that I'm awash with it.'

'Oh, I see.' Beth hesitated but she really didn't want anything to drink either. It had been more a delaying tactic, but perhaps it would be better to get this over with. The sooner Callum had said his piece, the sooner he would leave and things would get back to normal. It was a relief when he carried on.

'I got here as quickly as I could, Beth. Once I received your letter, I contacted the agency and told them that I needed to return to England immediately.' He shrugged. 'All right, I'll admit that it took a couple of weeks to make the arrangements but there was nothing I could do about that. It was out of my hands.'

He sounded sincere enough and Beth found herself wavering. Was he telling her the truth or was it merely some elaborate tale he had dreamed up to explain his absence? The Callum she had known in the past had never lied to her. Or at least she had *thought* he hadn't done so, she amended swiftly. She didn't want to think that he was lying to her now but how could she trust him after what he had done? He had walked away even though he had claimed to love her. He had even told her that on their last night together, told her that he loved her and that he would always love her. She had taken it to mean that he had changed his mind, that the divorce had been a mistake, and that he wanted them to get back together.

Tears filled her eyes as she recalled how devastated she had felt when she had woken in the morning to find him gone. No, if Callum had truly loved her then he would have *stayed*.

* * *

Callum could tell things weren't going well. Beth had tears in her eyes now and he didn't imagine they were tears of joy either. He searched his mind for the right words, words that would convince her he deserved another chance, but in his heart he knew there was nothing he could say to make up for what he had done. He hadn't been here when she had needed him. He hadn't been here for her or their daughter and there was no point explaining how bad he felt about it when she wasn't interested in anything he had to say. Beth didn't want him in her life any more and the pain that thought caused him made him suck in his breath.

He stood up abruptly, his legs trembling so hard that he wasn't sure if they would hold him, but he refused to let her think that he was playing for sympathy.

'I didn't come here to upset you, Beth. It's the last thing I want to do. I've told you the truth but I can see that I was wrong to expect you to believe me.' He spread his hands apart in frustration. 'If there was anything I could do to convince you then I'd do it, but I doubt if you'd be interested even then. I'm no longer part of your life and I accept that, but I hope you will allow me to be part of our daughter's life in some way.' His voice caught then, the words all jammed up inside him as emotion took over, and he stared at the ceiling, not wanting her to guess how agonising it was to know that he might be excluded from his child's future.

'I'll think about it, although I'm not making any promises.'

Beth sounded as choked up as he did and Callum

lowered his eyes. His heart scrunched up inside him when he saw the tears that were now trickling down her beautiful face.

'I'm so sorry,' he began, but she held up her hand.

'Don't! I don't want to hear anything else.' She stood up, making it clear that she wanted him to leave.

Callum didn't say another word as he let himself out. He made his way back to the pub, went up to his room, and lay down on the bed, feeling more wretched than he had felt in his entire life.

Even when he had asked Beth for a divorce, he hadn't felt this depth of despair. It had been hard then, heart-wrenchingly hard, but he had been so sure it was the right thing to do. With him out of the way, she would be forced to stop trying to conceive and allow her mind as well as her body to rest. That thought had kept him focused, given him strength. He had loved her *so* much, but he'd had to leave for her sake. Now she didn't want anything to do with him and even though he understood why she felt that way, the thought ripped a hole right through his heart.

CHAPTER THREE

BETH SPENT THE next few days thinking about what Callum had asked her. The question constantly whizzed around her brain: should she allow him to have access to Beatrix? Her gut reaction was to refuse but she knew that she needed to take her time and think about it. It wasn't fair to Beatrix to make a snap decision when it could have such a huge impact on her life.

When Daniel Saunders, the senior partner at the practice, phoned to ask her if she would consider returning to work earlier than planned, it was a relief because it gave her something else to think about. Apparently, Sandra Nelson, one of the other GPs, had been rushed into hospital with appendicitis. With Daniel's wife, Eleanor, on maternity leave, it meant the practice was currently under a huge amount of pressure.

Beth agreed immediately, even though she hated the thought of leaving Beatrix. She went into the surgery on the Monday morning, realising in surprise that she felt a little bit nervous. Even though she had worked there for a number of years, it felt strange to be back, almost as though she was the new girl. However, she soon got over that feeling when Marie, the receptionist, greeted her in delight.

'Beth!' Marie shot round the desk and enveloped Beth in a hug. 'It's great to have you back. We've missed you!'

'Thank you. I've missed you too,' Beth replied, and realised that she meant it. Although she loved Beatrix to bits, she enjoyed her job and had missed the daily contact with her colleagues and patients. She glanced around the waiting room, smiling when she spotted a couple of early arrivals. 'Not much has changed, I see. The early birds are still here.'

'Too right!' Marie agreed, laughing. 'It's business as usual, although Eleanor's on maternity leave and Bernard has finally retired, though I expect you know that already.'

'I do, but it's nice to be reminded.' Beth rolled her eyes. 'I'm suffering from a bad case of baby brain and keep forgetting things.'

'Don't worry, it will get better, although it could take some time before you're functioning properly,' Marie replied wryly. 'I remember how long it took me to feel halfway normal after I'd had my two.'

'Don't!' Beth laughed. 'You're scaring me to death.' She looked round and smiled when she saw Daniel coming along the corridor. 'Marie was just explaining the pitfalls of motherhood to me.'

'A bit late for that, I'd have thought,' he answered, laughing. He kissed Beth on the cheek. 'Thank you so much for doing this. When Sandra's husband phoned and told me what had happened, I didn't know what we were going to do. I can't tell you how relieved I was when you said you'd come back to work earlier than planned.'

'It isn't a problem,' Beth assured him as they headed to his room. 'I dropped Beatrix off at the childminder's house and I have to say that she didn't appear to be the least bit worried about me leaving her. She was more interested in playing with the other children to miss her mum.'

'Good. It's never easy when you leave them for the first time, whether it's with a childminder or on their first day at school. Why, I even got all choked up when we saw Nathan off to Australia,' he admitted, referring to his nineteen-year-old son who was currently away on his gap year. 'How daft is that?'

'It isn't daft at all,' Beth assured him, smiling. 'Although you'll have to toughen up now that you have Mia. It won't be long before she has a whole load of "firsts" to get through.'

'Don't!' Daniel shuddered at the thought of going through it all again with his baby daughter. 'Anyway, enough of that. I just wanted to check that you're up to speed. You'll be covering Hemsthwaite Surgery while Sandra's off. I don't think you've worked there before, have you?'

'No. I'd gone on maternity leave when you introduced the new system so that the staff here could take turns working there.'

'I thought so. It's been very useful, I have to say. Although some patients use both surgeries, the majority tend to stick to one or the other. The new system gives everyone a chance to get to know all our patients and that can only be a good thing. Obviously, you'll have access to everyone's notes via the computer so if one of our patients does turn up there, it won't be a problem,' he added.

'It sounds great. I'm looking forward to getting back to work,' Beth explained, truthfully.

'Good. I'm delighted to have you back too. We've been really pushed recently, although I'm hoping that things are going to improve. If you're agreeable, of course.'

'You want me to do some hours here as well?' Beth queried, wondering why Daniel sounded so grave all of a sudden.

'No, not at all. Covering for Sandra is more than enough at the moment.' He paused and Beth felt her nerves tighten. She was actually holding her breath as she waited for him to continue.

'We desperately need more cover here, though. It was hard enough when there was just Eleanor and me, but now that I'm on my own, it's impossible to keep on top of all the work. I've been trawling the agencies to find a locum but there's nobody suitable willing to work in this part of the world.' He sighed. 'Beautiful countryside can't hold a candle to the bright city lights, it seems.'

'It must be difficult,' she murmured, wondering where this was leading. Daniel rarely prevaricated and that he was doing so now set all her internal alarm bells ringing.

'It is. Which is why I was delighted when I had a phone call from someone I not only know can do the job, but who will also get on with the rest of the team.' He looked her straight in the eyes. 'Callum has asked if he can have a job here, Beth. While I know he's ideal, I don't want to cause any problems for you, so it's your call. What shall I tell him?'

Callum switched off his phone, stunned by what he had just heard. Daniel had called to say that the job was his if he still wanted it. Daniel had been quite blunt when Callum had asked him if there was a vacancy. He had made no bones about the fact that he would need to ask Beth how she felt about Callum working at the surgery. It was the fact that she had agreed that surprised him most of all. Did it mean that she was willing to give him another chance?

He cut that thought dead. There could be a dozen different reasons why Beth had agreed to him working at The Larches, so he shouldn't go jumping to conclusions. He had spent three wretched days, too wrapped up in his own misery to think clearly. Then, gradually, his mind had started to clear and he had realised what he needed to do. He wasn't going to give up. He was going to find a way to convince Beth that he cared about their daughter. Maybe he would never be able to convince her that he cared about *her* too, but he had to accept that.

Staying in Beesdale was the first step and he couldn't believe his luck when he heard someone mention in the pub one night that the surgery was desperately in need of another doctor. He had phoned Daniel immediately and explained that he was back in Beesdale and looking for a job. Although he hadn't gone into detail, he had also explained about the delay in receiving Beth's letter. It had obviously reassured Daniel to some extent, but he had still added the proviso that he would need to consult Beth before he could take Callum on. And it appeared she hadn't raised any objections. Even though Callum had told himself not to leap to any conclusions, he couldn't help it.

If Beth had hated the idea of him staying in Beesdale then she would never have given the go-ahead for him to work there.

Beth found herself starting to relax once she had seen her first patient. Whether it was the shock of hearing that Callum intended to stay in Beesdale or first-day-back nerves, she had felt incredibly tense when she had arrived at the Hemsthwaite surgery. However, focusing on her patients' problems had soon taken her mind off everything else, even if it was only a temporary reprieve. She buzzed in her next patient, smiling when Diane Applethwaite came into the room. Diane and her husband, Phil, ran a highly successful sheep farm. Their lamb was renowned throughout the Dales for its quality and flavour. With seven children, plus a brand new grandson on the way, Diane was a very busy woman. She was always full of life so Beth was surprised to see how down she looked that day.

'Hello, Diane. Come and sit down.' Beth waited until the other woman was comfortably settled. 'So what can I do for you?'

'I'm not sure what to tell you, Dr Andrews. I just feel so tired all the time, as though I've got no energy left.' Diane sighed. 'It's not like me at all. Phil must be sick of me moping about all over the place. That's why I came to see you.'

'I see. Do you have any other symptoms apart from feeling tired?' Beth asked, mentally running through a list of possible causes. Anaemia was a possibility as a lot of women suffered from that, especially if their monthly periods were heavy. She glanced at Diane's notes and checked her age: forty-eight. It could be the menopause, of course; that could cause a wide range of symptoms from tiredness through to mood swings. Hormone replacement therapy could help if that were the case, although it was too soon to make a diagnosis.

'Not really.' Diane hesitated. 'Although I've felt sick a few times too.'

'Anything else?' Beth prompted when Diane paused again.

'Well, I've not had a period for a while.' She grimaced. 'I used to be regular as clockwork but in the past year, I've been all over the place. Do you think it's the change, Dr Andrews?'

'It's possible, Diane. You're forty-eight and it could very well be the start of the menopause. We'll do some tests, check your hormone levels, and see what they show.'

Diane nodded. 'I thought it might be that. To be honest, I've been dreading it. My mum was terrible when she went through the change, had these awful hot flushes and she was so bad tempered too. I'd hate to think that I'll be like that.'

'There's no reason why you should take after your mother,' Beth said consolingly. 'Every woman is different, plus there's HRT these days, which can help enormously to alleviate the worst symptoms.'

'Is it safe, though? I've read so many conflicting reports about HRT that I'm not sure if I want to take it or not.'

'That's your decision and I certainly wouldn't try to force you to take it,' Beth assured her. 'However, in my opinion, it's extremely safe and very helpful too.' She stood up, not wanting to appear to be pushing Diane into making a decision right then. 'Let's take some blood and see what that shows before we go any further.'

Beth took the sample, deciding it was easier to do it herself rather than ask Diane to wait to see Jane Barton, their practice nurse. Once the tubes were clearly labelled, she popped them into an envelope ready for the courier to collect at lunchtime. 'We should have the results back in a week or so. In the meantime, I'm going to prescribe a course of iron tablets to help with the tiredness. I think you may be a little anaemic—the blood results will show if you are—and the iron will help.'

'Let's hope so. It's a busy time of the year for us and I could do with a bit more energy. I'll definitely need it when our Sam and Lauren have the baby,' Diane declared, sounding much brighter than when she had arrived.

'It won't be long now,' Beth agreed, thinking how much it could help to talk through a problem. She sighed inwardly, wondering if she should have talked to Daniel about the problem she had with Callum before she had agreed that he could work at The

Larches. Maybe it would have helped a bit, she acknowledged, but at the end of the day it was something she had to resolve by herself. She fixed a smile to her mouth, not wanting to think about her own worries. 'Are you looking forward to being a grandmother?'

'That I am. It seems an age since there was a little one running around the place,' Diane said with a laugh. 'Steven, my youngest, is seventeen now and at least a foot taller than me. He's certainly not a baby any more!'

Beth laughed as she saw Diane out. She worked her way through the rest of the list then went to Reception to wait for the courier. There were several more tests that Jane had collected so she handed them over as well. They closed for lunch but there was an open surgery in the afternoon, plus a visit by the local optician. Hemsthwaite Surgery might be smaller than The Larches and open for fewer hours, but it was still very busy and she would enjoy working there, she decided as she went to lock the door after the courier left.

Her hand was hovering over the catch when she saw a car turn into the car park and she frowned, hoping it wasn't an early arrival. It was only when the driver got out that she realised it was Callum and her heart seemed to skip a beat. What on earth was Callum doing here?

Callum wasn't sure if he should be doing this. He had intended to give Beth some space but the urge to see her had been too strong to resist. He locked the car then started to walk towards the surgery, his stomach lurching when he saw Beth standing by the door. It was hard to read her expression from this distance but he had the feeling that she wasn't exactly thrilled to see him. It was only the thought of how it would appear if he turned around and went back to the car that kept him walking towards her.

'What are you doing here, Callum?'

There was no welcome in her voice and he sighed under his breath. Obviously, the situation hadn't improved as much as he had hoped it had. Beth was still loath to have anything to do with him and although he could understand it in a way, it was starting to grate on him. His tone was harsher than it might have been, less conciliatory. Beth wasn't the only one who had suffered: he had too.

'I came to thank you for not raising any objections about me being offered the locum post,' he said flatly. 'However, I can see that I'm wasting my time. Jack the Ripper would probably receive a warmer welcome than me!' He swung round, deciding that it would be better if he got back in his car and left. He wasn't helping his case, was he? He was simply putting Beth's back up and that was the last thing he could afford to do.

'Wait!'

Callum slowed, although he didn't stop altogether. Glancing over his shoulder, he saw that Beth had stepped outside and was standing on the path. There was such a look of indecision on her face that he felt his heart suddenly go out to her. That she was torn between sending him packing and talking to him was obvious and he hated to know that he had put her in this position. He didn't want to make life difficult for her but unless they found a way to resolve this situation, it was going to continue to be stressful for both of them. The thought made him turn round and retrace his steps.

'Look, Beth, I didn't come here to start an argument,' he said quietly. 'I simply came to thank you. Daniel told me that I could have the job as long as you didn't raise any objections and I'm just grateful that you agreed.'

'Why? That's what I don't understand, Callum. Why do you want to work here? Why do you want to stay in Beesdale for that matter?'

There was a tremor in her voice that made Callum feel worse than ever. That she was upset was obvious and there was absolutely nothing he could say that would help...apart from telling her the truth, perhaps?

The thought of baring his soul made his stomach clench. Was he prepared to do that, to admit how he felt about becoming a father in the hope that it would convince her to let him see their daughter? What if he said too much? What if the words somehow slipped out and he found himself admitting how he felt about *her*? The thought gave him hot and cold chills because he wasn't sure if he could cope if Beth rejected him.

'Callum...?'

'Have you had lunch yet?' Callum cut her off, knowing that he needed time to work out what he was going to say if he was to avoid a disaster.

'Lunch,' Beth repeated, blankly.

'Mmm. I've got to drive over to Leeds this afternoon to pick up the rest of my stuff from the airport.

There wasn't room for it in the plane I flew back on so it had to be sent as freight. I was planning to have lunch on the way so do you fancy joining me?' he said, as though inviting her to have lunch with him was the most natural thing in the world to do. Maybe it should be, he thought suddenly. After all, if they could forge some kind of *normal* relationship then surely it would help?

'I'm not sure it's a good idea,' she said flatly.

'Why not? Look, I know you're angry with me, and I understand why, but I want this to work, Beth. I want to be here for Beatrix, not just now but in the future as well. Maybe I had doubts about becoming a father in the past, but now that it's happened, I know it's what I want.' Callum felt a wave of emotion rise up and almost choke him but he forced himself to carry on. 'The last thing I want is Beatrix growing up, thinking that I don't care about her. I know how destructive that can be, believe me!'

CHAPTER FOUR

BETH SAT ON the old settle and watched as Callum made his way to the bar to order their lunch. It was a beautiful day and the pub was busy with tourists enjoying a day out but she had no problem picking Callum out from the crowd. With his thick dark hair, his tanned skin and that air of authority he exuded, he stood out and she noticed several women glance his way. Callum had always possessed the ability to turn heads, just as he had turned hers when they had first met.

'Right. That's all sorted.' He came back and dropped down beside her.

'What do I owe you?' Beth edged away when she felt his thigh brush against hers. She would have dearly loved to move but every seat was taken and they'd been lucky to find these. She bent down to pick up her bag, steeling herself when her knee accidentally knocked against his. She could feel ripples of sensation running under her skin and bit her lip. She didn't want to feel anything for him, didn't want to be aware of him in any way at all, but it was impossible when even the slightest contact made her skin tingle and her blood heat.

'It's my shout. I invited you, don't forget.'

Callum dismissed her offer to pay her share with a shake of his head. Beth was sorely tempted to argue with him but she decided that it wasn't worth it. She needed to keep things on an even keel and not allow emotions to get in the way. She placed her bag back on the floor, taking care not to touch him this time.

'Have you left Beatrix with the childminder?'

She jumped when he shot the question at her. 'Well, I certainly haven't left her at home on her own,' she replied tartly.

'I didn't think you had,' Callum said quietly. 'I was only asking, Beth. I wasn't having a go at you.'

'No. Of course not. Sorry.' Beth flushed, knowing that she had been far too sharp with her answer. She took a quick breath to calm herself but her nerves were jangling. It wasn't easy being with Callum like this but she had to try to maintain some kind of a balance. 'I left her with Alison Lewis. One of the mums I met at my antenatal classes recommended her and she's very nice—she has a real affinity with the children she minds.'

'I remember her from when I last worked here,' Callum said thoughtfully. 'Doesn't she have twins, a boy and a girl?'

'That's right—Molly and Max. They're three now and Beatrix adores them. She was so excited when I dropped her off this morning because she knew they'd be there to play with.'

'Good. It must make it easier if you know that she's happy,' he observed.

'It does,' Beth agreed, somewhat surprised by his astuteness. 'I have to admit that it was a wrench to leave her but she didn't seem the least bit worried. She was more interested in playing with the other children than in the fact that Mummy was leaving her!'

'It sounds as though she's got loads of confidence,' Callum said with a smile.

'Oh, she has. She's just like you in that respect.' The words rushed out before she could stop them and she saw an expression of pain cross Callum's face.

'I wish I could see her, Beth. Oh, I know you need time to decide what you intend to do but it would mean such a lot if I could see her.' He stared down at his hands. 'After I received your letter telling me you were pregnant, I spent hours wondering if you'd had a little boy or a little girl. Then ever since I found out she was a girl, I've spent even more time imagining what she looks like.'

He suddenly looked up and Beth felt a lump come to her throat when she saw the yearning in his eyes. 'I mean, is she blonde like you or dark like me? Does she have brown eyes or hazel? At the moment she's just this shadowy little figure who I can't picture clearly and I can't tell you how much it would mean to me to just see her, touch her, *smell* her even. Then I'll really feel that she's my daughter.'

Callum hadn't meant to let his emotions get the better of him. On the contrary, he'd been determined to project a calm front. However, thinking about the daughter he had never seen had let loose a host of feelings, most of which he had never expected to experience. He had never yearned for a child of his own, never longed to procreate even when he and Beth had been trying so hard to have a baby. But now that his daughter was a fact, he found it impossible to take a step back from her.

'Here. I have some photos of her on my phone.'

He jumped when Beth pressed her phone into his hand. He stared at the screen, feeling his emotions multiply a hundredfold as he looked at the fair-haired moppet smiling up at him. She had Beth's colouring and his eyes. She also had his nose if he wasn't mistaken.

Words failed him as he flicked through the photos, one after the other. They were a record of his daughter's life to date, the first one taken straight after her birth and the last one only a couple of days ago. All those months that had passed without him being there, he thought wretchedly. All that time during which she had grown up and he had known nothing about her existence.

How he longed to turn back the clock, to have been there for her from the very first moment, but it was impossible. He could never recapture that precious time he'd lost; all he could do was to make sure that he was there for the rest of her life. The thought stiffened his resolve, made him see just how important this was to him. He wasn't going to give up. Even if Beth refused his pleas then he would find a way to maintain contact with his daughter.

'She's beautiful,' he said, reluctantly relinquishing the phone. 'She has your colouring and my eyes.'

'Yes.' Beth bit her lip and he could sense her hesitation before she hurried on. 'I think she has your nose as well, although babies change so quickly that it's hard to be certain. One minute they look like one parent and the next they look like the other.'

'It must be fascinating, seeing all the changes,' he said, struggling to control the emotions that kept welling up inside him. He cleared his throat when he saw Beth glance at him, not sure if he felt comfortable about laying himself bare this way. It would have been different if they'd still been together; he wouldn't have felt nearly as self-conscious then. But they were no longer together, no longer involved apart from through their child, and he needed to protect himself.

'It is. Every day Beatrix seems to change. It's not just how she looks either but what she can do.' She smiled, her beautiful face lighting up with delight. 'I swear she said "dog" the other day when I took her out for a walk.'

'Sure it was "dog"?' Callum asked, adopting a deliberately sceptical tone because he couldn't afford to think about how much he wanted her at that moment.

'Well, I'm not sure exactly, but it sounded very much like it,' she said defensively.

Callum laughed. 'I'll take your word for it. After all, you know her better than anyone else does.'

'I do.' She took a quick breath and he steeled himself for what he was about to hear. 'It's been just Beatrix and me right from the very beginning, Callum, and that's how I want it to continue.'

'Meaning there's no place for me?' he said harshly

as his worst fears coalesced into one terrible thought: Beth was going to refuse to let him see his daughter. She wasn't going to allow him to have any contact with her. Oh, maybe he could go through the courts and apply for visitation rights, but how would that help? Beth would only resent him if she was forced to grant him access and Beatrix would soon realise there was something wrong. Could he do that to her, could he put his child through that kind of trauma, make her suffer at the hands of two warring parents? Of course not!

'Why do you want to play a part in her life, anyway?'

Beth answered his question with a question of her own and Callum drew himself up short. Was it a sign that she hadn't completely made up her mind about this? That she was willing to reconsider if he could prove his case? The thought made his insides churn with nerves but if there was one occasion when he needed to appear confident, it was now.

'Because I know how important it is, not just for me but, more crucially, for Beatrix.' He had never told Beth about his unhappy childhood. Whenever the subject had come up, he had brushed it aside. However, now it was time to tell her the whole story. His tone was flat when he continued because he had long since come to terms with the past and it no longer had the power to affect him.

'My parents never really wanted me, you see. They're both lawyers and run their own firm, specialising in international property rights. They spend a lot of time flying to one place or another, so my arrival was merely a hindrance. I spent my early years being looked after by a succession of nannies then, once I was old enough, I was sent away to school.'

'How old were you then?'

Callum heard the shock in her voice but he didn't dwell on it. His past no longer mattered apart from if it helped to make his case to see his daughter. 'Seven.'

'So young!' she exclaimed.

He shrugged. 'Most of the boys were the same age as me when they started at the school, so it was quite normal.'

'Did you miss them, your parents, I mean?' she queried, obviously finding it difficult to understand.

'Not really. I'd had very little to do with them so it really didn't worry me. In fact, it was holidays that were the worst times. It was obvious that they resented spending time with me when they could have been working. In fact, it was a relief when I was old enough to go away on holiday on my own and do various activities like skiing or diving.'

'I can't imagine what it must have been like,' she admitted. 'My family has always been close and we enjoyed spending time together.'

'You were lucky.' Callum smiled at her. 'Not everyone has such a good relationship with their parents.'

'So it seems,' Beth replied, her voice wobbling. 'Do you see much of them nowadays?'

'No.' Callum could tell that she fighting back tears and felt dreadful about it but he couldn't afford to weaken if he was to plead his case. 'We go our separate ways and that suits us fine. However, there's no denying that my childhood had an effect on me. That's why I was so reluctant when you suggested we should have a baby. I was afraid that I'd turn out like them and not really be interested in my child, but I was wrong.'

He held her gaze, knowing that this was the most important moment of his life. He had to convince her that he meant every word. 'As soon as I learned that we had a child, everything changed. Maybe I don't know how to be a proper father yet but I'll learn—I promise you that. Just give me a chance, Beth. Give *Beatrix* a chance to get to know me because I swear on my life that I'll never let her down.'

Beth collected Beatrix from Alison's house and drove home. The afternoon had passed in a blur. Callum's revelation about his childhood had answered so many questions she had wondered about but he'd never wanted to talk about it before. How awful it must have been for him to feel unwanted! Coming from a loving home herself, it was hard to understand how anyone could behave that way towards their own child, but she knew that he had been telling her the truth.

He hadn't made up some sob story to persuade her to let him see their daughter; every heartbreaking word had been true. She couldn't begin to explain how much it hurt to know how he must have suffered.

She let them into the cottage and set Beatrix on the sitting room floor so she could play with her toys while Beth made her tea. She boiled an egg and made toast soldiers to go with it then fetched Beatrix through to the kitchen and popped her in the highchair. The little girl was at the messy stage of wanting to feed herself but it was all part and parcel of growing up.

Beth helped her spoon some egg into her mouth then handed her a finger of toast. Some of it ended up in Beatrix's hair, which she seemed to think was the perfect spot for wiping her hands, but Beth didn't mind. Beatrix was happy and healthy and loved and they were the things that mattered most.

Tears suddenly welled to her eyes again as she thought about Callum and what he had told her, *how* he had told her. There'd been no sadness in his voice, no anger, no pain. It made her see just how awful it must have been for him to live through a childhood like that. No wonder he was so determined to be there for their daughter.

Standing up, Beth went into the sitting room and found her phone. Maybe she wasn't one hundred per cent certain that she was doing the right thing but she knew that she would never forgive herself if at some point in the future Beatrix thought that her father hadn't wanted anything to do with her. She bit her lip as she pressed the dial button. She didn't want to add to Callum's pain either.

Callum had just taken a shower when his phone rang. Digging through the pile of clothes on the bed, he finally unearthed it, his heart racing when he saw Beth's name appear on the screen. He still wasn't sure if he had done the right thing by telling her about his childhood. What if it had simply confirmed her fears that he wasn't fit to be Beatrix's father? By his own admission he knew nothing about being a parent and he couldn't blame her if she had decided to cut him out of their daughter's life.

'Hello,' he said, hoping she couldn't tell how nervous he felt.

'I was wondering if you were busy this evening,' she said quietly, although he heard the tremor in her voice that she was trying to disguise.

'Not unless you call going down to the bar to sample yet more pub grub busy,' he replied with forced levity. 'I'm not exactly fussy when it comes to food but if I have to eat another pie then I might just keel over!'

'Oh, dear.' She laughed and Callum felt his spirits lift. Beth had the most wonderful laugh, warm and genuine, just like her.

'Well, I can't promise cordon bleu cooking but I can rustle something up for us and it won't be a pie, I promise you.' She took a quick breath and then hurried on. 'I thought you might like to come round and meet Beatrix.'

Beth opened the sitting room door but Callum didn't move. She glanced at him, feeling her heart ache when she saw the expression on his face. Beatrix had already had her bath and she was wearing her favourite pyjamas, the ones printed with pink bunny rabbits. She looked so adorable as she sat on the rug playing with a toy car that Beth's own heart melted. It wasn't hard to understand how Callum must feel at that moment, just how overwhelming it must be for him.

Without pausing to think, she took hold of his hand and led him into the room. His fingers were icy-cold and her emotions see-sawed once more. She had intended to keep this first meeting low-key but it was impossible to pretend that it wasn't of major importance for both him and Beatrix. For if it was the first time that Callum had seen his daughter then it was the first time that Beatrix had seen her father too. Tears stung her eyes at the thought but she blinked them away. Letting go of Callum's hand, she went over and knelt down on the rug beside Beatrix.

'There's someone here to see you, darling,' she said softly. 'Say hello.'

Beatrix looked up, her big brown eyes fastening on the stranger standing by the door. Just for a moment her lower lip wobbled ominously before Callum stepped forward. Crouching down, he picked up a car and ran it across the rug.

'Broom, broom. Beep, beep,' he said as he steered it towards the little girl.

Beatrix's face broke into a huge smile as she took the car from him and pushed it across the rug, making appropriate beeping noises. Callum laughed. 'She's obviously going to be a racing driver when she grows up.'

'Looks like it.' Beth felt a wave of relief wash over her. There'd been a moment when she had thought that Beatrix might get upset at seeing a stranger in their home but, somehow, Callum had immediately struck the right note with her. Was it a sign that it would be easier than she had feared to let him into their lives? She sighed softly. It was too soon to speculate about that. Far too soon either to know if his interest would last.

The doubts rushed in before she could stop them and she scrambled to her feet, not wanting to go down that route at this moment. There would be time for that later, time when she would have to weigh up the pros and the cons of this situation, although there could be only one outcome. Beatrix's happiness came first and if she had any concerns at all about her precious daughter then she would call a halt, even if it meant disappointing Callum.

'I've done salmon and new potatoes for us. I hope that's all right. It's just about ready so I suggest we eat while madam here is happily engaged with her cars.'

Her tone was overly bright and she saw Callum shoot an assessing look at her. He didn't say anything, however; he simply ran his hand over Beatrix's hair as he stood up, and the very simplicity of the gesture moved Beth more than she could say.

It was obvious that he wanted this to work, but was wanting enough? It wasn't easy being a parent. He'd need to make some massive changes to his life and she wasn't sure if he understood that. After all, he had very little experience of what it took to be a father after the less than ideal childhood he'd had. It was a worrying thought and Beth's mind was racing as she served their meal. Callum sighed as he took his first bite.

'This is delicious. You shouldn't have gone to so much trouble, although I'm glad that you did. My arteries will be able to have a day off from all that grease.'

'Eating out is fine but not when you have to do it

every day,' she agreed, finding it easier to stick to a more neutral topic. Maybe they both needed to take a step back from all the heavy emotional stuff, she mused. It had been full-on ever since Callum had re-appeared and it might help if they found some kind of balance so she carried on in the same vein. 'Are you going to continue staying at the pub or do you plan to find somewhere else to live while you're covering for Eleanor's maternity leave?'

'I'm going to move into the flat over the surgery. Daniel asked me if I'd like to move in there and I jumped at the chance.' He speared a piece of fish then looked at her. 'It will give me time to look around for somewhere permanent.'

'Permanent?' Beth echoed, unable to hide her surprise. 'You mean that you intend to *stay* in Beesdale?'

'Of course.'

'But what about your aid work?' she asked, her heart racing. Callum was planning to live here permanently—could it be true? He had lived here once before, of course, when he had first moved to Yorkshire to be with her. Although he had never said so at the time, she'd had the impression that he hadn't really settled into the role of country GP. The thought set all her internal alarm bells clanging and she hurried on. 'I know how much you enjoy the work you do, so are you sure you'll be happy switching careers?'

'Yes. Oh, don't get me wrong, I love my job, but my priorities have changed. I have a child now and there's no way that I intend to go trekking off around the globe when she needs me.'

There! He'd said it, actually put into words all the

vague ideas he'd had since he had returned to England. He intended to be here for Beatrix, not just for a few months, either, but permanently. He wanted to watch her growing up and have some real input into her life. He had no idea how Beth would feel about the idea, but he would worry about that later. For now it was enough to make his position clear.

'I don't know what to say, Callum. When you turned up, I thought it was just going to be…well, a brief visit.'

'So did I at first. Oh, not too brief. I did plan to stay around to sort things out—' He broke off. Admitting that he had hoped to sort things out with her seemed like a pipe dream now. It was obvious that she didn't want him back and, although it upset him terribly, he had to accept it. He would be Beatrix's father—no more and certainly no less than that. If Beth would let him.

The thought that even now she might not allow him to have any contact with his daughter in the future sent a rush of panic shooting through him. He pushed away his plate, all thoughts of food forgotten. 'I know it very much depends on you, Beth, but I hope you'll believe me when I say that I'm serious about this. I want to be a real father to Beatrix.'

'But for how long, though?'

The scepticism in her voice cut close to the bone but he didn't dare show it. He couldn't afford to let her see that he had his own doubts about his ability to live up to the role. 'For ever. There's no time limit on being a parent as far as I'm aware.'

'No, there isn't. It's a lifetime commitment,

Callum—are you really prepared for that?' She gave a brittle laugh. 'You don't exactly have a good track record when it comes to commitment, do you?'

'Meaning when we split up?' He sighed, wishing he could explain why he'd had to leave her. Should he tell her the truth, that it had been just too painful to watch her torturing herself, that he'd hoped she would find some kind of balance if he was no longer around? He had left because he had loved her, but how could he tell her that when it was unlikely she'd want to hear it? The last thing he wanted was for it to lead to another destructive argument. 'That was different, Beth.'

'Was it? Really? You got tired of me and left, so who's to say you won't get tired of being Beatrix's father and decide to leave her too?'

'I won't. I swear on my life that it won't happen,' he said hotly, hating the fact that she had such a poor opinion of him. 'She's my daughter and I'll never abandon her!'

'You say that now, Callum, but I'm not totally convinced.'

It was obvious that she wasn't prepared to give an inch and he sighed in frustration. 'Then I'll have to prove that I mean it. That's all I'm asking for, Beth, a chance to prove to you that I can be a proper father to our daughter. Oh, I don't expect to jump straight in and become a major part of her life. She needs time to get to know me first. But I want to be involved, take her to the park, teach her how to ride a bike—do all the things that fathers do.'

'And what about the other times, like when she's

sick or just being a typical toddler and throwing a tantrum? Will you still want to be her father then?'

'Yes, I will,' he said firmly. Maybe he did have doubts about his ability to take on the role but he wouldn't fail through lack of effort. He intended to put his heart and his soul into making a success of this. If Beth would let him. He stared down at his hands, willing himself to say the words even though they hurt so much.

'I know it didn't work out for us, Beth, but that's all in the past. You'll meet someone else one day and put it behind you. It's the future that matters now, your future, my future but, more importantly, Beatrix's future.' He looked up, trying to hide his devastation at the thought of Beth loving anyone else. 'And I intend to be part of her future.'

CHAPTER FIVE

'So what's happened? Have you seen Callum again?'

'Yes. He's coming round tonight, in fact.' Beth unfastened the sphygmomanometer cuff and rolled it up. Now that Polly was pregnant, she had offered to do her friend's antenatal check-ups. She noted down the blood pressure reading then smiled at her. 'Close your mouth. You look like a goldfish, gaping at me like that.'

'Is it any wonder?' Polly grumbled, rolling down her sleeve. She fixed Beth with a piercing stare. 'I've only been away for two weeks on my honeymoon and look what's happened. You and Callum are getting all cosy again!'

'That's where you're wrong.' Beth got up and took the sample of urine over to the workbench to test it for sugar. Peeling off one of the chemically coated strips, she dipped it into the pot. 'Callum is coming to see Beatrix, not me.'

'If you expect me to believe that,' Polly began, but Beth didn't let her finish.

'Well, you'll have to believe it. He isn't interested in me. He's only interested in his daughter.' She tossed the test strip into the bin then sat down again. 'Everything's fine—blood pressure, sugar level all normal.'

'That's good,' Polly said distractedly. She leant across the desk, her pretty face filled with concern. 'Are you sure he's telling you the truth, Beth? I mean, I wouldn't be at all surprised if he was feeding you a line because he can't bring himself to admit that he's still crazy about you. After all, he came back, didn't he? That has to prove something.'

'He came back to see Beatrix,' Beth corrected her. 'It didn't have anything to do with me. If he hadn't found out that we had a child then he wouldn't have bothered, believe me.'

'It's so sad. I always thought you two would make a go of it eventually,' Polly declared. 'Oh, I know how awful it must have been for you when Callum didn't reply to your letter, but now you know what happened, are you sure there isn't any chance of you getting back together?'

'No. The only reason Callum would want us to get back together is if he thought it would benefit Beatrix,' Beth said baldly. 'He isn't interested in us having a relationship again and neither am I.'

'I see.' Polly sighed as she stood up. 'Well, you know best, Beth, but I still think it's a crying shame if you two don't try to work things out. You went through such a lot together and I find it hard to believe that you don't still have feelings for one another.'

'I'm not saying that,' Beth said quietly, feeling a lump come to her throat. It was difficult to admit that she still cared about Callum when he obviously didn't feel anything for her any more. She held up her hand when Polly went to speak. 'I do care about him but he's made it very clear that what we had is over. He even mentioned me meeting someone else.'

'Maybe you should,' Polly conceded. 'After all, if you and Callum really are history then it's time you moved on. You can't live in the past for ever, Beth.'

Beth sighed after Polly left. She knew that her friend meant well but the thought of meeting anyone else held very little appeal after what had happened between her and Callum. She had thought that they would be together for ever, that their love could overcome any obstacle, but she had been so very wrong. Did she really want to risk going through that kind of heartache again? Of course not!

'Right, Mr Brimsdale, you can put your shirt back on.'

Callum helped the old man into his shirt then went and sat down behind the desk. Arnold Brimsdale was his first patient that morning. At over ninety years of age, Arnold had come into the surgery for his six-monthly check-up. Now Callum smiled as the old man came to join him. 'Well, I have to say that I wish more of our patients were in as good health as you are, Mr Brimsdale. Your blood pressure is spot on and you've got a good strong heartbeat. The only thing slightly amiss is your breathing but so long as you keep using your inhaler, it shouldn't cause a problem.'

'That's good to hear, Doctor.' Arnold sat down in front of the desk and laughed. 'I'm hoping to get my telegram from the Queen before I pop me clogs. It'll look right nice on the mantelpiece, it will.'

'It will indeed!' Callum laughed as well. He had forgotten how much he enjoyed the Dales people's dry sense of humour. He filled in a repeat prescription for Arnold's inhalers and emailed it to the on-site pharmacy. 'Unless you have any problems I'll see you in six months' time. Don't forget to collect your prescription on your way out, will you?'

'I won't,' Arnold assured him, standing up. 'I take it that you're staying around here then from what you just said.'

'Yes. I'm covering for Dr Saunders while she's on maternity leave, but I'm hoping to be taken on permanently after that,' Callum explained, thinking about the conversation he'd had that morning with Daniel. Although Daniel hadn't actually offered him a permanent post, it was definitely on the cards and now he just needed to tell Beth. The thought of how she would react to the news made his stomach churn but he managed to hide his unease. 'The practice could do with another doctor now that Dr Hargreaves has retired.'

'Aye, that it could, plus that little lass of yours needs her daddy,' Arnold observed before he took his leave.

Callum sighed as the door closed. Everyone in Beesdale knew he was Beatrix's father and they were probably waiting to see if he measured up to the job too. He hadn't exactly got off to a flying start but, hopefully, they wouldn't hold it against him. At least his colleagues at the surgery knew about Beth's letter failing to reach him. It could have been very awkward if they'd all thought he had deserted her when she had needed him most. He would never have left if he'd thought there was a chance of her getting pregnant, though. He would have stayed right here and they could have looked forward to the birth of their baby together. How different his life would have been then.

He blanked out that thought because it was pointless thinking like that. He'd done what he had thought was right at the time, and now he had to live with the consequences. Would Beth follow his advice and move on? he wondered suddenly. Part of him hoped that she would while another part rebelled at the thought of her meeting someone else. He sighed as he buzzed in his next patient. If some passing genie could grant him a wish then it would be to have Beth back in his life, Beth *and* Beatrix, but genies were few and far between in the Yorkshire Dales!

Beth just had time to tidy up before Callum arrived that evening. They had slipped into a routine whereby he called round after work and spent an hour or so playing with Beatrix. She hadn't invited him to dinner again, however; it had seemed wiser to keep things on a less familiar footing. After all, Callum wasn't coming to see her, he was coming to see their daughter, and there was no reason to turn his visits into anything more than they actually were.

Beatrix was delighted to see him each day and held up her arms to be picked up. She had accepted his presence in her life with an ease that Beth envied. Now she sighed as she picked up a pile of clean baby clothes and took them up to the nursery. Even though she knew how silly it was, she was always on edge when Callum was there.

Oh, he never said anything to alarm her. On the contrary, he always confined their conversations to what Beatrix had done. However, just having him in the house made Beth feel very self-conscious. She couldn't help remembering when they had lived there together and how different it had been. Even though their relationship had been under a lot of strain, there had been good times too. Lots of them.

She pushed that thought aside, not wanting to dwell on it. Leaving the clothes on the changing table, she ran back downstairs, forcing a smile when she found Callum playing a game of peek-a-boo with their daughter. Beatrix was giggling in delight, loving every second of it too. 'It looks like you two are having fun,' she observed as she went to join them.

'We are.' Callum covered his face with his hands then peeped through his fingers. 'Peek-a-boo!'

Beatrix laughed so hard that she tumbled over. Beth quickly righted her, placing a steadying hand under her arm as she scrambled to her feet. 'She managed to walk all the way to the chair on her own this morning,' she told Callum as Beatrix shuffled her way to the basket of toys.

'Really?' Callum sounded impressed. 'Some babies don't even attempt to walk until they're much older, do they?'

'No, apparently not,' Beth agreed. 'Obviously, Beatrix is keen to explore the big wide world.'

'It must be in her genes,' Callum replied, laughing. 'I was always eager to see something of the world.'

'Yet you ended up here in the Dales,' Beth said flatly. She sighed but there was no way that she could let the comment pass unchallenged. 'Are you sure you know what you're doing, Callum? Moving here to live is going to be a huge change for you.'

'I've lived here before,' he pointed out.

'Yes, and it wasn't exactly a roaring success, was it?' she shot back as all her doubts came flooding back. She had tried her best to ignore them but it was impossible. At the back of her mind the thought that Callum would eventually grow tired of living in the town nagged away at her. Beatrix would grow to love him and then he would suddenly disappear from her life.

'I'm not sure I understand what you mean,' he said flatly. 'I certainly didn't have any complaints about my work at the surgery. In fact, Daniel has made it clear that he's more than willing to offer me a permanent post once Eleanor's maternity leave has finished.'

It made perfect sense. Daniel would be keen to offer Callum a post at the surgery because he knew that Callum could do the job and that he fitted in. However, it wasn't that which worried her. 'I wasn't talking about whether or not you can do the job, Callum. That isn't an issue.'

'Then what's the problem?'

'The problem is whether you'll grow tired of being tied to one place. I got the feeling that you found it rather restricting working here the last time.'

'Did I ever say so?' His tone was hard and she sighed. She didn't want to start an argument but he needed to take a good hard look at what he was planning.

'No, you didn't, but I could sense how you felt, tell that you were getting fed up with being in one place all the time.' She shrugged. 'I'm sure it was a contributing factor as to why you left. You'd not only had enough of me but you'd had enough of living here as well.'

Callum wanted to refute what she was saying but how could he? The reason he had left Beesdale—left her!—had nothing whatsoever to do with him growing bored with country life. He had got over his desire to move around all the time by then, worked the wanderlust out of his system. However, if he told Beth that then he would have to tell her the truth, that he had left because watching the woman he loved putting herself through such torment month after month had been unbearable.

'People change,' he said neutrally.

'Do they?' She shrugged. 'I've never really believed that, I'm afraid. You are who you are and that's it.'

'Meaning that I'm never going to settle down and one day I'll decide I've had enough and pack my bags and leave again?' He shook his head, wishing that he could make her understand how wrong she was. 'It's not going to happen, Beth. Especially now.' He looked pointedly at Beatrix.

'So you're going to stay purely for Beatrix's sake?'

'Yes,' he said curtly, hating the fact that she didn't

believe him. What made it worse was the fact that he knew it was his fault too. He had left her, so she was bound to have doubts.

'And how long will it be before you come to resent it, resent *Beatrix* because you feel that you have to stay for her sake?' She shook her head, the soft blonde curls dancing around her face. 'Don't say it won't happen, Callum, because I know that it will.'

'You know no such thing!' he exploded because it hurt to know what she thought about him. He leant forward, feeling his senses whirl as he inhaled the scent of her shampoo and was suddenly transported back in time. The familiar fragrance unleashed a flood of memories as he recalled all the other times he had smelled it when Beth had stepped out of the shower each morning and into his arms…

'Just because I left you, Beth, it doesn't mean that I'll leave our daughter,' he said harshly, needing to rid his mind of such dangerous thoughts. 'I love her and I'll always be here for her.'

She drew back abruptly and he frowned when he saw the pain in her eyes. 'Then let's hope you mean what you say this time, Callum. Now I think it's time you left. I have to be in work early tomorrow for the team meeting and I need to put Beatrix to bed.'

Callum wasn't sure what he'd said, although it was obvious that he had upset her. However, short of trying to prise it out of her, there was little he could do. He said his goodbyes and left, taking his time as he walked back to the surgery. He headed straight round to the back where there were steps leading to the flat above. He had moved in the previous week and was slowly settling in. Fortunately, the flat was fully furnished so he hadn't needed to worry about furniture, although he would have to do so when he bought a place of his own.

He sighed. He had moved around such a lot that he had never collected many belongings. When he and Beth had got married she had been amazed to find how little he owned apart from some personal items—clothing and books, that kind of thing. However, if he bought a house then he would have to furnish it and make it comfortable for Beatrix when she came to stay with him—*if* she came to stay with him, he amended swiftly.

He frowned. What on earth had he said to upset Beth so much?

Beth arrived at the surgery the following morning just as Daniel was unlocking the doors. He waved to her then went inside to switch off the alarm. Beth took a deep breath as she got out of her car. She'd hardly slept and she felt tired and drained. Although she knew how stupid it was to have let it affect her, that comment of Callum's had really thrown her. He couldn't have made it any plainer if he had spelled it out for her that he had never really loved her at all. It made her wonder if everything she'd thought they'd had together had been a sham. The idea that she had been fooling herself about how Callum had felt about her was excruciating, but she had to face up to it. She may have loved him with every fibre of her being but it appeared that he had never felt the same way about her.

Daniel had the kettle on by the time Beth made her way inside. He looked round and grimaced. 'Mia had us up all night so I'm in need of a strong dose of caffeine to get me going.'

'Me too,' Beth agreed fervently, earning herself a quizzical look. 'It was one of those nights when you just can't seem to settle,' she explained hastily, not wanting to go into the whys and wherefores of why she'd been awake. 'What was wrong with Mia anyway? I saw Eleanor at the shops the other day and she told me that Mia was sleeping through the night now.'

'Normally, she does, but she had a touch of colic and we couldn't get her settled.' Daniel spooned coffee into the machine and switched it on. 'Needless to say, she was fast asleep this morning when Eleanor and I had to get up.'

'Typical!' Beth drummed up a laugh, hoping it didn't sound as forced to Daniel as it did to her. She looked round when she heard footsteps coming along the corridor and felt her heart jolt when Callum appeared.

'Ah, coffee. Great stuff,' he declared, coming into the kitchen. He nodded to Beth then turned to Daniel and started to tell him about a call he had made the previous day.

Beth frowned. Although she had been upset when Callum had left her house last night, she was sure that she had hidden it. However, there was no denying that there seemed to be a definite atmosphere all of a sudden. Despite the way he was regaling Daniel with the tale of what had gone on, Callum looked uneasy and it wasn't like him. Beth chewed it over but she was no closer to finding an explanation by the time the rest of the team arrived. Once everyone had a drink they adjourned to the meeting room. Beth found herself sitting next to Owen Walsh, who had recently taken over the running of the on-site pharmacy. He smiled when she sat down beside him.

'Hi, you must be Beth. It's nice to meet you at last.'

'And you too,' she replied, taking an immediate liking to his open and friendly manner. 'How are you settling in?'

'Fine. Everyone's been very welcoming, I'm relieved to say.' He grinned at her. 'I was a bit worried in case people saw me as an incomer and were a bit sniffy about me taking the job, but they've been great.'

'Beesdale is a really friendly little town,' she assured him. 'I found everyone very welcoming when I moved here. The only downside is that the locals love to know everything about you, so if you have any skeletons in your cupboards then be warned. They will find out!'

'Thanks for the advice.' Owen laughed. 'I'll make sure I fit some strong locks to my cupboards.'

Daniel called the meeting to order then so Beth turned her attention to what was being said. There was always a lot to get through and there was no time to waste. Marie was having problems with the computer and Daniel asked her to phone the IT specialists so they could check it out as it was vital to the smooth running of the surgery.

Beth's gaze moved on around the rest of the group, coming to a halt on Callum, who was sitting off to

her right, and she felt her breath catch when she realised that he was watching her. Just for a moment
their eyes met before he looked away but she could
feel her heart racing. What had she seen in his eyes?
For a second it had looked almost like pain but that
couldn't be right. Callum didn't care about her; he
never really had cared. Yet no matter how many times
she told herself that, it was hard to believe it.

Callum couldn't believe the agony he felt as he
watched Beth laughing with Owen Walsh. He
clenched his hands, forcing down the pain. He knew
he should be glad that she looked so happy as she
sat there, listening to what Walsh was saying, but it
was impossible. He didn't want to see her enjoying
some other man's company. He wanted her to enjoy
his! And it was pure unmitigated torture to have to
sit there and pretend that he didn't care. When Daniel asked him a question, it took a tremendous effort
just to string together an answer.

The meeting came to an end at last and Callum
made his escape. He went straight to his room and
brought up his morning list on the computer, sighing
in frustration when halfway through the screen went
blank. Leaving his desk, he went through to Reception where Marie was struggling to get the system
working again.

'It's no good,' she declared, turning to him. 'I can't
get it going. I'll have to phone the IT guy to see if
he can sort it out. In the meantime, we'll have to go
back to the old system of giving everyone a number
when they arrive.'

'Can we still access their notes?' Callum asked, glancing over his shoulder when he heard voices in the corridor.

'I doubt it,' Marie admitted. 'The whole system seems to have gone down. I'll have to dig out everyone's paper file, although I'm not sure how up to date they are.'

'What's happened?'

Callum steeled himself when he heard Beth's voice. It took every scrap of willpower he could muster to turn and face her. 'The computer's packed up completely now so Marie's going to get straight on to the IT guy. In the meantime, we'll have to use the paper files to check the patients' notes.'

'I'd better check the pharmacy computer,' Owen Walsh declared anxiously. He touched Beth's arm. 'I'll give you a call at the weekend, if that's all right?'

'Yes. Fine. I'll look forward to it,' Beth replied, smiling at him.

Callum counted to ten but he still couldn't manage to hold back the question that was clamouring to get out. 'Why is Walsh going to phone you?'

'To make arrangements for us to go out for dinner some time,' Beth replied coolly. 'Although I really don't see what business it is of yours, Callum.'

'It's my business if it impacts on Beatrix,' he said harshly.

'I think it's up to me to worry about that, don't you?' She turned to Marie, ignoring him as she asked the receptionist's advice if any patients from the Larches turned up at the Hemsthwaite surgery and she couldn't access their notes.

Callum went back to his room, his temper soaring. Why, for two pins he would ban Beth from going out with Walsh, he thought furiously, then sighed when he realised how ridiculous it was to think he could do that. He had no control over what Beth did or with whom she did it either and the thought cut right through him. The idea of her meeting someone else might have been fine in theory, but the reality was very different. He took a deep breath, knowing that he had to rein in his emotions. If he didn't do so then Beth might decide to cut him out of her life altogether and he would never see her or Beatrix again.

CHAPTER SIX

BETH WAS GLAD to see a long queue when she arrived at the Hemsthwaite surgery. She needed to keep busy in the hope that it would take her mind off the strange way Callum had behaved that morning. Mandy Stephens, their receptionist, had been alerted to the problems with the computer and was busily hunting out paper files for those patients who had turned up. She grimaced when Beth went into the surgery.

'I'm not sure how up to date these are now everything's done on the computer,' she explained anxiously, blowing the dust off a couple of buff-coloured folders.

'We'll just have to do the best we can and hope the IT chap can sort out the problem,' Beth told her, deliberately downplaying any problems they might encounter when she saw how flustered Mandy looked. She glanced around the waiting room, smiling when she spotted Diane Applethwaite. At least Diane's test results should be available as the lab they used always sent through a printed report rather than rely solely on email.

'I suppose so.' Mandy handed her the folders.

'They're in order and I've given everyone a number so they know who's next.'

'Thanks. That's really helpful,' Beth declared, smiling at her. Leaving Mandy to carry on finding files, she went to her room and got settled in. Just for a moment her mind flicked back to Callum's reaction about Owen asking her out. He had sounded decidedly put out about it but why? He'd been the one to raise the subject of her meeting someone else, so why should he care if she went out with Owen? It was a mystery, although she didn't intend to dwell on it. She and Callum were divorced and it was none of his business what she did.

The morning flew past with very few problems, thankfully enough. Most people had come with new complaints rather than long-standing conditions that would have required an in-depth study of their case histories. Beth asked anyone she wanted to double-check on to make an appointment on their way out and was confident that she hadn't overlooked anything vital. By the time Diane Applethwaite came into the consulting room, she was feeling far more relaxed and smiled at her.

'Sorry about the wait but the computer's packed up so we're having to go back to the old-fashioned way of doing things. I hadn't realised how much extra time it took.'

'Computers are great when they work but a real pain when they have a hissy fit,' Diane agreed, sitting down. 'Phil has a real love-hate relationship with ours. I've had to rescue it a couple of times from the barn after it's failed to give up some vital bit of infor-

mation. Mind you, I think it's more Phil's fault than
the machine's. He's not what you'd call technologi-
cally minded.'

Beth laughed. 'Oh, dear. It's a good job you're
there to sort things out. Right, let's have a look at
those test results and see what they say.' She took the
printed sheet out of Diane's file and scanned through
it then read it a second time, more slowly.

'What's wrong, Dr Andrews? I can tell from your
expression that something's happened,' Diane said
worriedly.

'There's nothing wrong. But the results aren't exactly what I thought they would be.' Beth put the sheet
on the desk and looked at Diane, wondering how to
break the news to her. However, there really was only
one way. 'Far from being in the early stages of the
menopause, Diane, it appears that you're pregnant.'

'Pregnant?' Diane repeated, sounding shocked.
'But I'm forty-eight. How can I be pregnant at my
age?'

'It's unusual, yes, but it isn't unheard of,' Beth said
gently. 'There have been cases of women becoming
pregnant well into their fifties, in fact.'

'I don't know what to say… ' Diane broke off and
gulped.

'It must be a lot to take in,' Beth said, sympathetically. 'Maybe you should speak to your husband before you decide what you want to do.'

'What I want to do… What do you mean?' Diane
asked in confusion.

Beth chose her words with care. 'In case you decide not to go ahead with the pregnancy.'

'Oh, no. I couldn't do that,' Diane declared. She took a deep breath. 'If it's right and I am having a baby then I'll just have to get on with it.' She suddenly laughed. 'Although what Phil's going to say about us having another little one keeping us awake at night, I have no idea!'

Beth laughed too, delighted that Diane had taken the news so well. 'I'm sure he'll cope brilliantly, the same as you will. After all, you've had a lot of practice. Right, we need to establish how far along you are with this pregnancy. As your periods have been so erratic lately, it's difficult to work out when the baby's due. Are you still feeling sick, dizzy, tired?'

'No. In fact, I've felt better than I have for a long time,' Diane declared.

'Hmm. It could be a sign that you're over twelve weeks or thereabouts. After that stage, a lot of women find that they no longer feel as sick or as tired, although everyone is different, of course.' She picked up her pen and made a note on Diane's file. 'I'll book you in for a scan, although the hospital usually prefers to do them at around sixteen weeks so they may decide to wait.'

'I'm happy to wait if it's better for the baby,' Diane said firmly and then frowned. 'There's a bigger risk of there being something wrong with it because of my age, isn't there?'

'Yes.' Beth knew that Diane would appreciate the truth rather than have her put a positive spin on the situation. 'The risk of having a child with Down's syndrome, for instance, increases with the mother's age. You will be offered tests to check for that.'

'I see.' Diane sounded momentarily worried before she rallied. 'Well, we'll have to wait and see what happens. There's no point borrowing trouble, is there?'

'Definitely not,' Beth agreed, thinking how well Diane was coping with the shock of it all. She could remember how she had felt when she had discovered she was pregnant, she thought as she saw Diane out. It had been a lot to take in, even though she had wanted a baby for so long. She sighed. Of course, it would have been different if Callum had still been there. They could have celebrated together, although *would* Callum have seen it as something to celebrate when he had no longer loved her? Now that Beatrix was a living, breathing human being, she didn't doubt that his feelings had changed about having a child but, back then, would he have seen her pregnancy as a hindrance that would stop him leaving her?

Beth felt a chill envelop her. Although she didn't doubt that Callum would have stayed with her if he'd known she'd fallen pregnant, it would have been out of a sense of duty and not out of love.

The computer problems slowed everything down so it was after seven before Callum left the surgery. He debated going round to see Beatrix but in the end decided not to risk it. He was still smarting at the thought of Beth going out with Owen Walsh and he needed to get a firm grip on his emotions before he spoke to her again.

He went up to the flat and made himself a meal of pasta and ready-made sauce then sat slumped in front of the television while he ate it. He felt tired and out of sorts and he knew that he had to shake himself out of this mood. Beth wasn't his any longer and he couldn't dictate what she did even if she would listen, which he very much doubted.

Part of her charm had always been her independence, her willingness to stand up for herself as well as for other people; why would he want her to change, even though he hated the thought of her seeing another man? He should be pleased that she was getting her life back on track but it was impossible to feel anything other than this bitter disappointment. It was a relief when the sound of his phone ringing cut through his unhappy thoughts and he snatched it up.

'Callum O'Neill.'

'It's me—Beth.'

'Beth,' he repeated as his thoughts spun even faster. He wouldn't change a single thing about her, apart from how she felt about him, of course. If he could make her love him again, as she had loved him once before, then he would do so in a trice. It was a revelation to realise how much he longed for it to happen so that it was a moment before he discovered that she was still speaking. 'Sorry, can you say that again?' he asked, forcing down the surge of pain at the sheer futility of hoping that she would ever feel that way about him again.

'Joe Thorne's just been on the phone. There's an elderly couple been reported missing. Apparently, they were planning to walk to the Witch's Cauldron and told the owner of the guest house where they're staying that they would be back by four but they've not appeared yet. Joe needs someone medically trained

to go with the team. I can't go because of Beatrix and
Daniel is at a meeting in Leeds so I suggested you.'
She paused when he didn't reply. 'You don't have to
go if you don't want to…'

'Of course I'll go.' Callum finally managed to drag
his thoughts together, lining up the facts like ducks
in a row: Joe Thorne, leader of the local search and
rescue team; missing walkers, lost and possibly injured out on the hills; no one else available except
him. 'Where are we meeting?' he demanded, dump-
ing his plate on the coffee table.

'The car park at the lower edge of the Cascade,
although Joe said he can pick you up on the way, if
you want him to,' she informed him.

'Right,' Callum said, switching off the television.
'Can you phone Joe back and tell him I'm coming and
that I'd like a lift? I don't have his number.'

'Of course.' She paused then rushed on. 'Take care,
Callum.'

'I shall,' he replied, his heart swelling with joy
because it seemed that she did care about him, after
all. He opened his mouth to say something else, although heaven knew what, but realised that she had
already hung up.

Hurrying into the bedroom, he gathered together
what he would need, telling himself that it was ridiculous to get his hopes up like that. *Take care* was on
a par with the equally anodyne *Have a nice day*—a
trite comment that meant absolutely nothing. However, despite knowing that, he couldn't shake off the
thought that Beth might actually *care* about him. A
huge smile lit his face as he swung his backpack over

his shoulder. Quite frankly, he couldn't think of a better inducement to get back safely!

Beth paced the sitting room floor, unable to settle. Although it was past midnight, she knew it was pointless trying to sleep. She kept thinking about Callum being out on the hills. Maybe he had worked in all sorts of places around the globe but the Yorkshire Dales were an unknown quantity to him. He had very little experience of the rough terrain he would encounter and she couldn't help worrying. He could so easily find himself in serious trouble.

The sound of a car drawing up outside had her flying to the window and she felt her heart leap with relief when she saw Callum getting out of the search and rescue team's four-wheel drive. Beth saw him glance towards the cottage and held her breath, wondering if he would knock on her door when he saw the light was on. It was only when she saw his shoulders slump as he turned away that she realised she couldn't let him leave without speaking to him. Hurrying to the front door, she called after him.

'Callum, wait! What happened? Did you find the missing walkers?'

'Yes, we did.' He came back and she could see the lines of strain etched on his face. Without pausing to think about what she was doing, Beth held the door wide open.

'Come in and tell me about it,' she said quietly. She led him into the sitting room and waved him towards a chair. 'I can see you're upset so what happened?'

He sighed heavily as he sat down. 'The woman

was already dead when we found them. She had Alzheimer's disease, apparently, and had wandered off on her own and fallen over the edge of the Cauldron. Her husband had managed to climb down to her and he was just sitting there, holding her hand, when we arrived.'

'Oh, how tragic!' Beth declared, feeling her eyes sting with tears. 'It must have been horrendous.'

'It was. It took me ages to convince the husband that she was dead. He kept insisting that she'd be all right if we got her to the hospital.' He shook his head. 'Even after we'd loaded her body into the back of the car, he couldn't seem to take it in.'

'Where is he now?' Beth asked, her heart going out to him. A situation like this was always stressful and it was obvious that Callum had been deeply upset by what he had witnessed.

'Still at the hospital. He was in no fit state to be sent back to the B&B on his own,' he explained. 'The police have contacted his son and he's driving up here. He lives in Surrey, though, so it'll take him a while to get here.'

'At least the old man will have someone with him,' Beth said, softly. 'That will help.'

'Yes. He's lucky in that respect. At least he isn't completely on his own now and has a family who cares about him.'

There was something in his voice that made Beth's heart ache all the more. Was Callum thinking that *he* didn't have any family who cared about him? She knew it was true and the urge to comfort him was too strong to resist. Reaching out, she gripped his hand. 'There are people who care about you, too, Callum.'

'Are there?' He gave a bitter laugh. 'If you mean my parents then forget it. They didn't care about me when I was a child and they certainly don't care about me now that I'm an adult.'

'You have friends,' she began but he shook his head.

'I've lost touch with most of my friends in the past year. I doubt they even spare me a thought these days. They have their own lives, their own problems—why should they worry about me?'

'Because they care about you! Maybe you haven't seen them for a while but it takes more than that to end a friendship.'

'Does it? Really? All it took to end our marriage were a few words, Beth. I told you I wanted a divorce and that was it.'

'That was different,' she murmured painfully. 'It was clear that you didn't want to be with me any more.'

'Was it? What if I only asked you for a divorce be-cause I felt it was the right thing to do?'

'What do you mean?' She gripped his hand when he went to draw it away. 'Tell me, Callum!'

'Nothing. I'm just rambling, that's all.' He stood up, effectively breaking her hold on him. 'I'd better go. We've got work in the morning and it's late. I'm sorry if I woke you, Beth, but it was easier for Joe to drop me off here than drive to the surgery.'

'It doesn't matter,' she managed, her head reeling as she tried to make sense of what he had said.

What had Callum meant about it being the right thing to do? Right because he had stopped loving her? Or right for some other reason? She followed him into the hall, wishing that she could make him explain even though she knew it was pointless. The facts were clear, after all. Callum had stopped loving her and had asked her for a divorce.

And yet the nagging thought that she was missing something wouldn't go away. When he turned towards her, she searched his face, feeling her heart quicken when she saw the regret in his eyes, but regret about what? About divorcing her? But why would he regret it when it had been his decision?

'Callum,' she began.

'Don't.' He touched her mouth with his fingertips, stopping the question before it could emerge, and his expression was infinitely sad. 'There's really nothing more to say, Beth, believe me.'

He let himself out without another word. Beth watched until he disappeared from sight and only then did she let out the breath she hadn't realised she was holding. Closing the door, she leant back against it, feeling her whole body trembling. Raising her hand, she touched her mouth, but the warmth of Callum's fingers had already faded. She couldn't hold onto it any more than she had held onto him and it was the most bitter thought of all. She hadn't been enough for him and she never would be. Any interest he showed in her from now on was purely because she was the mother of his child. She took a deep breath, letting that thought seep into every cell in her body because she must never forget it.

* * *

Callum telephoned the hospital the following morning to check on the man he had helped to rescue and was relieved to hear that his son was now with him. He thanked the ward sister and hung up, wondering why the incident had had such an impact on him. Was it the fact that it had brought it home to him just how alone he was in the world? His only real family link was with Beatrix, his daughter, and he resolved to spend as much time as possible building a relationship with her.

When he went into work, he put through a call to Beth, meaning to start the way he needed to continue. Maybe the thought of her seeing another man devastated him, but if that was how things had to be, then he would use it to his advantage.

'Beth, it's me. I won't keep you because I'm sure you're busy, but I just wanted to say that if you need a babysitter any time then ask me. I'll be more than happy to mind Beatrix if you want to go out.'

'Oh. Right.' She sounded surprised, as well she might, Callum thought wryly. He had never imagined himself making such an offer.

'I know you said that you and Walsh might go out for dinner one night, so I thought I'd mention it,' he said, stamping on the spurt of jealousy that suddenly reared up inside him.

'I…er…yes, although we've not made any arrangements yet,' she said hurriedly.

'Well, when you do there's no need to worry about finding someone to look after Beatrix,' Callum said, hoping she couldn't hear the edge that had crept into his voice despite his best efforts to avoid it. 'I'll be happy to do it.'

'Um, thank you. Anyway, I'd better get on. Are you calling round tonight to see her?'

'If it's all right with you,' he said levelly.

'It's fine. I'll see you later then.'

With that she hung up, leaving Callum in a quandary. Whilst he was glad that he had made the offer, he couldn't claim that he was happy at the thought of her going out with Walsh, or anyone else for that matter. He sighed wearily. He couldn't have it both ways, could he? He couldn't offer to babysit and then behave like the proverbial dog in a manger. Beth was free to see whoever she liked, no matter how he felt about it. One thing was certain: Beth wasn't interested in having *him* back in her life in any capacity other than that of Beatrix's father. And even that wasn't guaranteed.

Beth was still reeling from the shock of Callum's phone call when she set out to visit one of the outlying farms that afternoon. It was a wet and windy day, the previously fine weather having changed in the space of a few hours as it often did in the Dales. Rain lashed against the windscreen as she headed out to Outhwaite's Farm.

Jenny Outhwaite had requested a home visit because she was worried about her youngest child, two-year-old Tilly, who was running a high temperature. It was the most remote of all the farms on their books and the journey there took time even on a good day. Now with the wind and rain slowing her down, Beth realised it was going to take her even longer than usual and sighed, wishing that she had phoned Alison to warn her that she might be late collecting Beatrix.

Maybe she should phone Callum and ask him to fetch her, she mused, and then just as quickly dismissed the idea. While she didn't doubt that he would take good care of Beatrix, was she really ready to make him an accepted part of her daughter's life? Apart from the concerns she had about his commitment, there was the fact that Callum unsettled her.

Take today, for instance. She'd felt on edge ever since he had offered his services as a babysitter. She wasn't sure why but it felt wrong to even think about asking him to look after Beatrix while she went out with another man. She sighed, knowing that she was overreacting. Hopefully, the situation would improve in time, but at the moment it seemed safer not to involve him in her affairs.

It turned out that little Tilly Outhwaite had chickenpox. The rash had appeared since Jenny had telephoned the surgery so Beth was quickly able to diagnose the problem. The little girl's chest and thighs were covered in spots, some of which had already turned into the fluid-filled blisters so characteristic of the illness. Beth advised Jenny to give Tilly paracetamol liquid for her temperature and to dab calamine cream on the spots to stop them itching. Cutting Tilly's nails would also help to prevent scarring if she scratched the scabs that would form once the spots started to heal.

Beth left the farm a short time later, having refused a cup of tea. The storm was getting worse and she was eager to get back to Beesdale. Rounding a bend in the road, she gasped when she was suddenly confronted by a huge pile of rocks blocking the way. She ground to a halt, her heart racing at the near miss she'd had.

Opening the car door, she went to investigate, hoping there would be room to drive around the landslide, but the ground beside the road was far too wet to risk it. Getting bogged down in the mud wouldn't help so her only option was to phone the surgery and see if Daniel could come out to collect her. Hurrying back to her car, she took her mobile phone out of its holder, groaning when she discovered that she didn't have a signal. There were blank spots all over the Dales and, typically, she was in the middle of one.

Beth got out of the car again and headed back along the road, holding up the phone in the hope that she could find a signal. Maybe it would help if she tried climbing up the hillside, she decided. She was in a dip here but if she was higher up then she might be able to connect to the nearest mast. Stepping off the road, she started to scramble up the hill. She was still staring at her phone and never even noticed the patch of loose rocks until her feet skidded out from under her. A searing pain shot through her right ankle as she fell heavily onto the ground and she cried out. Sitting up, she checked the damage, grimacing when she rolled up her trouser leg and discovered that her ankle was already swelling up. Whether it was sprained or broken, she couldn't tell, but the moment she tried to stand up and put her weight on it, the pain became unbearable.

Beth sank back down onto the ground, forcing

back the tears as she suddenly realised her predicament. She couldn't get back to her car and return to the farm and she couldn't summon help either. It looked as though she was going to be stuck here until someone came looking for her.

If anyone did.

CHAPTER SEVEN

CALLUM WAS CLEARING up when Daniel came to find him. It had been a busy afternoon with appointments as well as the antenatal clinic. Polly had taken the clinic, but one of her mums had had a problem with her blood pressure and he had been drafted in to deal with it.

It had been a stark reminder of how easily things could go wrong during pregnancy. He knew from a comment Polly had passed that Beatrix had arrived several weeks early and it must have been a very worrying time for Beth. To say that he felt guilty about not being there was an understatement, even though he'd had no idea what had been happening at the time. He sighed because it all boiled down to one thing, didn't it? If he hadn't left in the first place, then he would have been here when Beth had needed him.

'Have you spoken to Beth recently?' Daniel asked him now without any preamble.

'Not since this morning, although I'm calling round to hers tonight to see Beatrix, as it happens.' Callum frowned when he saw the concern on the older man's face. 'Why? What's wrong?'

'I'm not sure,' Daniel replied. 'Alison has just phoned. Apparently, Beth hasn't collected Beatrix yet. Alison's quite happy to keep her there, but she's worried about Beth not turning up.'

'That's strange!' Callum exclaimed, glancing at his watch. 'It isn't like her to be late.'

'It isn't,' Daniel agreed. 'Apparently, she was doing a home visit this afternoon at Outhwaite's Farm. I've spoken to Jenny Outhwaite and, according to her, Beth left there a couple of hours ago.' He glanced out of the window and shook his head. 'The weather's atrocious so maybe that's what's delayed her.'

'I take it you've tried phoning her?' Callum said, his anxiety mounting. Maybe it was too soon to start panicking but it was hard not to do so.

'I have, but it's going straight to voice mail.' Daniel grimaced. 'The signal is patchy around there so it doesn't mean very much. She might just be out of range.'

'Or she could have had an accident.' Callum knew that he was merely voicing what Daniel was thinking and his heart turned over. He came to a swift decision, knowing that he wouldn't rest until he was sure that Beth was safe. 'I'll drive over there and see if I can spot her. Can you mark the route on the map for me? I've not been to the farm before and I don't want to end up getting lost.'

'Of course.' Daniel sounded relieved. 'I'll copy the map we have in Reception—all the farms are marked on there. Satnav's useless around here—you'll find yourself driving round in circles if you try to follow it. Stick to the map and you'll be fine.'

'Shall do.' Callum unhooked his waterproof jacket off the back of the door, thanking his lucky stars that he had left it there in case he ever needed it. The rain was lashing down now and the trees at the bottom of the car park were bent double from the force of the wind.

'Maybe I should come with you,' Daniel suggested suddenly. 'It's a filthy day and I don't want you going missing as well.'

'No, it's better if you stay here. That way you can alert the search and rescue team if you don't hear from me in a reasonable length of time.'

'Good point, although I hope that won't be necessary,' Daniel said grimly. 'I'll also phone Tim Outhwaite and ask him if he'll check if there's any sign of Beth thereabouts.'

'That would be a big help,' Callum agreed, heading for the door. They walked through to Reception where Daniel photocopied the section of the map that Callum needed, placing it in a plastic sleeve to keep it dry.

'Keep me posted, won't you?' he said, clapping Callum on the shoulder. 'I don't want anything happening to you.'

'Me neither,' Callum replied lightly, although there was no denying that Daniel's concern had sounded genuine. It reminded him of what Beth had said the other day about people caring about him. Maybe it was true, he conceded as he ran out to his car. However, the one person he really wanted to care about him was the most unlikely of all. After all, why should Beth care about him after the way he had behaved, even if he had believed that he was doing the right thing?

The thought stayed with him as he drove out of the town. The route was clearly marked and he had no difficulty following it, although he knew that he would have had problems if he hadn't had the map. The roads became increasingly narrow as he drove on, twisting and turning through the countryside. This part of the Dales was sparsely populated, with only the odd farm here and there, and he grew increasingly anxious when he saw no sign of Beth's car along the way. By his reckoning he was only a couple of miles away from Outhwaite's Farm now so where on earth was she?

He rounded a bend and had to slam on his brakes when he was confronted by a huge heap of rocks and soil blocking the road. It was obvious that the rain had caused a massive landslide and there was no way that he could drive around it. Leaving his car where it was, he hurried towards it, his feet slipping and sliding as he scrambled over the top, and felt his heart surge in relief when he saw Beth's car parked on the other side. He ran straight over to it, his relief rapidly disappearing when he discovered that it was empty. Fear knotted his guts as he turned in a slow circle and scoured the surrounding countryside. Where on earth was she?

Beth wasn't sure how long she had been stranded out on the hillside. The noise of the wind as it tore across the hills made it difficult to think clearly. All she knew was that the combination of the wind and driving rain had chilled her to the bone. The light-weight jacket she was wearing provided little protection from the elements and she knew that she needed to find shelter or she would be in real danger of developing hypothermia.

There was no way that she could walk so she tried scooting along on her bottom instead. It was sheer agony as even the slightest jolt sent a shaft of red-hot pain shooting through her ankle. In the end she couldn't do it any longer and was forced to stop. Pulling the collar of her jacket around her neck, she tried to conserve what little body heat she had left, but she was so cold now that her teeth were chattering. Glancing at her watch, she was shocked to see that it was gone seven o'clock. Hemsthwaite Surgery had closed after she had left to do the callout, and it was unlikely that anyone would have missed her. Although Alison was bound to wonder where she was when she didn't collect Beatrix; would she have raised the alarm? And if so, would people know where to look for her? Tears welled in her eyes when it hit her that she might be stuck out there all night long.

'Beth!'

All of a sudden Callum was there beside her and Beth stared at him confusion. 'What are you doing here?'

'Looking for you, of course.' Stripping off his rain-coat, he wrapped it around her. 'Explanations can wait for now. We need to get you out of this rain. Can you stand up?'

'No. I've injured my ankle.' She bit her lip, but

it was impossible to hold back the sobs that rose up inside her.

'Shh, it's all right. You're safe now.' He drew her into his arms and Beth cried all the harder. Between the pain from her ankle and the fear that she might have been stranded on the hillside all night long, it was just too much.

'It's okay—you're safe now,' he repeated as he drew her closer. 'I know how scared you must have been, Beth, but it's all over now. We just need to get you to my car then I can drive you to the hospital and get your ankle seen to.'

'I didn't think anyone would miss me,' she muttered, brokenly.

'Of course we missed you,' Callum said hoarsely. He tilted her chin and Beth felt her heart leap when she saw the expression on his face, all the fear mingled with something else, an emotion that she had never expected to see. Callum was looking at her as though the thought of losing her was more than he could bear, but that couldn't be true. Could it?

When his head suddenly dipped, Beth closed her eyes. She didn't want to see anything else, didn't want to know if she was mistaken. She simply wanted him to kiss her and make her feel safe even though it defied all logic. Callum had left her. He had left her because he had no longer loved her. Those were the facts but she wasn't interested in facts at that moment, only in feelings: how Callum felt; how he made *her* feel. His lips found hers and she shuddered when she realised how cold they were—the coldness of fear. When he parted her lips, she didn't resist. She wanted to feel that chill turn to warmth, feel fear turn to desire...

'Hello! Can you hear me? Where are you?'

The sound of a man's voice broke the spell. Callum let her go and leapt to his feet as Tim Outhwaite appeared. Beth took a shaky breath but her heart was racing. She knew that in another second there would have been no turning back. She would have given herself to Callum right here on the hillside with the storm raging around them. Had she learned nothing from what had happened in the past? she thought, bitterly. Apparently not!

'Thank heavens!' Tim came hurrying over to them. 'I was starting to fear the worst when I saw the cars and no sign of you both.'

'Beth's injured her ankle,' Callum informed him tersely. 'I don't know if it's fractured or sprained but we need to get her to hospital.'

Beth shivered when she heard the grating note in his voice. Was Callum regretting what had happened just now? she wondered, sickly. Wishing that he hadn't behaved so impulsively? Maybe he had been tempted to kiss her but had it been the heat of the moment that had led him to behave that way? Callum hadn't wanted *her*. He had simply reacted to events.

Even though she knew it was foolish, she couldn't help feeling as though it was yet another rejection of her. It was only the thought of him guessing how devastated she felt that helped her hide her feelings as he and Tim carried her back to the road and got her settled in his car. Hurrying round to the boot, Callum took out an inflatable splint and carefully fitted it around her injured ankle.

'This should help protect it,' he said, steadfastly avoiding her eyes.

'Thank you,' Beth murmured, her heart aching all the harder when she realised she was right. Callum regretted what had happened because he was afraid of finding himself caught up in a situation he wouldn't welcome. It was a relief when he turned away to speak to Tim.

'Can you phone Dr Saunders and let him know that I'm taking Beth straight to the hospital? Her ankle will need X-raying and it's easier to go straight there.'

'Of course.' Tim grimaced. 'We've put you to an awful lot of trouble, Dr Andrews. I'm so sorry.'

'It isn't your fault,' Beth assured him, trying not to think about how hurt she felt. After all, nothing had changed. Callum may have reacted to the heat of the moment but it didn't alter the fact that he no longer loved her. She hurried on, determined not to go down that route. 'Can you ask Dr Saunders to phone Alison and explain what's happened and that I'll collect Beatrix as soon as I get back from the hospital?'

'I will.'

Beth sank back against the seat as they set off, feeling more exhausted than she'd felt in her entire life. Between the stress of being stuck out in the storm and what had happened with Callum, she felt completely drained. She glanced at him, studying the shape of his head and the set of his shoulders. Every detail was familiar to her. It had all been logged away in her brain, stored there for eternity. She had loved him so much but her love had meant nothing to him. Tears pricked her eyes. Even if they hadn't been interrupted, that kiss wouldn't have meant anything either.

What on earth had he been thinking?

Callum stood up and paced the corridor outside the X-ray department. Beth was inside having her ankle X-rayed. There was a red light above the door, warning people not to enter, and he sighed. If only there'd been a red light warning him of the danger of being so close to Beth again then he might not be in this situation now. However, the moment he had held Beth in arms, all sensible thoughts had fled. He had wanted to hold her and never stop. Wanted to kiss her and promise that she would never be in danger again as long as there was breath in his body. The urge to protect her had been overwhelming—so was that why he had behaved the way he had?

His heart lurched as he recalled what had happened. It might have started out as an attempt to comfort her but there had been other emotions brewing, far stronger ones too. Holding Beth in his arms had unlocked all the feelings he had tried so desperately to forget. However, the thing that shocked him more than anything else was that he knew Beth wouldn't have stopped him kissing her. She hadn't tried to push him away, hadn't shown any sign at all that she hadn't wanted him to kiss her. She had simply looked at him and then closed her eyes...

The red light turned to green and Callum desperately tried to pull himself together as the radiographer wheeled Beth out. Allowing thoughts like that to fill his head was only asking for trouble. Maybe she hadn't pushed him away but it didn't mean anything. After everything she had been through, she had needed comforting, and he'd just happened to be on hand.

'I have to see the doctor about my results,' she informed him tersely. 'I'm not sure how long it will take so don't feel that you have to wait for me. I can get a taxi home.'

'Of course I'll wait for you,' Callum said hotly, hurt beyond all reason that she should think that he would leave her to make her own way home. He pushed her back to A&E, his heart sinking when he realised once again what a poor opinion she must have of him. It made him see how foolish it would be to read anything into what had happened tonight. Beth had been scared and upset, and he'd been there. That was all.

It turned out that her ankle wasn't fractured but badly sprained. It would take a couple of weeks for it to heal and in the meantime Beth was not to put any weight on it. The doctor asked one of the nurses to strap it up then gave them a note for a pair of elbow crutches to be collected on their way out and that was that. Callum insisted on pushing her back to his car in the wheelchair then went back to fetch the crutches and stowed them in the back.

'Would you mind stopping off at Alison's so I can collect Beatrix?' Beth asked him as they set off.

'Of course not.'

Callum left the hospital, taking the ring road that skirted around the city centre. It would be quicker this way and he was eager to get home. Tonight had been tough and he needed time to get himself back on track. Telling Beth how he felt was out of the question: he could see that now. It was guaranteed to make her reconsider her decision to allow him to spend any time with Beatrix, so he needed to batten down his feelings no matter how difficult it was.

Thoughts flowed in and out of his head as he drove and he was thankful that Beth didn't seem to want to talk any more than he did. It was gone eleven when he drew up outside Alison's house. Beth immediately went to open the car door but he stopped her.

'You stay here—I'll fetch her. Remember what the doctor said about staying off your ankle.' He didn't wait for her to reply as he got out of the car and knocked on the door. Alison answered almost immediately, looking relieved when she saw him.

'Oh, good. You made it. I was wondering what to do if you didn't get back tonight. I don't have a cot now that the twins are that bit older, you see.'

'I'm sorry we're so late but it took quite a bit of time at the hospital,' Callum explained, following her inside. Beatrix was in the sitting room, listlessly playing with some toys. She smiled when she saw Callum and held up her arms to be picked up.

Callum swung her up into the air, feeling a whole rush of emotions hit him. He already loved her so much, this tiny miracle he had known nothing about until a few weeks ago. Losing her now would be unbearable and he would do anything to stop it happening. If he had to hide his feelings from Beth for ever then that was what he would do, because he simply couldn't risk losing his daughter for any reason.

It was a painful thought but one that needed to remain at the forefront of his mind, he realised as he carried Beatrix out to the car. Alison had offered to lend him a car seat as there wasn't one fitted in his car so he handed Beatrix to Beth while he secured it in the back. Once he was sure it was safely installed, he strapped Beatrix in and drove back to the cottage. Beth handed him the keys to the front door so he could carry a now sleeping Beatrix inside. He took her straight upstairs and placed her in her cot then went back to help Beth.

Using the crutches proved a bit of a problem so in the end he picked her up and carried her inside as well. He put her down next to the couch, quickly steadying her when she wobbled.

'Thanks,' she said, ruefully. 'I'll have to practise with these crutches. Obviously there's a knack to using them.'

'They probably need adjusting so they're the right height for you,' Callum said, trying to sound upbeat even though he couldn't help wondering how on earth she was going to manage. The stairs in the cottage, for instance, were extremely steep and he really couldn't see her being able to get up and down them even with the aid of the crutches.

Beth was obviously thinking the same as him because she sighed. 'I hope you're right, although I don't know how I'm going to make it up the stairs, let alone carry Beatrix up and down them. Maybe if I try doing it on my bottom, with her on my knee, it might work.'

'Would it be safe, though? I mean, if she starts squirming around then are you sure you can hold onto her?' Callum replied, anxiously.

'No. I'm not.' She frowned and he could see the worry on her face. 'I don't want to put her at risk in any way but what else can I do? I need to be able to bath and change her, put her in her cot—all the normal things I do each day.'

Callum took a deep breath. He had a bad feeling about what he was about to suggest but what choice did he have in the circumstances? 'Then it seems to me there's only one solution.'

'And that is?'

'That I move in here and help you.'

CHAPTER EIGHT

THE SKY OUTSIDE the sitting room window was grey and leaden, perfectly reflecting her mood. Beth lay on the couch thinking about what had happened and what she should do about it. Last night she had been too exhausted to argue when Callum had put his proposal to her but she knew that having him living in the cottage was the last thing she needed after what had happened yesterday. Maybe it had been a reaction to the stress of the situation, but there was no way that she was prepared to risk it happening again.

A light tap on the door made her jump and she pressed a hand to her throat to stem the sudden pounding of her pulse. 'Yes?'

'Can I come in?' Callum said quietly from the other side of the door. 'Then I can make us some tea.'

'I...erm...yes,' Beth replied because it would be churlish to refuse. She pulled up the quilt, tucking it under her arms to hold it in place, then sighed. Did she really think that Callum would be so overcome with passion by the sight of her wearing her night-clothes that he wouldn't be able to control himself? Fat chance of that!

'How did you sleep, or did your ankle keep you awake?' he asked politely as he came into the room. It had been his idea that she should sleep on the couch. It converted into a double bed and was quite comfortable. The cottage had a downstairs loo plus a shower and it meant that she had everything to hand without needing to negotiate the stairs.

'It wasn't too bad,' Beth answered in the same vein. Maybe that was the key, she decided. Behave politely and steer clear of anything that could be construed as personal. It was worth a try so she carried on. 'I took another couple of painkillers around three a.m. and that seemed to settle things down.'

'Good.' He turned to go into the kitchen then paused. 'What time does Beatrix normally wake up? I popped my head round her door but she's still fast asleep so I left her.'

'She's usually wide awake by now!' Beth exclaimed. She tossed back the quilt as a rush of panic hit her. 'She is all right, isn't she? You did check that she was breathing properly?'

'There was no need,' he said quietly. 'It was obvious that she was asleep.'

'Obvious to you, maybe, but I need to check on her myself.' Beth swung her legs off the couch, completely forgetting about her ankle in her need to see her daughter. Pain shot through it when she tried to stand up and she gasped.

'For heaven's sake, Beth, be careful!' Callum caught her as she slumped forward and helped her sit down. 'If you keep putting pressure on that ankle, it will never heal.'

'I know but I need to see Beatrix and make sure she's all right,' she said, raising haunted eyes to his face. 'You read about cot deaths and I have this awful fear that she might not wake up one day...' She broke off and Callum sighed.

'Oh, Beth, don't torture yourself. You know how rarely something like that happens.'

'Yes, but I can't help worrying. She means the world to me, Callum, and if anything happened to her, I just couldn't bear it.'

'That's how I feel too.' He bent so that he could look into her eyes. 'I've only known about her existence for a few weeks but I love her, too, Beth. She's the best thing that's ever happened to me.'

Beth knew what he was saying, that he was asking if she had made up her mind about allowing him to take on a more permanent role in their daughter's life. It was on the tip of her tongue to tell him that he could, but something held her back. Maybe he *did* love Beatrix, and maybe he *did* want to be her father, but would his interest last? She simply didn't know and it was the uncertainty that stopped her saying anything.

Disappointment crossed his face as he straightened up. 'I'll fetch her down then you can see for yourself that she's perfectly fine,' he said, his deep voice suddenly grating.

Beth watched him go with a heavy heart. She hated to know that she had upset him but she couldn't risk Beatrix's feelings. She had to be sure that Callum would stay the course before she allowed him to play a major role in their daughter's life. He came back a few moments later with Beatrix in his arms and placed her on the couch next to Beth.

'Here she is, a little grumpy 'cos she's been woken up, but otherwise she's fine. Give me a shout when you've finished having a cuddle and I'll take her into the kitchen for her breakfast. What does she normally have?'

'Porridge and a sliced banana,' Beth told him, hugging the baby close to her.

'Right. I'll go and get it ready.'

He turned to leave but Beth knew that she had to try to make amends for his disappointment.

'Thank you for doing this, Callum. You didn't have to stay and I appreciate it.'

'It's the least I can do.' He turned to look at her and there was a wealth of sadness in his eyes. 'I'll do anything it takes to prove to you that I can be a proper father to her, Beth, but, at the end of the day, it's your call. You have to decide if it's what you want too.'

He didn't wait to hear what she had to say, not that there was anything she could think of. Until she was one hundred per cent certain about his commitment then she couldn't make any promises and how could she ever be completely sure? Callum had sworn that he had loved her, hadn't he? That was why they had got married, because they had loved one another so much. Even though she had been devastated when he had told her that he'd wanted a divorce, a tiny bit of her had still believed that he'd cared about her. When he had come to see her after the divorce was finalised, and they had slept together, she had honestly thought that he had changed his mind and wanted her back. However, when she had woken up the following morning, he had gone.

Her heart ached as the memories came rushing back as bitter and as painful as ever. How could she believe a word he said after betraying her like that?

With Beth out of action, it put even more pressure on them at work. Callum agreed immediately when Daniel asked him if he would drive over to Hemsthwaite and work there until lunchtime. Anyone with an afternoon appointment would be offered the chance to be seen at The Larches instead. It wasn't ideal but it was the best they could do in the circumstances, although it was obvious that they couldn't continue running both surgeries with so few staff.

Callum left Daniel phoning around the agencies and drove over to Hemsthwaite. Hopefully, Daniel would find someone to cover until Beth returned to work, although he didn't want her rushing back and end up hindering her recovery. He frowned. He didn't want her doing too much at home either. She had insisted on keeping Beatrix with her instead of taking her to Alison's, but he should have insisted that she stick to the arrangements. After all, childcare wasn't all down to Beth; he should take an active role in it too. He grimaced. Thinking like a parent didn't come easily to him.

Thankfully, he got through the morning without any major hiccups. One of his patients was a three-year-old boy who had chickenpox. It turned out that he went to the same playgroup as Tilly Outhwaite so no doubt he had caught it there and there would be other cases too. Although chickenpox was a fairly mild childhood illness and rarely caused complications, it could be extremely serious in the latter stages of pregnancy. Callum put through a call to the woman who ran the playgroup and explained what was happening so she could warn any expectant mums. There was no point putting people at risk.

He drove back to Beesdale after he had finished, pausing at the crossroads as he wondered if he should check on Beth. Although she had assured him that she would be fine, he didn't like to think of her being on her own with Beatrix all day. He drew up outside the cottage a few minutes later and let himself in, heading straight to the sitting room where he was met by a scene of chaos. There were toys everywhere—on the couch, on the coffee table, all over the floor. Beatrix was lying on the rug, fast asleep, while Beth was slumped on the couch. She looked up and he saw the tears in her eyes.

'I'm sorry it's such a mess. I've never known Beatrix to throw everything around like this before.'

'Hey, it's only some toys,' he said gently, going over to her. 'It won't take more than a few minutes to put them away.' He bent down, his heart aching when he saw how weary she looked. 'How are you doing? That's the main thing. Is your ankle all right?'

'Yes,' she began then grimaced. 'Not really. I didn't like to take the painkillers in case they made me feel a bit woozy and my ankle is throbbing like crazy now.'

'You need to take them every four hours,' Callum

said firmly. 'If you let the pain get too bad then it will just take longer for it to die down.'

'I know.' She sighed. 'I was just worried in case I wasn't in a fit state to look after Beatrix.'

'I can understand that but you still need to take them.' Callum lifted them down from the shelf and handed them to her. 'I'll fetch you some water.'

He went into the kitchen and filled a glass with water, wishing that he had thought about this before. Beth was bound to be wary of taking the tablets if she thought they could affect her ability to look after their daughter. A fine doctor he was not to think about that, he thought wryly, not that he wanted to be Beth's doctor, of course.

The thought of exactly what he would like to be was something he knew that he mustn't dwell on. The situation was volatile enough as it was. Although Beth had spent the night on the sofa, he had been very conscious of the fact that he'd been sleeping in the bed they had once shared. He wouldn't have been human if he hadn't recalled how different life had been before the strain of trying for a baby had affected them.

Making love with Beth had been everything he could have dreamed about, their passion for one another reaching heights that he had never known existed before. He had loved her with both his heart and his soul and the thought filled him with a deep sense of regret for all he had lost. It was an effort not to show how he felt as he took the glass of water through to the sitting room. However, the last thing he needed was Beth noticing he was upset, and wondering about it.

'Here you are.'

'Thanks.' Beth downed the tablets then leant back against the cushions with another sigh. 'I can't wait for them to kick in.'

'I bet you can't,' he said, sympathetically. 'Right, now that's sorted, how about I make you something to eat? What do you fancy?'

'Anything. I'm famished, but are you sure you've got time?' she said, glancing at her watch.

'Yes, well, enough time to make you a sandwich. The cordon bleu meal will have to wait until another day, I'm afraid,' he replied, drolly.

Beth laughed out loud. 'Since when did you start cooking cordon bleu meals? Eggs and bacon were your speciality. It's the only thing you ever made for us.'

Beth knew she'd made a mistake the moment the words were out of her mouth but there was nothing she could do about it. She couldn't *un*say them, couldn't pretend that she remembered nothing about the time when they had lived together.

'Hmm, cooking's definitely not one of my major accomplishments,' he agreed, ruefully. 'It's a good job you could cook, Beth, or we'd have starved.'

'I doubt it,' she said quickly, not wanting to go down the slippery slope of remembering all the cosy evenings they had spent, enjoying meals she had made for them. It would only lead to the next memory about how those evenings had ended, with them in bed together. Pain seared through her and she hurried on. 'I'm sure you would have managed to make something, even if it was only beans on toast.'

'Maybe. Anyway, I'd better go and rustle something up for you,' he said flatly, and she had a feeling that he was as keen as she was to change the subject. 'Should I make something for Beatrix as well?'

'No, she's already had her lunch,' Beth explained, quietly. Had Callum been thinking the same as her? she wondered as he disappeared into the kitchen. Remembering how wonderful their life had been? She knew it was true and it hurt to know how much things had changed. She had honestly thought that they would be together for ever but she'd been wrong. Their love hadn't been strong enough to withstand the pressures of them trying to conceive. How ironic that what had led to the break-up of their marriage had brought them back together. If she hadn't given birth to their daughter then Callum would never have contacted her again.

It was hard to shake off the feeling of melancholy that thought aroused when he came back with a plate of sandwiches and a mug of coffee but Beth knew that she had to keep things on an even footing. She frowned when he set the plate and mug on the table beside her. 'Aren't you having anything?'

'I've not got time. I covered Hemsthwaite Surgery this morning but I'm needed at The Larches this afternoon so we've had to close Hemsthwaite early.' He shrugged. 'We simply don't have enough staff to run both surgeries.'

'It's a nightmare, isn't it?' Beth said, worriedly. 'Is Daniel trying to find locum cover?'

'He was phoning around the agencies this morning when I left,' Callum explained.

'How on earth will you manage if he doesn't find anyone? I suppose I could come in. I mean, if I just sit at my desk then it won't affect my ankle, will it?'

He shook his head. 'You know it isn't as simple as that, Beth. You'll have to get up to fetch things and examine patients. All it needs is for you to go over on that ankle and you could be out of action for months. No, you need to be sensible and rest it, which is why I was going to suggest that I drop Beatrix off at Alison's on my way to the surgery. It would be easier if she was there, wouldn't it?'

'I suppose so,' Beth conceded. 'I thought I could cope but after this morning, I'm not so sure. She's run me ragged!'

Callum laughed. 'Don't sound so disgusted. You aren't the only mum who needs a helping hand, especially at a time like this.'

'Maybe not but I just feel that I should be able to cope.'

'You can and you do cope wonderfully. But sometimes you have to accept that you can't do it all yourself and this is one of those times.' He paused then carried on. 'It isn't just down to you, Beth, or it shouldn't be. Beatrix is my responsibility too.'

'But for how long, though? Until my ankle's better? Or until you grow tired of being responsible for her?'

'You still don't believe that my interest will last, do you?' he said harshly.

'No, I don't, if you want the truth.' She spread her hands wide open. 'Oh, you seem keen enough right now but who knows how you'll feel in six months' time?'

'I don't know how to convince you that I mean what I say,' he began, but she cut him off.

'Oh, I'm sure you mean it at this very moment, but you could change your mind. After all, it wouldn't be the first time, would it?'

'Meaning when I asked you for a divorce? You're never going to believe that I had my reasons for doing what I did, are you, Beth?'

The bitterness in his voice surprised her and she frowned. After all, it had been Callum's decision to end their marriage, so why should he sound so upset about it? It was on the tip of her tongue to ask him but she managed to hold back. Did she really want to go down that route again, start looking for excuses for his behaviour? She had done that in the months after he had left, dreamt up increasingly bizarre explanations as to why he had gone, and she refused to do it again. Callum had left because he had stopped loving her, and that was all she needed to know.

'Quite frankly, I don't care what your reasons were, Callum. The only thing that concerns me now is making sure you don't do the same thing to Beatrix.'

'I won't.'

'No, you won't because I won't let you.'

'So that's it then, is it? You're not even going to give me a chance to prove that I mean what I say?' he said, hotly.

'Do you blame me?' she countered, just as hotly. 'Why would I want to take the risk of Beatrix getting hurt?'

'Because I will never, *ever* hurt her! She's my

daughter and I'll do whatever it takes to make sure she's safe and happy.'

'Even if it means staying in Beesdale for the rest of your life?' she said, sceptically.

'Yes! If that's what it takes then that's what I'll do.' He bent so that he could look into her eyes and Beth shivered when she saw the anguish on his face. 'This is more important than anything else and I only wish I could convince you of that.'

'And I wish I could believe you, but I can't.' Beth could feel her own emotions bubbling up inside her, all the pain and heartache she had felt after Callum had left her coming together to form a huge torrent that threatened to overwhelm her.

'Then it seems we've reached an impasse.' He straightened abruptly. 'I just hope you don't regret your decision when Beatrix is old enough to start asking why she doesn't see her father. Admitting that you stopped me having any contact with her might not go down too well with her.'

'If that's a threat—' she began.

'It isn't. It's merely a statement of fact. Maybe you need to think about it.'

He didn't say anything else as he picked up Beatrix and carried her out to his car. Beth watched them go with a heavy heart. She didn't want to be at odds with him but it was obvious that they saw the situation from two very different perspectives. She sighed as she started to clear away the toys. Callum seemed so sure that he would stay the course but would he? He had spent most of his life since he had qualified working overseas and she simply couldn't imagine him settling down to life as a rural GP. He might be content enough for a while but at some point the need to move on was bound to surface and she could imagine how devastated Beatrix would be if he disappeared from her life when she had grown to love him. Even if it was difficult to answer Beatrix's questions in the future, it was a risk she wasn't prepared to take for any reason. Or anyone.

The days flew past and the spell of bad weather gradually improved. Callum woke to blue skies on the Saturday morning but it did little to improve his mood. Relations between him and Beth had hit an all-time low and they were barely speaking now. Fortunately, her ankle was healing and she was much more mobile now, although she still had difficulty negotiating the stairs. He knew that once she was able to manage them, she would insist she didn't need his help, so his time at the cottage was limited.

Although he loved the fact that he got to spend so much time with his daughter, he couldn't deny that he found it stressful. Being in the cottage had brought back a lot of memories, both good and bad, and he wouldn't have been human if he hadn't found himself thinking about what had gone on there and regretting it.

Beatrix didn't go to Alison's at the weekend. Callum knew that Beth would claim that she could manage on her own and didn't need his help, but he had no intention of leaving her to fend for herself all day long. It was just gone seven when he went into the nursery, smiling when he discovered that Beatrix was wide awake.

'Good morning, madam, and how are you this fine day? Full of beans from the look of you.'

Lifting her out of the cot, he dropped a kiss on the top of her head, feeling his insides scrunch up with love. Although he had treated many children in the course of his work, he'd had very little to do with them on a personal level, and he hadn't expected to feel this way. It made him see how important it was that he and Beth resolve their issues. He needed to be part of his daughter's life, not just for her sake but for his as well, and to do that he had to convince Beth that she could trust him, although how he was going to achieve that was a mystery. He was still mulling it over when he carried Beatrix into the kitchen and popped her in her high chair.

'Oh, I didn't know you were in here.'

Callum swung round when he heard Beth's voice. Just for a second his senses whirled as he took stock of what she was wearing, which was very little. In a fast sweep his eyes ran over her, drinking in the sight she made as she stood there dressed only in a pale blue bath towel. It was only when he realised that she was waiting for him to say something that he managed to drag his thoughts together, but it was an effort. The sight of her near-naked body was definitely having an effect on him!

'I...er... I thought you were in the shower,' he murmured, desperately trying to clamp down on the surge of desire that was racing through him.

'I just got out,' she said, then suddenly seemed to realise her state of undress. Colour bloomed in her cheeks as she swung round and hobbled out of the kitchen. 'I'd better get dressed.'

Not on my account, Callum wanted to say, but managed to stop himself. He needed to heal this rift between them, not make it bigger. 'And I'd better give this little lady her breakfast.'

He got everything ready, forcing himself to concentrate on what he was doing and nothing else. Thinking about how beautiful Beth had looked in that scanty little towel certainly wouldn't damp down his raging hormones. By the time Beth reappeared, Beatrix had finished her porridge and was eating a banana, squeezing the fruit so that it oozed between her fingers.

'I think she prefers mashed banana,' he said, desperately trying to keep his thoughts on his daughter's antics. Maybe he did want Beth but it wouldn't help his case one iota if he let her know that.

'So I can see.' Beth tore off a length of kitchen roll and wiped the baby's hands. 'You're supposed to eat it, darling, not squeeze it to death. You're such a mucky little thing!'

Callum laughed as he took the empty cereal bowl over to the sink. 'She'll grow out of it eventually, I expect.'

'I hope so.'

Beth rolled her eyes as she sank down onto a chair and Callum felt his heart lift just a little. She didn't appear quite so hostile this morning and he had to admit that it was a relief not to be treated like a pariah for once. Maybe they could arrive at a compromise, he thought as he washed the bowl and put it back in the cupboard. If they tried talking to one another rather than arguing all the time, then surely she would start to trust him? It was that thought that made him make a suggestion he had never planned on making.

'How would you feel about having a day out?' He turned to face her, feeling his emotions swirl once more. It had nothing to do with how she was dressed this time but how she had always affected him. Right from the beginning he'd only had to look at her to want her and it was disconcerting to realise how little his feelings had changed.

'A day out,' she repeated. 'You mean go somewhere, together?'

'Yes.' He shrugged, trying to keep a tight grip on his emotions. 'Your ankle's a lot better and so long as you don't do too much then it should be fine. I'm sure Beatrix would enjoy a change of scene so why don't we take her out for the day?'

'I'm not sure if it's a good idea,' she began.

'It's just a day out, Beth. I'm not suggesting that we bury the hatchet, although I'm more than willing to do so if that's what you want.' He sighed when she

didn't say anything. 'I just feel it might make things…
well, easier if we at least tried to get along. So what
do you say?'

CHAPTER NINE

THEY WENT TO a petting zoo the other side of Hemsthwaite. Callum had found it online and suggested that it would be the perfect place for Beatrix. She certainly seemed to be enjoying herself, Beth thought, listening to her daughter squeal with excitement when she saw the goats. Callum lifted her out of the pushchair and held her close to the fence so that she could stroke their whiskery faces, and Beth frowned. For someone who knew very little about children, Callum seemed to have struck just the right note by bringing them here.

It was an unsettling thought, especially when it made her realise how hard she had been on him lately. Maybe she did have concerns about his ability to commit to being a father, but there was no doubt that he was making a huge effort to live up to the role. She summoned a smile when he brought Beatrix over to where she was sitting, feeling guilty all of a sudden. She hated to think that she was being unfair to him.

'She's certainly enjoying herself. I've never heard her squeal like that before.'

'The goats are obviously a big hit,' Callum agreed,

laughing when Beatrix started wriggling around, demanding to be put down. 'Oh, off we go again. Are you all right sitting there for now? There's llamas over there but the ground looks rather rough and I don't want you coming a cropper.'

'I'm fine,' Beth assured him, trying not to read anything into the way he was treating her with such concern, but it was impossible not to do so. A rush of warmth invaded her and it took all her effort not to let him see how touched she felt. 'I'll sit here till you come back then maybe we can go to the café. It's almost time for Beatrix's lunch so we may as well have something to eat as well.'

'Good idea.' He set Beatrix on the ground and took firm hold of her hand. 'Come on then, sunshine, let's see what you make of those llamas. You won't see many of them roaming around the Dales!'

Beth watched him lead Beatrix towards the llamas' pen. There were a lot of families there enjoying a day out and she couldn't help thinking how well Callum fitted in. Nobody watching him and Beatrix would guess that he had only known about his daughter for such a short time. She sighed because it would be a mistake to allow appearances to influence her. Although he seemed to be adapting to the role of doting father, she still wasn't convinced his interest would last. And nobody, not even Callum himself, could guarantee that it would.

The café was crowded but Callum managed to find them a table outside on the terrace. He got Beth seated then fetched a highchair for Beatrix and popped her in it. 'Right, what do you fancy?'

'Just coffee and a sandwich is fine for me, thank you. I've brought Beatrix's lunch with me. There's a jar in the bag and it just needs warming up.'

'I'll do that first then,' he said, taking the jar of baby food out of the bag. There was a flask of juice in there as well and he handed it to Beth to open, smiling when Beatrix immediately reached for it. 'I expect she's thirsty after all the excitement.'

'I expect she is.' Beth loosened the top on the flask and handed it to her daughter. She laughed when Beatrix began to gulp it down. 'Hmm, you're right. All that squealing has obviously built up a thirst.'

'I could do with a coffee myself,' Callum admitted and rolled his eyes. 'I didn't realise it was such thirsty work, having fun.'

He grinned at her and Beth felt her heart give a little bounce when she realised how handsome he looked when he smiled like that. Ever since Callum had come back to Beesdale they had been at loggerheads, it seemed, and there had been very little to smile about. Now she could feel her pulse racing and it was unnerving to know that he still had this effect on her. It was a relief when he went to heat up the baby food because it gave her a breathing space. Maybe she was still attracted to him but nothing would come of it. She wasn't foolish enough to risk having him break her heart a second time.

Callum could feel his heart pounding as he paid for their lunch. He couldn't rid himself of the memory of how Beth had looked at him. Had he made a mistake or had there been genuine awareness in her eyes just now? A shudder ran through him as he took his change from the cashier. He knew how dangerous it was to think like that. It would only lead to other thoughts, ones he couldn't afford to harbour. It wasn't how he felt about Beth that mattered; it wasn't even how she felt about him. It was whether she would allow him to be Beatrix's father that was the issue. He simply couldn't risk alienating her by doing or saying the wrong thing.

His heart was heavy as he carried the tray outside to their table. It wasn't going to be easy to hide his feelings but he knew it was what he needed to do. He had hurt her badly when he had left, even though he had truly believed it had been the right thing to do. However, even if he explained it all to her, would she believe him? It was obvious that she didn't trust him and she could think that he was simply spinning her a tale. Although he longed to tell her the truth, he was afraid that he might end up making the situation worse. He sighed. It would be better not to say anything than run that risk.

'Here we go. I'm afraid there wasn't much choice, so it's tuna mayo or cheese and pickle—take your pick,' he said with forced cheerfulness as he placed the tray on the table.

'I'll have the cheese if you don't mind,' Beth replied, taking one of the cardboard cartons of sandwiches.

'No problem.' Callum doled out coffee and paper napkins then sat down. Beatrix had finished her lunch and was eating some strawberries now. Picking up

a napkin, he wiped away a dribble of juice that was
trickling down her chin. 'There you go, poppet. All
beautiful again.' He dropped a kiss on the end of her
nose and picked up his coffee, only then realising that
Beth was watching him with the strangest expression
on her face. 'What's the matter?' he said, wondering
what he had done wrong this time.

'Nothing.' She bit her lip but he could tell that she
was holding something back and it made him more
determined than ever to make her tell him.

'Oh, come on! It's obvious that you want to say
something, so out with it. It's not like you to pull your
punches, Beth. Or not lately, at least.'

She flushed bright red. 'If I haven't pulled my
punches then it's because I wanted to make the situation perfectly clear to you, Callum. You came back
here expecting to step into the role of Beatrix's father,
but it isn't as simple as that.'

'So I've gathered,' he replied, tartly.

'Good.' She tilted her head and looked him straight
in the eyes. 'At least we've made some progress.'

'You may have done but I certainly haven't. And
I won't until you accept that I'm serious about this.'
He held up his hand when she went to interrupt. 'No,
I've heard it all before, Beth. You've made it perfectly
plain that you don't believe I'll last the course. But
you can't prove that I'm going to jump ship any more
than I can prove that I won't.' He laughed harshly, unable to hide his frustration.

'I knew it wasn't going to be easy when I came
back here but I never thought you'd have such a closed
mind. You're so determined to punish me for leaving

you that you don't care about the impact it's going to have on our daughter if you won't allow me to be a father to her!'

The accusation cut her to the quick. Beth reeled back, appalled that Callum could even think that. Beatrix was her first and only concern…wasn't she? The doubt rushed in before she could stop it, growing stronger by the second. Was she thinking solely about her daughter or was she also thinking about herself, about how devastated she'd been when Callum had left her? She couldn't put her hand on her heart and swear it wasn't true and she felt sickness well up inside her at the thought that she might be guilty of basing her decision on her own feelings rather than on Beatrix's needs.

'I'm sorry. I shouldn't have said that.'

Beth looked up, unable to hide how upset she felt. 'Why not if it's what you believe?' she replied, brokenly.

'It isn't. Well, I suppose I do think it's partly true. What happened between us is a huge sticking point, although I suppose it's only to be expected.' He sighed as he reached over the table and caught hold of her hand. 'I know you feel that I let you down, Beth, but I did it for the very best of reasons.'

'What reasons? You keep hinting that there was more to your decision to ask me for a divorce than the fact that you'd fallen out of love with me, so tell me what it was. You owe me that much, at least, Callum.'

She snatched her hand away, not wanting him to touch her. Her heart was pounding as she waited to hear what he had to say, even though she couldn't imagine what it would be. It was all quite simple to her mind: if Callum had loved her, he would never have divorced her and left. So how on earth was he going to explain what he had done?

'It wasn't an easy decision,' he began then stopped when another family came and sat down at the table next to theirs. There were four young boys in the group and they immediately started squabbling over a plate of giant cookies. The youngest boy grabbed one of the cookies and bit into it then suddenly toppled off his chair, clutching his throat. The two adults appeared rooted to the spot with shock, so Callum leapt to his feet. Kneeling down beside the child, he rolled him over and checked his airway, although he could see the piece of cookie lying on the floor next to him. It was obvious that the boy hadn't swallowed it but there was no doubt that he was having difficulty breathing.

Callum turned to the couple. 'I'm a doctor. Is he allergic to anything? He didn't eat any of the cookie—the piece he bit off is here on the floor. I think he must be allergic to something it contains.'

'Nuts.' The woman suddenly seemed to rouse herself. She shot to her feet. 'He's my nephew, you see, and my sister keeps going on about him being allergic to nuts. I just thought she was fussing...' She broke off and Callum sighed. However, now wasn't the time to point out how foolish it had been to ignore the warning. The boy's breathing was becoming even more laboured as his airway went into spasm.

'Did your sister give you anything in case this ever

happened?' he demanded. 'Something that looks like a pen and contains a drug you can inject him with.'

'Yes, yes, she did! It's in my bag.' She grabbed hold of her bag and emptied it onto the table. 'Help me find it, Don,' she shouted to her husband, scrabbling through the heap.

'There it is.' Reaching over, Callum grasped the preloaded injection of adrenaline and plunged it into the child's thigh, praying that it would work. His heart sank when he realised that the boy's breathing wasn't improving. He was obviously going to need a second shot and there was always the danger that he could arrest in the meantime.

Glancing around, he spotted the girl who worked on the till and called her over. 'I'm a doctor and I need you to fetch my bag out of my car.' He told her the registration number and where it was parked then handed her the keys. 'Before you go, do you know if there's a defibrillator on site? He's a very sick little boy and we may need it.'

'I think there is, but I don't know where it's kept,' the girl explained. 'I'll get one of the others to ask the manager.'

She hurried away as Callum turned back to the child. He looked up when Beth came to join him.

'I've phoned for an ambulance.'

'Let's hope it gets here in time,' he said, quietly, as she knelt down beside him. 'I don't like the look of him at all.'

The words were barely out of his mouth when the child's eyes suddenly rolled back and he stopped breathing. Callum bent over him, shaking his head as he checked for a pulse. 'Nothing. We'll have to start CPR. Apparently, there's a defibrillator somewhere in this place but only the manager knows where it is.'

'Not much use hiding it away,' Beth said, tartly. 'I'll do the breathing if you'll do the compressions.'

She placed her mouth over the child's mouth and gave two sharp inflations. Callum followed them up with the necessary chest compressions. A crowd had started to gather now and they fell silent when they realised what was happening. They carried on like that for several minutes before the manager appeared carrying the portable defibrillator.

'I keep it locked up in the office,' the man explained importantly, placing it next to them. 'It'd be such a shame if people started messing around with it.'

'It'd be an even bigger shame if someone died because nobody knew where to find it,' Callum stated, bluntly.

He and Beth carried on performing CPR while the manager set up the defibrillator. The young cashier had come back with his bag and, without him even needing to ask, Beth took over the compressions while he drew up a second shot of adrenaline. Callum plunged the needle into the child's thigh then picked up the defibrillator paddles and applied them to the boy's chest, sending up a silent prayer. With the ambulance taking so long to reach them, he didn't rate the child's chances if this didn't work. When the boy suddenly coughed, Callum felt his heart lift in relief.

'It's all right,' he said soothingly when the boy

started to cry. 'You're going to be fine now. Just try to breathe nice and steadily for me.'

He checked the boy's pulse again and was reassured to find that it was growing stronger by the second. He moved aside when the boy's aunt came and knelt down beside them. Beth looked exhausted as she struggled to her feet and he helped her back to their table where Beatrix was still sitting happily in the highchair, playing with a toy.

'I don't want to go through anything like that again in a hurry,' she declared, running a trembling hand over her face.

'Me neither,' he agreed. Performing CPR was both physically and emotionally draining and it didn't get any easier no matter how many times you were called upon to do it.

'I really thought we were going to lose him at one point,' she said, her voice catching.

'So did I.' Callum put his arm around her, feeling more than a little choked up himself. Now that he had a child of his own, he understood just how awful it must be to lose a precious son or daughter. 'But we didn't, Beth, and it's mainly thanks to you. You did a great job just now. It isn't easy doing both the breathing and the compressions.'

She shook her head. 'No, it was a team effort.'

'We always did make a great team,' Callum said without thinking. It was only when she lifted anguished eyes to his that he realised what he had said, but it was too late to take it back by then. Far too late to pretend that he hadn't meant it either.

'Then why did you leave me, Callum? If we were

such a great team, what made you change your mind about us? I think I deserve to know the answer, don't you?'

The ambulance arrived some thirty minutes later, by which time the little boy, Harley Mitchel, was breathing steadily and seemed none the worse for his adventures. It was obvious that his aunt and uncle were loath to spend the rest of the day at the hospital, but Callum insisted that Harley needed to be checked over. Beth had never heard him take such a tough stance before and it was a surprise, yet why should it be? Callum could be ruthless when the need arose, as she knew to her cost.

The thought sent a shiver of apprehension racing through her as they gathered up their belongings and left. Although she'd been the one to demand an explanation from him, she was no longer sure if she wanted to hear what Callum had to say. After all, what would it achieve at this point? There was no guarantee that it would make the situation any easier, although it could make it a lot worse.

For one thing, she had never even considered the idea that Callum had left her for another woman. They had both lived and worked together, so how would he have found the time for an affair? However, they had started leading separate lives after he had asked her for a divorce and she suddenly wondered if she could have met someone then. Her heart scrunched up inside her because she could imagine how devastated she was going to feel if he told that he had fallen *out* of love with her and *in* love with someone else. By the time they arrived back at the cottage, she was beginning to wish that she had never started this conversation.

'Shall I take Beatrix straight upstairs and bath her?' Callum asked as he carried the little girl inside. He grimaced. 'She's completely worn out after all the excitement today.'

'Please. She can have an early night,' Beth said, struggling to stay calm. Although the idea of Callum loving another woman was terrifying, she would have to deal with it if it turned out to be true. However, there was no denying that it could have a huge bearing on what happened in the future. If he was in love with someone else, and thinking about marrying her, then she needed to know.

It was hard not to panic at the thought of some other woman being added to the equation. She tried to push the thought to the back of her mind as she went into the kitchen to make Beatrix's tea but it was impossible. Even if Callum wasn't involved with anyone at the moment, it could happen in the future.

How did she feel about Beatrix having another family, a stepmother and possibly even half-siblings? What if Beatrix found herself pushed to one side? One heard about such things and it could very well happen. By the time Callum came back downstairs with Beatrix, Beth had worked herself up into a real state. No way was her daughter going to be made to feel that she was second best.

Callum made a pot of coffee while Beth helped Beatrix eat her tea. By tacit consent, neither of them mentioned the subject uppermost in their minds. Beatrix's eyelids were drooping by the time she had finished the last fish finger and Beth sighed.

'I think we'll skip dessert tonight. She's too tired to bother eating it from the look of her.'

'I'll take her up and put her in her cot,' Callum said gruffly.

Beth shivered when she heard the strain in his voice. Was he thinking about their forthcoming conversation? she wondered, sickly. Feeling nervous about what he had to tell her? She knew it was true and it simply intensified her fears. Maybe it was foolish, but it was going to hurt unbearably if he had found someone else.

'I think you'd better.'

Beth dropped a kiss on her daughter's head, feeling all the love welling up inside her. Finding out that she was pregnant after Callum had left had been a huge shock. After everything they had been through to have a baby, it had seemed incredible that it should have happened like that. However, even if Callum had met somebody else, she didn't regret having Beatrix. She was her own little miracle, the child Beth had given up any hope of having.

No matter how painful this situation turned out to be, she was incredibly lucky to have her and she would keep that in mind. When Callum came back downstairs, she turned to face him because there was no point putting it off any longer.

'So, why did you really leave me, Callum? I think it's time you told me the truth.'

Callum picked up the coffee pot even though the last thing he wanted was anything to drink. It was merely a delaying tactic to give him time to work out what he should say. He sighed when it struck him that they had gone way beyond that point now. It was obvious that Beth was determined to get to the bottom of this mystery and no amount of carefully chosen words were going to help.

'Because I thought it was the best thing to do,' he said flatly, putting the pot back on the table. 'Things had become so fraught that I was afraid you could no longer cope.'

'Fraught,' Beth echoed, staring at him. 'I don't understand.'

'Of course you do!' he said hotly, then took a deep breath, knowing that he had to explain his reasons calmly and rationally. Getting upset certainly wouldn't help to convince her that he had done the right thing—the *only* thing possible in the circumstances.

His tone was gentler when he continued, his emotions held strictly in check. 'Getting pregnant had become, well, an obsession for you—you couldn't think about anything else. I was afraid that you wouldn't be able to handle it if it turned out that we could never have a child and that's why I left. With me off the scene, you'd have to stop and think about what you were doing.

'However, if I stayed, we'd be forever trapped on the merry-go-round, forever trying to have the child you longed for. I did it for you, Beth. I did it because I loved you and couldn't bear to watch you ruining your life any more.'

'And you really expect me to believe that?' She

laughed harshly, twin spots of colour burning in her cheeks. 'You left because you loved me and you wanted to save my sanity?'

'I didn't say that,' he began, his heart sinking because this wasn't going at all well.

'Not in so many words, but it's what you meant, Callum. I was *obsessed* with having a child and you thought I wouldn't be able to *cope* if it didn't happen. No wonder you wanted out. I mean, it wasn't as though you were ever that keen for us to have a baby. Oh, you went along with it but it was more to please me than out of any real desire on your part.' She smiled thinly. 'I can understand why you chose to leave when the going got tough.'

'That's not true!' How on earth was he going to convince her that she was wrong? he wondered desperately. He had left for *her* sake and not because he had grown tired of the situation.

'Oh, but I think it is true. You'd had enough and you wanted out. The fact that I got pregnant that last night we slept together is incidental. It certainly doesn't mean that you've changed. You would do the same thing all over again if it suited you.'

'You're wrong, completely wrong. I left for your sake, Beth, not mine, and that's the truth.' He took a deep breath, trying to clamp down on his emotions so that he could convince her. 'If I'd had any idea that you would find yourself pregnant after we slept together that night then I would never have left.'

'I'm sure you wouldn't. You'd have done your duty, wouldn't you, Callum, and stayed? Or at least stayed until the joys of fatherhood started to pall.'

'That would never have happened,' he declared. 'I would never have left you to bring up our child on your own.'

'No?' She shrugged. 'I suppose we'll never know now, will we? I can't prove that you would have left and you can't prove that you would have stayed. However, it does make me see what a risk it would be to ever rely on you again.'

'What do you mean?' he asked, his stomach churning because he had already guessed what she was about to say.

'That allowing you to be part of Beatrix's life is far too dangerous. To be blunt, I don't trust you, Callum, and nothing you've told me tonight has made me change my mind.'

Her voice caught on a sob as emotion suddenly got the better of her and Callum felt a huge great wave of guilt wash over him. He couldn't bear to witness her anguish and know that he was responsible for it. He got up, crouching down in front of her chair. Beth was hurting and all he wanted at that moment was to comfort her.

'Every word I said was true, Beth. I left because I honestly thought it was the best thing to do.' He captured her hands, overwhelmed by tenderness when he realised how small and fragile they felt in his. Everything he had done had been for one reason: to protect her.

His voice was rough when he continued but it was impossible to pretend that he didn't feel anything when he felt so much. 'If I'd had any idea that you were pregnant then I would never have left. I'd have stayed and looked after you, you and our baby.'

'Out of duty,' she repeated brokenly, her eyes welling with tears.

'No. Not out of duty. Because I wanted to.' He drew her into his arms because he simply couldn't see her suffering like this and not do anything about it. Her body felt stiff at first, resisting his attempts to comfort her, and he smiled sadly. Beth could be stubborn at times but there again so could he. Maybe that was why they had been such a perfect match.

The thought seemed to unlock the final barrier as memories of their past life together came flooding back. Although he had been out with a lot of women over the years, he had never felt for them what he had felt for Beth. Marriage had never been high on his agenda but when he'd met her, he had realised that it was what he wanted more than anything. Knowing that Beth was his and that he was hers had felt like a dream come true.

For the first time in his life, he had felt that he had belonged. And then Beth had told him that what she wanted more than anything was for them to have a child and everything had changed.

Sadness welled up inside him as he recalled her heartache when she had failed to conceive and he drew her closer, wanting in some way to make up for what she had suffered. Her body felt so tense as it rested against his, every muscle taut, and his heart ached all the more.

Beth didn't deserve this! She didn't deserve to suffer any more after what she had been through. He ran his hand down her back in an attempt to comfort her, following the rigid line of her spine. When he felt a tremor pass through her, he froze, expecting at any moment that she would push him away. He wasn't prepared when all of a sudden she relaxed against him.

Callum's breath caught when he felt her breasts brushing enticingly against his chest. His hand was shaking as it moved on, feeling the tension seep out of her with each gentle stroke of his fingers. When he reached her waist and paused, she looked up, her eyes holding his in a look that shocked him to the core. Far from wanting him to stop, he could tell she wanted him to continue!

Callum could feel the blood pounding through his veins as his hand slid over the rounded curve of her bottom. Beth didn't say a word but he could feel her nestling against him and the thought that she welcomed his touch was just too much. Bending, he took her mouth in a searing kiss. Her lips felt cool at first but he could feel the heat building beneath the chill, and groaned.

The rational part of his mind knew that he should stop what was happening. Beth was upset and she wasn't thinking clearly, but how could he stop when it was what he wanted so desperately? His tongue traced the outline of her lips and he shuddered when he felt them part for him. He hadn't kissed another woman since they had met and now he understood why. He only wanted Beth: no other woman would do.

The thought filled his head as his tongue mated with hers. When he drew her down onto the rug, she didn't protest. Callum ran his hands down her body, relearning its shape and feel. She was thinner than she had been, although her breasts were fuller, filling his palms when he cupped them in his hands. Undoubtedly, it was the result of giving birth to their daughter and he loved the thought that such a momentous event had caused these changes.

Bending, he drew her nipple into his mouth, lavishing it with love through her cotton blouse, wishing with all his heart that he had been here to watch her nurse their daughter. He had missed so much that was precious, missed making so many wonderful memories. Now all he could do was pray that he wouldn't miss any more.

A chill ran through him at the thought that nothing was guaranteed but even that couldn't dampen his ardour. His body was throbbing for release, but he didn't intend to rush things. He ran his hands down her body again, caressing the sweet, lush curves, before turning his attention to the buttons down the front of her blouse. Surprisingly he managed to undo them without any difficulty and he raised surprised eyes to hers.

'I must be getting better at this,' he said, ruefully, parting the blouse so he could drop a kiss on the warm curve of her breast. 'Buttons were never my forte.'

'It must be all the practice you've had,' she said flatly, and he frowned because that wasn't what he had meant to imply.

'Nope. I can honestly say that I haven't had any practice at all.' He waggled his fingers, opting to make a joke out of it as it made him feel incredibly vulnerable to admit that he hadn't slept with anyone else since they had parted. 'I must have discovered a natural talent somehow or other.'

'Oh.'

An expression of relief crossed her face before she reached up and drew his head down, but Callum had seen it and his heart swelled with joy. Beth was pleased that he hadn't slept with anyone else and it could only mean that she still cared about him. The thought filled his head as he stripped off her blouse and tossed it aside. The plain white bra she was wearing underneath was soon dispensed with as well, along with the rest of her clothes. Callum could feel his heart racing as he stared down at her naked body.

'You're so beautiful,' he whispered, hoarsely. 'So very, very beautiful.'

Beth didn't say a word as she waited for him to remove his clothes but her eyes never left him. Callum could feel her watching him as he dragged his sweater over his head, and shuddered. It was incredibly erotic to know that she enjoyed looking at him, that she wanted him.

He was trembling when he lay down beside her and drew her into his arms, letting her feel just how much he wanted her too. When he ran his hand down her body, seeking out the source of her heat, she shuddered, her breathing turning rapid and shallow as he caressed her. Callum continued to stroke her, his own passion rising until he couldn't hold back any longer. He slid into her with one smooth powerful thrust, felt her tighten around him, and gasped. All of a sudden nothing mattered but this—he and Beth, and the magic they were creating together.

CHAPTER TEN

IT WAS ALMOST midnight when Beth awoke. At some point they had moved upstairs to the bedroom and moonlight was streaming in through the open window. She lay quite still for a moment, savouring the unfamiliar feeling of peace that filled her. What had changed? Was she now willing to believe Callum? To trust him? To accept him as part of her and Beatrix's lives?

'Penny for them. Or are they worth a lot more than that?'

Beth felt her breath catch when Callum spoke. Rolling onto her side, she let her eyes drink in the familiar planes of his face. He had changed very little in the past year, she realised. Oh, there were a few more lines around his eyes, even a touch of silver at his temples, but he was still the most handsome man she had ever seen. Although she'd had a couple of relationships before they had met, she had never felt such desire for anyone else.

Was that why she had made love with him tonight, because she'd needed the fulfilment that only Callum could give her? All of a sudden the doubts came flooding back. Was she in danger of allowing desire to cloud her judgement?

'Beth? What is it? Tell me.'

Reaching out he touched her cheek, and she flinched. The thought that she had made a mistake made her feel sick. Maybe their lovemaking had been wonderful but it hadn't changed anything—not really. Callum was still the same person he had always been, the man who had run out on her. Maybe he had claimed that he had left to protect her, left because he had cared so much about her, but did she believe him? Could she be sure that he wouldn't do the same thing again?

'Nothing.' Beth tossed back the quilt and stood up. Picking up her dressing gown, she dragged it on, uncomfortable now with her nakedness when it just seemed to prove what a fool she had been.

'So that's it, is it?' He laughed shortly as he stood up. 'It's a bit late for second thoughts. You and I made love and there's no way that you can pretend it wasn't what you wanted, either.'

'I wasn't going to!' she retorted, hating to hear the mockery in his voice, especially when she knew that she deserved it. Callum would have stopped any time she had asked him to, but she hadn't wanted him to stop, had she? Colour flooded her face at the thought, but she refused to justify herself by lying. 'I'm as much to blame for what happened tonight as you are, Callum, but we both know it was a mistake. You and I are history and there's no way that we're going to get back together.'

'So tonight was what exactly? Some kind of nod to the past?'

'I doubt it. Let's face it, there's not a lot about the past that either of us would want to remember.' She shrugged, aiming for a nonchalance she wished she felt. 'No, it was nothing more than a combination of circumstances. I was upset, you tried to comfort me, and one thing led to another. We're both adults, Callum. We both know that these things happen. It's nothing to get worked up about.'

'I'm glad you can be so reasonable about it,' he said flatly, pulling his sweater over his head. 'Just so long as it doesn't have a knock-on effect.'

'What do you mean by that?' Beth asked, frowning.

'That you don't use what happened tonight to stop me seeing Beatrix.' He looked her straight in the eyes. 'As you just pointed out, we're both adults and this shouldn't have any bearing on my being allowed to see her.'

'I...um...no, of course not,' Beth murmured, her heart sinking at the thought of being put on the spot this way. If she refused him access then he would think that it was because of what had happened tonight, and she didn't want that hanging over her. She wanted to forget what they had done and not be constantly reminded about it. 'You can see Beatrix whenever you want, although I don't think you need to stay here any longer now that my ankle is so much better.'

'Of course not.' Callum slipped on his shoes, his expression impossible to read in the moonlight. 'In that case, I'll sleep at the flat tonight, if that's all right with you. I'm sure we could both do with a bit of breathing space.'

'It's fine,' Beth assured him, although the thought of him moving out of the cottage was upsetting for some reason. She forced herself to focus on practicalities as it seemed safer than looking for explanations. After all, Callum had never planned to stay here on a permanent basis and she wouldn't have wanted him to, either. 'What about your clothes and everything?'

'I'll collect them tomorrow. It's a bit late to start packing at this time of the night.'

'Of course.' Beth followed him out to the landing, knowing that she should say something. 'I appreciate everything you've done for us recently. Thank you.'

He gave a little shrug. 'I was happy to help, Beth. After all, Beatrix is my daughter too.'

He didn't say anything else as he ran down the stairs and a moment later Beth heard the front door open and close again. She bit her lip as she went back into the bedroom and stared at the rumpled sheets. She could think of a dozen different reasons why she had made love with Callum tonight but in her heart she knew that only one of them was true: she had wanted him. Tears filled her eyes because now she would have to get used to being without him all over again.

Callum did his best but it was impossible to blot out the memory of that night. What made it worse was that Beth had now returned to work. With Sandra back as well, it meant that Beth was working at The Larches and it was pure torture to have to see her each day. If she had left him with even the tiniest shred of hope that their lovemaking had meant anything to her then it might have made it easier, but he didn't even have that consolation. Beth had made it perfectly clear how she felt about what had happened.

He threw himself into his work in the hope that it would help if he kept busy. The outbreak of chickenpox had spread throughout the area and the surgery was busier than ever. It was the start of the new school year and almost half the pupils were absent as so many had gone down with the virus. They were inundated with phone calls from anxious parents and, in the end, he put together an information file, explaining the symptoms and how best to treat them, and posted it on the surgery's website. It helped a bit but there were still far more people than usual requesting home visits.

They took it in turns to go out on calls and he had to admit that he welcomed the opportunity to escape from the surgery. Although Beth was unfailingly polite whenever they needed to speak, there was a definite atmosphere when they were together. Callum knew that the others had noticed it too, but, mercifully, nobody asked him what was going on. Quite frankly, he would have been hard-pressed to come up with an explanation that he wanted to share.

He was on his way to a couple of calls when Marie popped her head round his door. 'There's someone on the phone who wants to speak to you urgently,' she explained. 'I didn't catch his name because the line's terrible—that's why I didn't want to risk transferring the call to you. He did say that he was from the agency, though, if that's any help.'

'Really?' Callum exclaimed, following her back to the reception desk. He picked up the phone, wincing when he was greeted by an ear-splitting series of crackles. 'I see what you mean,' he began then stopped when someone spoke at the other end. It was a colleague from Worlds Together, the aid agency he had worked for, and his heart sank when he discovered what the other man wanted. Apparently, one of their key workers had been taken ill and they desperately needed someone experienced to take charge of their next mission: would Callum do it?

Callum hung up a few minutes later in a real quandary. Heaven only knew what Beth would say if he went flying out to Africa, even if it was only for a couple of weeks. However, if he refused to go then the trip would have to be called off and that would cause a major disruption, not to mention the loss of a great deal of money. He groaned. Talk about being stuck between a rock and a hard place!

'So how are you, Diane? Although I don't think I really need to ask you that. You're positively blooming.'

Beth drummed up a laugh as Diane Applethwaite sat down in front of her desk. It was the monthly antenatal clinic and Diane was her last patient that afternoon. Normally, Beth enjoyed seeing the new mums but she was finding it hard to concentrate that day and it was all down to Callum. She had bumped into him as he was on his way out to do some home visits and he had asked her if he could have a word with her when he got back. She had no idea what it was about, but, knowing what had happened the last time they had had a serious conversation, it was little wonder that her internal alarm bells were ringing like mad.

'I feel marvellous, but then I always do when I'm pregnant,' Diane assured her. 'That's probably why Phil and I had so many children, although this little one has come as a complete surprise.'

'So how did your husband take the news?' Beth asked, trying not to think about that night. So she and Callum had made love—so what? As she had told him at the time, they were both adults and it was nothing to get worked up about. She sighed as she unravelled the sphygmomanometer cuff so she could check Diane's blood pressure, wishing that she actually believed that. 'Was he pleased?'

'Once he got over the shock, he was.' Diane laughed. 'I don't expect Phil thought we'd have another one at our age but, as I pointed out to him, we didn't do anything to stop it.'

Beth managed to smile but there was a sinking feeling in the pit of her stomach all of a sudden. She and Callum hadn't taken precautions the other night either, so was it possible that she might be pregnant? It was hard to hide her dismay as she finished the examination and saw Diane out. Polly had been talking to one of her new mums, working out a birthing plan with her, and she looked up when she saw Diane leaving.

'Is that it then? I think Diane was our last patient.'

'I...er...yes, she was.' Beth went back into her room and sank down on the chair, afraid that her legs were about to give way. Although she had always wanted more than one child, how did she feel about having another baby in these circumstances? More importantly, how would Callum feel about it?

'Are you all right? You look awfully pale, Beth. Shall I fetch you a drink of water?' Polly offered in concern as she followed her into the room.

'I don't think water's going to help,' Beth muttered, closing her eyes in despair. How could she have been so stupid not to have thought about the risk before now? She could have done something about it if she had, taken the morning-after pill and made sure that she wouldn't get pregnant again by accident as she had done with Beatrix. Now it was far too late for that.

'Is it Callum?' Polly asked quietly. She sighed when Beth nodded. 'I thought you two were getting along all right these days, so what's he done now?'

'It's not what he's done—it's what we've both done.' Beth shook her head. 'I can't believe we were so stupid!'

'Tell me to mind my own business if you want, Beth, but if there's anything I can do to help then just say so.'

'There's nothing anyone can do,' Beth replied brokenly. She bit her lip but the need to tell someone was too strong to resist. 'Callum and I...well, we slept together a few weeks ago.'

'You did? But that's good, surely? Especially if it means you're thinking about getting back together,' Polly declared.

'We're not. It was a mistake and it should never

have happened.' Beth put her head in her hands and groaned. 'The thing is that we didn't take any precautions and now I don't know if I might be pregnant.'

'Oh. I can see how awkward that would be,' Polly said, sitting down. 'Have you done a test yet?'

'No. I've only just thought about it,' Beth admitted. 'I can't believe I was so *stupid*!'

'There's no point beating yourself up,' Polly said firmly. 'You need to find out if you're pregnant first and then decide what you're going to do about it.'

'I don't think I could go through with a termination.' Beth felt tears well to her eyes. 'After everything we went through to have a child, I really couldn't do that.'

'That's something only you can decide, Beth.' Polly stood up. 'I'll go and get a pregnancy testing kit from the pharmacy.' She shook her head when Beth went to speak. 'Don't worry—I'll tell them it's for one of my mums. Nobody needs to know anything until you're sure what's happening.'

Polly hurried from the room, leaving Beth in the throes of despair. The thought that even now there might be a new life growing inside her should have filled her with joy but all she could think about was how Callum would react. While there was no doubt that he loved Beatrix, it that didn't mean he would welcome another child into his life, especially when there was no chance of them getting back together.

'Beth? Am I disturbing you? Only I need to have a word with you.'

Beth's head shot up in panic when she heard Callum's voice. 'I'm just waiting for Polly,' she said quickly, using the first excuse that sprang to mind. The last thing she needed at this moment was to have to talk to him.

'That's all right. It won't take long.' He came into the room and she felt her nerves tighten even more when she saw how serious he looked. She had a feeling that she wasn't going to like what he had to say, but before she could attempt to prepare herself, he carried on.

'There's no point me beating about the bush. The agency phoned today. They're sending a team out to Africa tomorrow but the team leader has been taken ill and is unable to go. It will cause chaos if they have to call it off at this late stage, not to mention the fact that a great deal of money will be lost if they have to re-book the flights.' He shrugged. 'Basically, I've agreed to go along.'

Callum could tell that the news hadn't gone down well but it was no more than he had expected. Beth had made no bones about her doubts as to his commitment to Beatrix and to his new life here, and this must confirm all her fears. He opened his mouth to explain that he would only be away for a couple of weeks but just as that moment Polly appeared.

'Oh, sorry! I didn't know you were here, Callum.'

She started to back out of the room but Callum beckoned her to come in. Quite frankly, he was sick and tired of being seen as the bad guy all the time: Mr Unreliable. If Beth wasn't convinced by now that he was serious about sticking around then she never would be.

'Don't leave on my account,' he said flatly, avoiding Beth's eyes. He didn't need to see the contempt they held to know it was there and the thought was so bitter that he had to wait a beat before he could continue. 'I've said what I came to say and that's it. I'll see you when I get back, Beth.'

He swung round, holding himself rigid as he made his way to his room. The urge to go back and beg her to understand that he'd had no choice in the matter was overwhelming, but he mustn't do it. Beth had to trust him. She had to know in her own heart that he would never let Beatrix down. He couldn't force her to feel that way: it had to come from inside her. And if it never happened then there was nothing he could do about it.

The thought that she might always doubt him hurt like hell but he knew that he had to accept it, somehow. He had already spoken to Daniel and received his blessing, so once he had handed Marie his notes, he left the surgery and went up to the flat. It didn't take him long to pack. He'd done it so many times before that he knew exactly what to take. Anyway, it wasn't what he was taking with him that mattered this time, but what he was leaving behind.

Callum took a deep breath, struggling to control the agony he felt. He was going to miss Beatrix so much while he was away and he was going to miss Beth too. Even if she didn't believe in him, she was the woman he loved with all his heart and it was going to be pure torture to be without her.

The test proved negative. Beth was overwhelmed with relief when she realised that she wasn't pregnant after all. After Callum's announcement, having another baby would have been a complete disaster. She told Polly the good news, cutting short her friend's attempts to talk about Callum's forthcoming absence. As far as she was concerned, there was nothing to talk about. Callum was simply behaving true to form.

The thought weighed heavily on her as she cleared up. It was her early finish so once she had collected Beatrix, she went straight home and set about the nightly routine. It was after seven before she allowed herself to think about what Callum had told her and her heart started to ache with a mixture of pain and disappointment. Even though she'd had her doubts all along about his commitment, it was still hard to face up to the fact that he had chosen his old life over their daughter.

It made her see that it would be a huge mistake to continue allowing him to have access to Beatrix. It was bad enough that he was leaving her now, but how much worse would it be the next time, when Beatrix was older and more aware of what was happening?

The thought of her daughter's confusion was more than Beth could bear. She knew only too well how it felt to be abandoned by the person you loved and she refused to let her daughter go through that kind of heartache. Once Callum came back then she would make it clear that he wasn't welcome any longer. Hopefully, he would have the sense to leave Beesdale for good then, and not put them through any more stress. Pain shot through her at the thought of never seeing him again, but she knew it was what she needed to do. It was better to put an end to it now than run the risk of Beatrix getting hurt even more in the future.

Callum couldn't sleep. He kept going over what he had said to Beth or, rather, what he hadn't said. Why in heaven's name hadn't he explained that he would only be away for a couple of weeks and that once the agency found someone else to take over, he would return to England? Why hadn't he reassured her that once he came back, he wouldn't go away again? He had already made it clear to the agency that this would be his last assignment but he had been too damned stubborn to explain all that to Beth. Too stubborn or just too proud!

He got up, pacing the floor as he tried to decide what to do. Should he go to see her and explain it all to her now? But would she listen to him? That was the question? He sighed wearily because he doubted it. Beth had made up her mind about him from the moment he had come back to Beesdale and he would be a fool to imagine that she was willing to give him the benefit of the doubt. He had left her: ergo he would leave their daughter too.

It was painful to have to face it, but what was even more upsetting was the fact that he had thought he was making some progress. Even after they had made love that night, she had allowed him to carry on seeing Beatrix, but would she let him see their daughter when he got back from this trip? He didn't think so! He would be right back to square one, and this time it would be even harder to convince her to trust him.

The thought made up his mind. He had to make Beth understand why he had agreed to go.

Callum dragged on his clothes and left the flat. It was after midnight and there was no traffic about as he drove to the cottage. He drew up outside, feeling his nerves jangling when he saw that the sitting room light was on. Was Beth still up, thinking about what had happened, about the way he had seemingly confirmed all her worst fears? He knew it was true and the thought of how difficult it was going to be to make her understand why he was doing this made him feel sick. He got out of the car and knocked on the door, feeling his heart start to race when she opened it.

'I wanted to explain,' he said softly, wishing she would say something rather than stand there, staring at him.

'What is there to explain?' She smiled thinly and he winced when he saw the contempt in her eyes. 'The lure of the job proved too much to resist. It must be far more exciting working overseas than working here.'

'You're completely wrong.' Callum took a deep breath to damp down the anger that shot through him at the knowledge that she thought he was so fickle. 'I only agreed to go because they were desperate for someone to take charge. I told you, if I don't go then the trip will have to be called off and that will cost the agency a great deal of money they can't afford to lose. It's only for two weeks and then I'll be back.'

'So it's Dr O'Neill to the rescue?' Her laughter echoed with scorn. 'How wonderful it must be to know that you're such a hero.'

'I'm not a hero,' he said through gritted teeth. 'I am merely doing what I think is right.'

'And you're very good at that, aren't you, Callum?'

'Meaning?'

'Meaning that you're very good at doing what's right.' She shrugged when he didn't reply. 'You left me because you thought it was the right thing to do, and now you're going on this assignment.' She gave a harsh little laugh. 'Not many people are as sure as you that they're doing the right thing. I know I'm not.'

'I can't believe that.' It was his turn to laugh now, although there was a hollow feeling in his stomach. Nothing he said was going to persuade her to trust him. 'You seem pretty sure about me, Beth. In fact, you don't appear to have any doubts at all that you might be wrong about me.'

'You haven't given me any reason to,' she shot back.

'No? So you don't believe that I love Beatrix and want only what's best for her?' He carried on when she didn't answer. 'Don't let your feelings about what happened between us blind you to the truth. I love our daughter and I would never hurt her. I think you know that, only you're too afraid to admit it.'

There was nothing else he could think of to say. Callum drove back to the flat and fetched his bag then went out to the car. It was far too early to catch his train so he would drive down to London instead. It would be better than lying in bed, thinking about Beth and what else he should and shouldn't have said. It was down to her now, although if she thought she could use this trip to cut him out of Beatrix's life then she was mistaken.

His mouth thinned. He was going to be a proper father to his daughter—with or without Beth's blessing!

CHAPTER ELEVEN

'I THINK IT may have been a TIA,' Beth said gently, looking at the middle-aged couple sitting in front of her desk. Penny and Michael Halthorpe had been rushed into the surgery by their son. They had been at a family gathering, celebrating their twenty-fifth wedding anniversary, when Michael had been taken ill, so she could appreciate what a shock this must be for them. 'A transient ischaemic attack—a kind of mini-stroke, in other words.'

'A stroke,' Penny echoed. 'My dad had a stroke and he was never the same...' She tailed off, too upset to continue.

Beth sighed softly. Michael Halthorpe ran the local building firm and he was well known in the town. It was a family concern and his son, Alistair, worked with him while Penny dealt with the paperwork. They were currently working on an extension to the junior school, adding an extra classroom as well as a new gymnasium.

This was going to be a blow for them on many levels and she chose her words with care. 'You said that you realised something was wrong when Michael spilled your drink—is that right, Penny?'

'Yes. We'd gone to The Fleece for lunch, you see. Everyone was there—our son, Alistair, and Cathy, our daughter-in-law, the grandchildren, Michael's parents. There was wine on the table but I wanted a soft drink so Michael went to the bar. It was as he was on his way back that I noticed he was holding the glass so that the tonic water was spilling out. Someone made a remark about him being one over the eight but I knew it wasn't that. Then when he sat down, he couldn't lift his hand up onto the table. That's when Alistair said that he'd drive us here to the surgery.'

'Which was exactly the right thing to do,' Beth assured her. She turned and smiled at Michael. 'So how do you feel now? Can you raise your arm?'

He shook his head. 'No. I keep trying but it still won't work properly.'

'Don't worry about it.' She could tell that his speech was a little bit slurred as well but, apart from that, he appeared relatively well. 'I've given you the recommended amount of high-dose aspirin and now it's simply a case of waiting for the ambulance to get here. They'll run a series of tests at the hospital to check if it was a TIA and then they'll put you on medication to prevent it happening again.'

'They can do that?' Penny exclaimed.

'They can indeed. It's very different these days from when your father had his stroke,' Beth explained. 'There's a range of medication that can and does work wonders.'

'Thank heavens.' Penny closed her eyes in sheer

relief at hearing that. Michael used his good hand to reach for hers.

'You're not getting rid of me that easily,' he declared, smiling at his wife with such love in his eyes that Beth felt a lump come to her throat. Once upon a time she had thought that she and Callum had the kind of relationship that would last a lifetime but she'd been wrong. He'd got bored after only a few years of being married to her.

It was a painful thought so it was a relief when Marie knocked on the door and ushered in the paramedics. Michael and Penny went in the ambulance, with their son following on in his car. The emergency had set her back so it was way past the time she should have finished before Beth had seen everyone.

She hurried out to her car, not wanting to be late collecting Beatrix. The little girl had been very unsettled recently, crying when Beth left her each morning. Although she knew that a lot of children went through a clingy stage, Beatrix seemed very unsettled at home too and she could only put it down to one thing: her baby was missing Callum.

Beth's mouth compressed as she drove out of the surgery. Callum had been gone for three weeks now and she'd had no contact with him since he had left. It shouldn't have come as a surprise. After all, he was doing what he loved best and he didn't have time to worry about his daughter or anyone else. However, if he thought he could get away with such behaviour, he was mistaken. When he came back then she intended to make it clear that there was no place for him in Beatrix's life.

* * *

Callum had never felt so frustrated in his life. So far the agency had failed to find a replacement for him so he'd been forced to stay on far longer than he had expected. Add to that the fact that they were working in one of the remotest areas of the planet, which made communications virtually impossible, and he was consumed with impatience.

He could just imagine what Beth must be thinking. Not only had he gone haring off to the other side of the globe, but he hadn't even bothered to get in touch with her and he hadn't returned when he'd said he would. If she'd had doubts about his suitability as a parent before this, they must have multiplied a hundredfold!

When word finally came that a replacement had been found, he was overjoyed. He packed up and made the long journey back to the capital where he wasted another couple of precious days hanging around the airport after his flight was cancelled. Eventually, he was on his way and arrived back at Heathrow in the early hours of the morning. He collected his car from the car park and set off. Although it was a long drive up to Yorkshire, all he wanted was to get home.

His heart lurched as the word slid into his head. He had never really considered anywhere as home before. Being sent away to school at such a young age had made it difficult to put down roots. Even after he and Beth had married and he had moved to the Dales, he had found it hard.

However, somewhere in the past couple of months

Beesdale had laid claim to him, although maybe it wasn't the town so much as the people who lived there, he realised suddenly. He had missed Beth and Beatrix so much while he had been away and he knew how empty his life would be without them. Even if Beth still had doubts about him, he had to find a way to convince her that all he wanted was to be with her and their daughter for the rest of his days.

Callum could feel his heart racing as he joined the motorway. He knew it was going to be extremely hard to make Beth trust him but he was determined to do so, determined that he would speak to her that very day. After all, she had trusted him enough to sleep with him, even though she had claimed later that it hadn't meant anything. He frowned. All of a sudden he didn't believe it. It was completely out of character for her to do such a thing. Beth would *never* have slept with him if she hadn't felt something for him!

The thought buoyed him up so that he barely noticed the miles passing. It was early morning when he reached Beesdale and there was a lot of traffic about. He slowed down as he approached the school. As well as parents dropping off their children, there was a truck delivering building materials for the new extension and he waited while it backed into the playground. Although the area around the site of the extension had been fenced off, children were entering the school through the main doors a few yards away.

Callum frowned when he saw the truck suddenly lurch backwards. To his mind, the driver was going far too fast and needed to slow down. The thought had barely crossed his mind when there was an almighty crash as the rear of the truck struck the building. Metal supports flew in all directions as they were ripped away and he gasped in horror when he saw the gable end of the old Victorian building start to give way. Huge blocks of stone began to rain down onto the playground as he leapt out of his car and ran across the road.

'Someone call the emergency services,' he shouted, running over to the truck. The cab had been partly crushed by the falling masonry and he could just make out the driver, slumped over the wheel. He climbed up to the cab and felt for the man's pulse but he couldn't find one. There was nothing he could do for him so he climbed back down and ran over to a woman who had a deep cut on her cheek. Taking a clean handkerchief out of his pocket, he pressed it against the cut to stem the bleeding then called over a man who was standing nearby.

'Keep putting pressure on it until the bleeding stops. It'll need stitching so make sure the paramedics see her when the ambulances get here.'

Callum moved on, checking the rest of the casualties who had been in the playground. Thankfully, nobody appeared to be badly injured, although one elderly man had a broken arm. He used a borrowed scarf to stabilise it then turned his attention to those inside the school. Some of the workmen from the site had started to clear a path to the main entrance, which had been blocked by falling stones. There was a young man directing operations and Callum hurried over to him.

'I need to get inside to see if anyone's been injured,' he explained.

'I'm not sure if that's possible,' the younger man replied. 'Some of those blocks of stone are barely holding in place and they could shift at any moment. I'm Alistair Halthorpe. It's my family's firm that is doing the building work.' He shot a worried glance at the truck. 'What about Ken, the truck driver? He and my dad have been friends for years...' He tailed off when Callum shook his head.

'Sorry. I'm afraid he didn't make it.' He waited a beat then continued, knowing that they didn't have time to grieve for the driver if they were to help the people trapped inside the building. 'Is there another way in?'

'There is, but it's in an even worse state than this.' Alistair made an obvious effort to collect himself as he led Callum around the building and pointed to what had been the back entrance. Callum's heart sank when he discovered that it had been completely blocked when part of the roof had caved in.

'There's no way you can get in that way—we won't be able to shift those beams for a start,' Alistair told him. 'We'll have to wait for the fire and rescue teams to get here. They'll have heavy lifting gear with them.'

'But how long will that take?' Callum shook his head. 'We can't afford to wait. If anyone's been seriously injured then they need help now. If we could manage to clear a passageway through the rubble then maybe I can get inside.'

They went back to the front of the building. News

of what had happened had spread and there was a large crowd milling about now. More men had joined the team shifting the stones away from the entrance and Callum went to help them. It was hard going but in a fairly short time a narrow passage had been opened up. Callum ran over to his car for his bag then hurried back and knelt down. There was just enough room for him to crawl through if he was careful.

'Try not to knock against any of those stones,' Alistair instructed, handing Callum a hard hat. 'One wrong move and the whole lot could fall on top of you.'

'That's reassuring to know,' Callum replied, drolly. He eased himself forward, taking his time so that he wouldn't inadvertently set off a landslide. It was highly uncomfortable crawling over the rough surface but he kept going until he reached the end of the passageway. There was a woman there, her face grey with worry, and she helped him to his feet.

'Thank heavens!' she exclaimed. 'I didn't know how long it would be before the emergency services arrived.'

'I'm afraid they aren't here yet,' Callum told her. 'It's just me for now. I'm Dr O'Neill from the surgery. Is anyone badly injured?'

'I'm Mrs Goulding, the head teacher,' the woman informed him, leading the way along the corridor. 'A couple of the children were hit by stones but, thankfully, they're more shocked than anything else. Mr Benson is my main concern. Nick was knocked out when a lump of stone fell on him. He's regained consciousness now but he seems rather confused.'

'I'll take a look at him first,' Callum said, his heart sinking. If the man had suffered a head injury then he would need immediate treatment at the hospital.

'He's in here. I know you're not supposed to move a casualty but I was worried in case the rest of the gable end came down, so we put him in the office. One of the other teachers is with him.'

Mrs Goulding opened the door and ushered Callum inside. He went straight over to the young man propped up against the desk and knelt down. 'I'm Dr O'Neill,' he explained, opening his bag and taking out a small torch. 'Mrs Goulding tells me that you've had a bang on the head.'

'That's right.' Nick Benson winced as he touched his temple. 'Something must have hit me, although I don't really remember what happened, if I'm honest.'

Callum's heart sank that bit more when he realised how slurred the other man's speech sounded. 'How long was he unconscious?' he asked, shining the torch into Nick Benson's eyes. Although the left pupil reacted normally to the light, the right one was very sluggish, an indication that Nick had concussion.

'About five minutes, although it could have been longer,' the young woman teacher, who had been delegated to sit with him, replied shakily. 'We were more concerned about getting the children to safety, you see, so it was a while before anyone realised that Nick had been hurt.'

'I see.' Callum nodded. 'I want you to keep a close eye on him. If his condition changes in any way, i.e. he lapses into unconsciousness again or has difficulty speaking, then I want you to come and get me straight away.'

The young woman nodded, obviously appreciating the seriousness of the situation. Callum followed Mrs Goulding out of the office and along the corridor to the hall where the children were gathered. An area in the corner had been cleared and he could see half a dozen or so children sitting there, along with a couple of mothers who must have been in the school when the accident had occurred. He was surprised when he spotted Polly amongst them.

'What are you doing here?' he asked, going over to her.

'I was dropping Joseph off,' she explained, looking equally surprised to see him. 'How about you? When did you get back?'

'First thing this morning,' Callum told her, and grimaced. 'I drove straight up here and was outside when the accident happened.'

'Does Beth know you're back?' Polly asked.

'No. I was going to surprise her, although whether it would have been a pleasant surprise is debatable,' he added wearily.

'Don't give up.' Polly smiled at him. 'No matter what Beth says, I know she cares about you, Callum. More than cares, in fact.'

Callum didn't get chance to say anything because Mrs Goulding interrupted them just then. However, as he followed the head teacher over to where a little girl was sobbing noisily, his heart was racing. Was it true? Did Beth care about him? He had no idea but he intended to find out as soon as he could.

* * *

Beth didn't hear about the accident until she went into work. Everyone was talking about it and she frowned in consternation. 'Was anyone badly injured?'

'Nobody knows yet,' Marie told her. 'Apparently, the children are still inside the school and they're having to wait for the emergency services to arrive. From what I can gather, it's too dangerous to try to get them out without the proper equipment.'

'How awful!' Beth exclaimed. 'Is there anything we can do?'

'Daniel's gone down there to find out. He said he'd phone and let us know what's happening...' Marie broke off when the telephone rang. She snatched up the receiver, listening intently to what was being said. 'That was Daniel. The fire and rescue teams have just arrived,' she explained after she'd hung up. 'They're going to shore up the building and make it safe. It appears that both entrances are blocked so they're going to get the children out through the windows.'

'Thank heavens for that.' Beth shuddered at the thought of the children being trapped inside. 'What does Daniel want us to do? Did he say?'

'Carry on as normal. Any minor injuries can be treated here while anything more serious will need to be ferried to the hospital,' Marie told her.

'Right, that's what we'll do then.'

Beth went to her room, wondering how many people had been injured. At least the emergency services were on site now and that would help. She saw a couple of patients then attended to a little girl who had been cut on the arm when a slate had dropped off the school's roof and hit her. Thankfully, the cut wasn't deep and only required butterfly stitches to hold it together.

By midday she had seen and treated at least a dozen more minor injuries. The children and their teachers had all been safely evacuated from the building now but she decided not to go for lunch in case she was needed. She was just making herself a cup of coffee when Polly appeared.

'Have you heard about the accident?' she asked, over her shoulder.

'Yes. I was there when it happened, in fact,' Polly replied.

'Really?' Beth swung round and stared at her friend in dismay. 'Are you all right?'

'I'm fine, so's Joseph. He thought it was great fun when the fireman carried him down the ladder to get him out.'

'Where is he now?' Beth asked, frowning.

'Waiting in the car.' Polly took a deep breath then hurried on. 'I'm about to take him home but I wanted to let you know something first. Callum's still inside the school. Apparently, one of the staff has been quite badly injured and he's stayed with him.'

'Callum? But he's in Africa,' Beth protested, unable to take it in.

'He got back in the early hours of this morning and drove straight up here,' Polly explained, then shrugged. 'I got the distinct impression that he was keen to see you, Beth.'

'I doubt it,' Beth said shortly.

'Why won't you give him a chance?' Polly held

up her hand when Beth opened her mouth. 'I know what you're going to say, that he let you down and you can't trust him not to do it again. But it's obvious that he cares about you otherwise he wouldn't have come haring back here as fast as he could.'

'So he cares, does he? Well, he has a funny way of showing it, that's all I can say.' Beth bit her lip when she felt tears well to her eyes. Even though she knew it was ridiculous, it had hurt to be ignored again. 'He never even bothered to contact me while he was away, not even to ask about Beatrix.'

'There could be a very good reason for that,' Polly pointed out. 'I mean, we have enough problems getting a signal at times, and we live in *Yorkshire*, not the depths of Africa!' She sighed. 'All I'm saying, Beth, is don't cut off your nose to spite your face. You'll only regret it.'

Beth picked up her mug of coffee after Polly left and took it back to her room. Was Polly right? Should she give Callum the benefit of the doubt? She took a sip of the hot liquid, thinking back over what had happened since he had first returned to Beesdale.

He had done everything he possibly could to convince her that he was serious about wanting to be a proper father to Beatrix, hadn't he? It was obvious that he loved Beatrix and that Beatrix loved him too, so why couldn't she accept that? Why wouldn't she trust him? Because it wasn't enough to know that he loved their daughter when she wanted him to love her too? Love her as much as she loved him?

All of sudden, she could see the situation clearly. She had never stopped loving him. Even when he had told her that he'd wanted a divorce, it hadn't changed how she felt about him. Oh, she had been hurt and angry but she had still loved him. That was why she had made love with him the night Beatrix was conceived. It was also why she had made love with him a few weeks ago. She loved him with every fibre of her being and knowing how she felt terrified her.

But Callum had never set out to upset her. What he had told her was true. He had left because he had been afraid for *her*. He had only asked her for a divorce because he had honestly thought it was the best thing he could do to protect her. How blind she had been not to understand all that before!

Beth stood up, her legs shaking as she hurried from the room. She didn't bother with her car but ran out of the surgery and along the road. All she could think about was Callum trapped inside the school. From what she could gather, there was every likelihood that it would collapse, and if that happened then she might never get the chance to tell him how she felt, how much she loved him.

The thought lent wings to her feet so that it took only minutes to reach the school. Barriers had been set up to keep people away and her heart raced when she saw the grim expressions on the faces of the firemen who were attempting to stabilise the building. All of a sudden there was a warning shout and she gasped in horror when she saw the front wall of the building start to bow out. Then with a tremendous roar, it collapsed. Beth pressed her hand to her mouth. Somewhere beneath all that rubble was Callum.

CHAPTER TWELVE

CALLUM WAS CHECKING Nick Benson's vital signs when he felt the building suddenly tremble. Nick had lapsed into unconsciousness again and Callum knew how urgent it was that they get him to hospital as soon as possible. If Nick had suffered a bleed on his brain, as Callum suspected, then pressure would be building inside his skull and he would need an operation to relieve it. Although it wasn't ideal to move him in this condition, Callum knew that he had no choice. He had to find a place that would provide them with some degree of protection if the building collapsed.

Looping Nick's arm over his shoulder, he half-dragged and half-carried him out of the office. He had no idea of the layout of the school but it seemed wiser to move away from the front of the building. Nick felt like a dead weight as he hauled him along the corridor, glancing into the classrooms as he passed, but none of them were suitable. He came to the kitchen and paused. Although the worktops would afford them very little protection, there was a walk-in refrigerator that might just do the job.

Callum didn't waste any more time debating its

merits. He dragged Nick across the kitchen and bundled him into the fridge, slamming the door behind them. He was only just in time too as there was a loud groaning noise followed by a mighty roar as the building collapsed. Callum could hear stone raining down all around them and flinched, expecting at any moment that they would be crushed by falling masonry.

He could scarcely believe it when the noise finally stopped and he and Nick were unharmed. Forcing open the door, he gasped when he saw the state of the kitchen. Everything had been destroyed and it was hard to believe that the refrigerator was still intact.

Leaving Nick in the relative safety of the refrigerator, Callum squeezed out of the door. Although it would be safer to wait there until the rescue team came to find them, he needed to get Nick to hospital. It wasn't easy finding his way through all the rubble and several times he had to retrace his steps when the way ahead was blocked, but finally he could hear voices up ahead.

He hurried towards them, so intent on getting help for Nick that he never noticed the broken beam dangling from what remained of the roof. He was directly underneath it when it fell, catching him squarely across his upper back. He slumped, face down, onto what had been the floor, hearing the anxious voices of the rescue team as they clustered around him.

'Nick…in the kitchen,' he managed to murmur. 'In the fridge….'

Blackness suddenly rose up to claim him and the last thing he saw before he slid into unconsciousness was Beth's face. A wave of sadness washed over him. Now he wouldn't get the chance to tell her how much he loved her.

It was the worst time of Beth's entire life. She went with Callum in the ambulance as it rushed him to hospital. Although he had regained consciousness, she wasn't able to talk to him because the paramedics were too busy checking his vital signs. All she could do was try to make sure he knew that she was there, although he was so woozy from the pain relief he'd been given that she doubted if he had registered the fact. He was taken straight to Resus and she was asked to wait outside. She paced the corridor, wondering when someone would come and tell her how he was.

It seemed like a lifetime had passed before the consultant appeared and her heart lurched when she saw how grave he looked.

'How is he?' she demanded. 'Do you know the full extent of his injuries yet?'

'No. We'll know more after he's had a scan.' The consultant led her into a side room. Beth sank down onto a chair, biting her lip as he continued. It wouldn't help if she gave in to the fear bubbling away inside her. 'As you know, the beam caught him across the upper back. There's extensive swelling in the area so it's difficult to tell how much damage has been done. I'll need to see the results of the MRI scan before I have a clearer idea.'

'So you don't know if he's suffered any spinal damage,' she said, her voice catching as she expressed her worst fear.

'No,' he replied. 'However, let's not assume the worst before we know what's going on.'

Beth stood up after he left, unable to sit there while she waited for news. Her heart caught because she couldn't bear to think that Callum might have suffered life-changing injuries. She took a deep breath, forcing down the panic. They would cross that bridge *if* and *when* they came to it. Right now she had to stay strong for Callum's sake.

Callum tried to keep a grip on the panic that filled him as he waited for the results of the scan but it wasn't easy. The thought that he might not be able to walk again was unbearable. He tried wriggling his toes but he couldn't tell if they had actually moved or not. His body felt numb from the shoulders down, plus he was still strapped to the spinal board, which made movement virtually impossible. Footsteps approached the bed and his heart started to race as he tried to prepare himself for bad news. When a figure loomed into view, it was a moment before he realised it was Beth.

'What are you doing here?' he exclaimed.

'I came in the ambulance with you—don't you remember?' She placed her hand over his and Callum felt his heart surge with relief and a whole lot of other emotions when he felt the warmth of her fingers on his. He could feel her touching him and that had to be a good sign, surely? He was still getting to grips with that thought when she bent and kissed him on the lips then drew back.

'I love you, Callum, and no matter what happens from here on, I want to be with you.'

Callum felt a wave of despair wash over him. It was what he had longed to hear her say but the circumstances were very different now. What if she was only saying that because she felt sorry for him and thought that he was going to need looking after? The thought was more than he could bear.

'I don't need your sympathy, thank you very much,' he snapped. He could tell that she was hurt by his response but better that than her thinking that she had to sacrifice herself for his sake.

'I'm not offering you sympathy,' she said, her eyes shimmering with unshed tears. 'I'm telling you how I feel, how I've *always* felt. I love you, Callum, and that's the truth, even if you don't believe me.'

'I don't.' He smiled thinly, deliberately hardening his heart because it was what he had to do. No way would he allow her to waste her life taking care of him. 'I think you're confusing pity with love, Beth, but, no, thank you. I'm not that desperate.'

Callum felt his insides twist with pain when she turned away. He longed to call her back and apologise but how could he? If it did turn out that he wouldn't be able to walk again then there was no way on earth that he was prepared to burden her with the task of caring for him. Beth deserved better than being tied to an invalid for the rest of her days.

The thought stayed with him as he waited for the consultant to return. He tried not to dwell on it but it was impossible. So much hinged on the results of this scan. If the prognosis was poor then he would have to accept that his whole life was going to change. And if it was good news then it meant that everything he had dreamt about might come true. By the time the consultant appeared, it was little wonder that his nerves were in shreds.

'I won't waste time, Dr O'Neill,' the consultant said briskly. 'The scan has proved to be less helpful than I'd hoped. The swelling around the area has made it difficult to get a clear idea of the full extent of the injury. Whilst it doesn't appear that your spinal cord has been damaged, we will still need to be extremely careful.'

'So what happens now?' Callum asked, his heart beating up a storm at such a mixed response. While it was good news that his spinal cord hadn't been damaged, he wasn't out of the woods yet, it appeared.

'Basically, we'll treat you as though you have an unstable spinal injury,' the consultant explained. 'The last thing we want is to risk the cord being damaged so we'll keep you in until the swelling subsides. Unfortunately, it means that you'll need to remain immobile during that time, but I'm sure you understand how vital it is with an injury like this.'

Callum nodded, even though his heart had sunk at the thought of being kept in hospital. 'How long will it be before you have a better idea about what's going on?'

'As soon as the swelling goes down, we'll do a second scan. That should tell us what we're dealing with.'

It was obvious that the consultant wasn't prepared to commit himself any further than that so Callum left it there. However, he knew enough about spinal injuries to guess that any damaged vertebrae would either need to be manipulated into place or surgically repaired. It all promised to take some time and he sighed as he thought about being out of action for weeks and possibly months to come.

There was so much he wanted to do, starting with telling Beth how he felt about her, although until he was certain that he was going to make a complete recovery, he didn't intend to say anything to her. His mouth compressed. He wasn't going to blight Beth's life in any way at all.

Beth had no idea what to do. Callum had made it perfectly clear that he hadn't welcomed her declaration of love and it hurt unbearably to know how he felt. It would have been much easier to hide herself away and escape the agony of rejection, but she couldn't bring herself to do that. No matter what he'd said, Callum needed her.

In the end, she phoned the hospital and discovered that he had been moved to the high dependency unit. She spoke to the sister there but, apart from saying that Dr O'Neill was comfortable, the woman wouldn't be drawn into disclosing any further information over the phone. Beth hung up in frustration. She would have to visit Callum if she wanted to learn more, although how he would feel about seeing her was debatable. It was a distressing thought but she couldn't just abandon him. She loved him far too much to do that!

Daniel agreed immediately when Beth asked him if she could take the following afternoon off to visit

Callum. Everyone had been shocked by what had happened and they were eager to help any way they could.

It was almost an hour's drive to the hospital and she grew increasingly nervous the nearer she got. What if Callum refused to see her—what should she do then? Even if he didn't want anything to do with her, *she* needed to know how he was. She made her way to HDU and was directed to a side room off the main ward.

Callum was lying flat on his back, his head and body supported by a metal frame to stop him moving. He didn't see her approaching and it was only when she stopped beside his bed that he realised she was there. Her heart leapt when she saw the light that suddenly appeared in his eyes. Was he pleased to see her, after all?

'I thought I'd come and see how you are,' she said, quickly squashing that thought before it could run away with her.

'You shouldn't have bothered,' he said gruffly. However, the brusqueness of his tone couldn't disguise another emotion, one that made her pulse race even faster. Despite his assertions to the contrary, he *was* pleased to see her.

'It's no bother,' Beth told him quietly, drawing up a chair. She laid her hand over his, felt him flinch, and knew that it wasn't because he hated her touching him. She squeezed his fingers, feeling her spirits lift as her confidence came surging back. It appeared that she still had an effect on him, even though he was doing his best to deny it. 'I wanted to come.'

'I don't know why. I thought we'd got everything

straight the other day.' The gruffness was seeping away and she smiled to herself. Callum was such a terrible liar.

'I disagree. I think there's a lot that needs sorting out, starting with what I told you.' She bent closer so she could look into his eyes, wanting there to be no mistake about what she was saying. 'I love you, Callum, and it has nothing to do with pity.'

'You're mistaken.' He closed his eyes as though he couldn't even look at her. 'Learning that I'd been injured must have come as a huge shock when you thought I was still in Africa. It's little wonder that you're confused about how you feel.'

His arrogance took her breath away. He had the nerve, the sheer *gall*, to tell her how she felt! 'I'm not confused. I know exactly how I feel, Callum, I assure you.'

'You may think you do but...'

'But nothing!' Beth felt her temper soar to dizzying heights. He was doing it again, telling her what was best for her. It was exactly the same as when he had asked her a divorce. *He* had decided that she'd needed protecting, and *he* had made the decision to end their marriage. Not once had he considered consulting her!

Bending forward, she kissed him on the lips, a kiss that was full of everything she was feeling, from anger to desire. His face was white with shock when she drew back but she didn't intend to apologise for that. 'Does that feel as though I'm confused?'

'Beth,' he began, but she didn't let him finish as she kissed him again.

There was a moment when he went rigidly still, a moment when she held her breath, wondering if she had made a huge mistake, and then all of a sudden he was kissing her back. Beth felt a wave of relief wash over her as his mouth claimed hers. Callum couldn't pretend any longer. He couldn't pretend that he didn't want her when she could *feel* and *taste* his desire.

They were both breathless when they drew apart, both aware that the truth couldn't be denied any longer. Beth could hear her voice trembling as she repeated what she had told him but this was an earth-shattering moment for both of them.

'I love you, Callum. I've always loved you and that's the truth.'

'I love you too, so much.' He broke off, overcome by what was happening. His voice was husky when he continued, filled with all the love he had tried so hard to deny. 'I never stopped loving you, either, Beth. Asking you for a divorce was the hardest thing I've ever had to do, but I was so sure that it was the only way to protect you.'

'I know.' Tears filled her eyes but they were tears of joy rather than sadness. 'I understand why you did it now, although at the time…' She broke off, not wanting to spoil everything by admitting how dev-astated she had been.

Callum obviously knew what she was thinking because he sighed heavily. 'I'll always blame myself for not finding a better way to convince you that we had to stop trying for a baby.'

'I doubt if there was any other way,' she admit-ted, sadly. 'Like you said, I was obsessed by the idea of us having a child and I couldn't think about anything else.'

'It was your dream, Beth, so don't blame yourself. Being a mother was what you wanted more than anything and I understood that.'

'It wasn't just becoming a mother that I wanted so desperately,' she said simply. 'It was having *our* baby, Callum, living proof of how much we loved each other.'

'Oh, sweetheart. That's why Beatrix means so much to me too. She's the embodiment of our love for one another.'

There were tears in his eyes now. Beth wiped them away then pressed a gentle kiss to his eyelids. That Callum had lowered his guard to this extent was incredibly moving. He had always seemed so in control of his emotions before and it was a revelation to know that he felt so deeply about her and their precious daughter.

'She's our own little miracle,' Beth said softly.

'She is.' He smiled up at her, all the love he felt shining in his eyes. 'I love her so much, Beth, just as I love you.'

'And we love you too. That's why I'm here. I want you to know that no matter what happens, we'll always love you.'

He closed his eyes. 'I'd made up my mind that I wouldn't ruin your life if it turned out that I couldn't walk again. That's why I said what I did.'

'The only way you'll ruin my life is by shutting me out,' she said firmly. 'I want to be with you, Callum, through the good times and the bad.'

'Thank you, although maybe there aren't going to be bad times as I feared.' He quickly explained what the consultant had told him and she gasped.

'But that's wonderful! Once the damage to your spine has been repaired then you should be fine.'

'It could take some time,' he warned her. 'And I could still have limited mobility at first...'

'It doesn't matter how long it takes. You're going to get better and that's the most important thing,' she insisted.

Callum laughed. All of a sudden the future that had seemed so bleak a short time before was filled with hope. 'You're right. I will get better because I have the best incentive in the world.'

'Do you indeed?' she said, teasingly.

'I do.' He smiled up at her, wishing with all his heart that he could sweep her into his arms but that would have to wait. For now. 'I have you and Beatrix in my life. And there can't be a better incentive than that.'

One year later...

It was like a case of déjà vu, Callum thought as he followed Daniel into the church. When he had first returned to Beesdale, he had come to the church and he could still remember the panic he had felt at the time. But today it was very different. Today there was no panic, just a deep sense of joy.

Callum took his place in the pew, thinking about what had happened in the past year. Finding out that he had a daughter had been a major event; it had changed his life for ever. He adored Beatrix and knew that she had accepted him as part of her life. One of his proudest moments had been when she had called him Dada for the first time. Although his contract as a locum had ended, Daniel had offered him a partnership when he had returned to work and Callum had eagerly accepted. He loved working in Beesdale and didn't want to work anywhere else.

The organist suddenly struck up the 'Wedding March' and the congregation rose to its feet. Callum rose as well and turned to watch Beth walking down the aisle towards him. She was holding Beatrix's hand and his heart overflowed with love when he saw them.

Although his recovery from his injuries had been frustratingly slow, Beth had been at his side every step of the way. Callum knew that he wouldn't have coped nearly as well if she hadn't been there to love and encourage him. Now he was ready to live his life to the full, a life that he would share with Beth and their daughter. They were the two people he loved most in the entire world and he couldn't believe how lucky he was to have them.

Beatrix suddenly spotted him, her face breaking into a huge smile as she pulled free and ran to him. Callum swung her up into his arms and kissed her then turned to smile at Beth. 'So you didn't change your mind,' he said softly, loving her with his eyes as he would love her with his body later.

'No. I won't ever change my mind, Callum. You're stuck with me for ever.'

'Good.' He dropped a kiss on her mouth, uncaring that everyone was watching them. They had come so close to losing one another and the thought was unbearable. They belonged together—him, Beth and their precious daughter.

Turning, he looked at the people who had come to help them celebrate this special day. They had welcomed him into their lives, made him feel part of their community, and he would always be grateful to them because it was the most wonderful feeling to know that he had found his rightful place in the world at last.

Polly was there, cradling little Angelica, with Elliot and Joseph sitting either side of her. Eleanor was keeping tight hold of Mia to stop her running to Daniel, who was Callum's best man. Diane and Phil Applethwaite had brought baby William to the church and were sitting next to old Arnold Brimsdale and his wife.

Nick Benson, now fully recovered from his injuries and back teaching, was in the next pew, along with Michael and Penny Halthorpe. Michael had handed over the family's building firm to his son and retired. Callum guessed that Michael's recent health scare allied to the death of his old friend, Ken, had made him reassess his priorities, especially when the post-mortem had shown that Ken had suffered a massive heart attack while he was driving the truck that day.

Owen Walsh was there as well, sitting next to his wife, Abby. Callum had no idea if Owen had ever asked Beth out on that date because it no longer mattered. However, he was pleased that Owen and Abby were trying to make their marriage work. Having just gone through the process himself, he only hoped they would achieve the same result.

He smiled as he turned back to Beth, took hold of her hand and lifted it to his lips.

'What are we waiting for? Let's do this!'

* * * * *

MILLS & BOON

Coming next month

REUNITED BY THEIR SECRET SON
Louisa George

Finn walked through to the waiting room and was just about to call out the boy's name when he was struck completely dumb. His heart thudded against his ribcage as he watched the woman reading a story to her child. Her voice quiet and sing-song, dark hair tumbling over one shoulder, ivory skin. A gentle manner. Soft.

His brain rewound, flickering like an old film reel: dark curls on the pillow. Warm caramel eyes. A mouth that tasted so sweet. Laughter in the face of grief. One night.

That night...

A lifetime ago.

He snapped back to reality. He wasn't that man any more; he'd do well to remember that. He cleared his throat and glanced down at the notes file in his hand to remind himself of the name. 'Lachlan Harding?'

She froze, completely taken aback. For a second he saw fear flicker across her eyes then she stood up. The fear gone, she smiled hesitantly and tugged the boy closer to her leg, her voice a little wobbly and a little less soft. 'Wow. Finn, this is a surprise—'

'Sophie. Hello. Yes, I'm Finn. Long time, no see.' Glib, he knew, when there was so much he should say to explain what had happened, why he hadn't called, but telling her his excuses during a professional consultation wasn't the right time. Besides, she had a child now; she'd moved on from their one night together, clearly. He glanced at her left hand, the one that held her boy so close—no wedding ring. But that didn't mean a thing these days; she could be happily unmarried and in a relationship.

And why her marital status pinged into his head he just didn't know. He had no right to wonder after the silence he'd held for well over two years.

They were just two people who'd shared one night a long time ago.

Continue reading
REUNITED BY THEIR SECRET SON
Louisa George

Available next month
www.millsandboon.co.uk

LET'S TALK
Romance

For exclusive extracts, competitions
and special offers, find us online:

f facebook.com/millsandboon

⦿ @millsandboonuk

𝕏 @millsandboon

Or get in touch on 0844 844 1351*

For all the latest titles coming soon, visit
millsandboon.co.uk/nextmonth